ALLEN COUNTY PUBLIC LIBRARY

P9-EDG-852

Fiction
Conrad, Helen
Jake's promise

K ... p
at ...

Jake nodded and waited, almost holding his breath.

A huge grin broke over the boy's face. "Right on," he shouted. "I told them you'd come for my birthday. Just like you promised. So can I go with you now?"

Jake stared at the child. He wanted to feel joy at the way Kenny had accepted him, but something didn't feel quite right. Paige's face floated in front of his eyes. *We are the only family the boy knows,* he could hear her say.

Blinking hard, he put his hand on Kenny's tousled hair. "Listen, Kenny," he said. "Do you remember me?"

Kenny nodded. "Of course. I always read your letters at night," he said, and Jake felt a stab of remorse that there hadn't been more of them. "And I always have your picture near me," Kenny added, gesturing toward the bedside table. "I always knew you would come for me," the boy said serenely. "I was just waiting."

There was a lump in Jake's chest and it was affecting his throat. This wonderful little boy was his son—his flesh and blood. And nothing Paige Kenton could say or do could change that fact.

Dear Reader,

A family man—exactly what every woman's searching for, even as she falls head over heels for "bad boys" and wild men. The point of the exercise is to turn those ruffians into family men, isn't it? No matter how liberated we become, we still have times when we want a pair of strong, loving, protective arms around us...and our children.

I got a family man when I married my husband of twenty-seven years. We have four boys—the oldest is in college, the youngest in junior high. And I hope some woman will turn each of them into a family man when the time comes.

Helen Conrad

Books by Helen Conrad

HARLEQUIN SUPERROMANCE
322—DESPERADO
544—JOE'S MIRACLE

Don't miss any of our special offers. Write to us at the following address for information on our newest releases.

Harlequin Reader Service
U.S.: 3010 Walden Ave., P.O. Box 1325, Buffalo, NY 14269
Canadian: P.O. Box 609, Fort Erie, Ont. L2A 5X3

Helen Conrad
Jake's Promise

Harlequin Books

TORONTO • NEW YORK • LONDON
AMSTERDAM • PARIS • SYDNEY • HAMBURG
STOCKHOLM • ATHENS • TOKYO • MILAN
MADRID • WARSAW • BUDAPEST • AUCKLAND

If you purchased this book without a cover you should be aware that this book is stolen property. It was reported as "unsold and destroyed" to the publisher, and neither the author nor the publisher has received any payment for this "stripped book."

ISBN 0-373-70617-0

JAKE'S PROMISE

Copyright © 1994 by Helen Conrad

All rights reserved. Except for use in any review, the reproduction or utilization of this work in whole or in part in any form by any electronic, mechanical or other means, now known or hereafter invented, including xerography, photocopying and recording, or in any information storage or retrieval system, is forbidden without the written permission of the publisher, Harlequin Enterprises Limited, 225 Duncan Mill Road, Don Mills, Ontario, Canada M3B 3K9.

All characters in this book have no existence outside the imagination of the author and have no relation whatsoever to anyone bearing the same name or names. They are not even distantly inspired by any individual known or unknown to the author, and all incidents are pure invention.

This edition published by arrangement with Harlequin Enterprises B. V.

® and TM are trademarks of the publisher. Trademarks indicated with ® are registered in the United States Patent and Trademark Office, the Canadian Trade Marks Office and in other countries.

Printed in U.S.A.

To the Jenkins Family—
Mary, the true romance lover;
Horace, the skeptic and skilled rebuilder
of my husband's knees;
and their children, some of the fastest
swimmers around.

CHAPTER ONE

"MY DAD IS *TOO* COMING." Kenny Winslow set his thin face at a stubborn angle, glancing up at his aunt with huge gray eyes that revealed the fear he refused to admit out loud. "He promised. I know he's coming."

Paige Kenton had to resist the urge to press her hand against her chest to ward off the pain that slashed through her, pain for this boy who had been cheated out of so much in his short life. Instead, she forced a smile.

"I'm sure he'll come if he can, Kenny," she said brightly, fussing with the magazines and baseball cards on his hospital tray, as though getting those things straightened out would put order back into his life. "Whether he comes or not, you know how much he loves you...."

"He'll come. 'Cuz he promised."

Because he promised. Paige bit her tongue and pushed her long, silver-blond hair back away from her face, trying to think of some way to change the subject. Jake's promise wasn't worth the air he breathed to make it. Someday Kenny was going to have to face that. But now was not the time.

"We've got big plans for your birthday party," she told him instead, wielding a smile that needed some propping up at the edges. "And if you're still here, we'll move the whole thing into this room with you. Dr. Holmes said it would be all right."

Kenny didn't answer. He stared out the window at the sky as though cloud formation was of great interest to him. She knew him well enough to know he was concentrating hard so as not to cry in front of her. How she wanted to take him in her arms and comfort him, just as she had when he was younger. But he was going to be thirteen on Saturday. He didn't want that sort of comfort any longer.

"Good morning." A hearty voice filled the air as Dr. Trent Holmes came into the room. "How's my favorite patient this morning?"

Paige and Kenny both turned to him with relief.

"I'm doin' great," Kenny maintained stoutly. "Can I go home today?"

"Home?" Trent grinned at him as he pulled back the covers and began gently manipulating the boy's legs. "What...and miss all this fun?" He wrote something on his chart and resumed studying Kenny's condition. "This is like a vacation for a kid like you. Food whenever you want it, television twenty-four hours a day. Visitors at all hours." Trent's engaging chatter was clearly meant to take the boy's mind off the examination.

"Yeah, nurses with needles," Kenny complained, but there was a glint of humor in his gray eyes.

"Hey, the nurses tell me you're their favorite pincushion. You can't deny them their fun." He pulled up the covers and grinned at Kenny. "But you know we've got all kinds of entertainment planned for you. Just say the word and we'll send in the dancing girls. We've got them lined up in the hall."

"Really?" he asked, sounding skeptical but intrigued.

"Sure. Of course, we couldn't get the Rockettes, so you'll have to make do with Nurse Cranston in a tutu and Nurse Tannemucca in strategically placed surgical masks. Think you can handle that?"

Kenny laughed, and the doctor gave him a wink. "See you later, Ken. I've got to go check up on the rest of my victims."

Paige followed him out into the hall, her arms tightly folded against her chest. "Well?" she asked impatiently. "What's the verdict?"

He turned and smiled at her, his hazel eyes full of kind intelligence. In his mid-thirties, he was a handsome man with sandy hair and the look of enduring youth. "Paige, I've told you all along I think he's going to be okay. The ribs are healing nicely, and I'm not too concerned about his legs any longer. But a concussion like the one he's had can be tricky. I'm not ready to let him go home just yet. I want to keep him where I can be sure he's lying still and we can watch him."

She nodded. "I know that." Sighing, she shook her head ruefully. "I'm just so anxious to see him back to normal, and with his birthday coming up on Saturday..."

"Ah, yes, the notorious birthday." His eyes darkened. "Heard anything from Jake?"

"No." Anger flared in her glance. "And I don't expect to, either."

He hesitated. "I don't know, Paige. The Jake I knew—"

"Would keep his promise to his son?" she demanded scathingly. "Be serious, Trent. What other promise has he ever kept? Why would this one be any different?"

The promise had been made long ago, but Jake had repeated it in the letters he occasionally wrote to Kenny. When he'd gone off and left his son behind, he'd sworn to be back on the boy's thirteenth birthday. She could still see him as he'd looked that day.

"I'll be coming back, Kenny," he'd said, his face hard, his blue eyes unreadable. She remembered searching those eyes for signs of pain, anguish, some emotion over the loss of his wife, the potential loss of his son. But there had been nothing there. Nothing she could read, anyway. "I'll be coming back to get you," he'd said again. "I swear it."

She hadn't believed him then, and she didn't believe it now. Jake had betrayed and disappointed everyone who ever loved him. Why would this time be any different?

Trent looked distressed at her obstinacy. "Maybe you're right," he said doubtfully. He touched her shoulder with quick affection. "We ought to get together more often," he said pleasantly. "Are you free tonight?"

She looked at him and smiled regretfully. "Sorry, Trent. I'm busy."

"Going out with Barry?"

"Yes, we...we have to go over plans for the Gold Rush Days parade."

"Ah. Of course." He grimaced and laughed softly. "Say, I've been meaning to thank you for giving San a job. She'd been a bit lost since she moved back home. Working for you has really perked her up."

"Oh, I'm glad to have her," Paige responded with sincerity. She'd always liked Trent's little sister and she was glad for the help at her gift shop. "She's a terrific addition to the crew."

He nodded, then glanced at his watch. "Well, have a good time," he said as he turned and walked away. "And don't you worry about Kenny. I'm sure he's going to be just fine."

She was counting on it. Anything else was too scary to consider. Suddenly, she thought of Jake again. For four years he'd left his son behind. So what if he'd promised to come back on Kenny's thirteenth birthday? She'd believe it when she saw it.

"A SMALL TOWN IS a lot like a whore. They both pretend to love you while they're stripping you of everything they can get."

Jake grinned and nodded his agreement as the middle-aged gas station attendant took his bill and rang up the sale. "If you hate small towns so much," he said as the older man laboriously counted out the change, "why do you stay?"

"I didn't say I hated 'em," the man answered, leaning against the oil-stained counter. "I didn't say I hated whores, either."

Jake laughed and waved a quick salute as he started for his truck. The dusty smell of spring was in the air. His blood was pounding a little faster through his veins. He was almost home.

Whatever that meant. Home was supposed to be where the heart lay. A man's castle. The place where they had to take you in.

His home wasn't like that. Which, he supposed, was why he never stayed there.

The outskirts of the town started too soon. There to the left, beyond the ditch, was where he'd played baseball on hot summer evenings. What used to be a field was full of houses now, tall, stucco houses with wide driveways and RVs parked out in front. There was a traffic light where he used to sit in the dust with Barry McDonald and count out-of-state license plates as the cars rolled by. And old man Lynch's cow pasture was now a shopping mall, filled with cheesy fast-food restaurants and beauty parlors.

Aberdeen. In the heart of California Gold Country. Home. Like they said, you can't get there from here.

He hated it, all the changes, and then wondered at his reaction. It wasn't as though he had many fond memories of this place, after all. All the best years of his life had been spent someplace else. Still…this was where he'd been born and where he'd gone to school. Rotten as it always was, he hated to see it change.

And would Paige have changed? If what he'd seen so far were any indication, the signs weren't good. But he would know soon enough.

Downtown looked a little more familiar, though more crowded than it used to be. Dunk 'n Go Donuts was still on the same corner. Martha's Cozy Kitchen was still open for business. The big old library still brooded under the sycamores and couples still lay about on the grass in front of it.

He pulled into an empty parking space across the street from Paige's shop, the Serendipity, and stared at the storefront. There were too many people in there right now. But it was almost closing time. They would clear out soon. And then, he would go in and have it out with her.

The door to the shop opened and she appeared, waving goodbye to a couple who were leaving. For one moment, his heart lurched in his chest. There were times when she looked so much like Carol.

Just as he was about to open the car door and go to her, another couple appeared, entering the shop and creating a stir. It would be a while yet. He settled back, pushed his Stetson down over his eyes and began the wait.

IT WAS AFTER closing time and she'd thought the place was empty, or else she would never have gone into that silly song-and-dance routine from *West Side Story*. She'd just made a great sale and it felt darn good, so as soon as the customer was out the door, she celebrated with a quick turn around the floor, holding a broomstick and bellowing out a tune at the top of her lungs—an act she'd quickly regretted with all her heart. Feeling pretty was okay as long as you didn't sing about it in front of the man you hated.

What business did he have sneaking up like that? And he could have moved. He didn't have to stand right there in the middle of the aisle and let her dance right into his arms.

"Oh!" she cried as she stumbled against him.

"Watch out," he said sharply, frowning fiercely. "Like they say," he muttered as he pushed her away, "pretty is as pretty does."

She was blushing to the roots of her hair, but she managed to frown right back as she regained her balance and set aside the broom. It took her only a few seconds to find her focus again.

"So the prodigal father has returned, after all," she said, not bothering to keep the slight sneer out of her tone. "I never thought I'd see the day."

"You're seeing it." He stood with legs apart and arms folded, looking cold and massive with his soft leather jacket and open shirt. "And you know damn well why I'm here."

Her heart was knocking back and forth in her chest like a wild thing. He really was back and she was very much afraid she did know why. But she had to pretend not to. And hope. And pray.

"No, Jake," she said coolly, staring at him from across the high bridge of her patrician nose. "I haven't got a clue."

His silver-blue eyes glittered dangerously. "I've come to get my boy, Paige. I'm taking him with me."

"No!" For a second, she was afraid she'd cried out loud. But no. It was still inside her, painfully inside her. Her worst nightmare was coming true. She had to think fast, find some way to prevent this from happening. She had to buy some time.

"That's very interesting," she said crisply, turning away and heading toward the office. She picked up a file and put it away, readying the shop for closing, as she did at this time every evening.

He followed her slowly, glancing at the display of old gold-mining paraphernalia she'd set up. The pans were bent and authentic-looking, the leather pouches worn and cracked. The gravel sparkled with muscovite instead of gold dust, but the effect was pretty good.

"How's he been?" he asked quietly, turning to look at her. "What's he like now?"

She hesitated, wanting to say something sharp and cutting about a father who abandons his son and then shows up four years later asking this sort of question. But she could see the hunger in his eyes, the need to know, the regret.

"He's fine," she said haltingly. "And . . . well, he's a great kid."

Jake nodded slowly. "He always was," he said softly. "I've missed him."

Had he really? She found that hard to believe. Four years was a long time. If he really cared, he could have showed up any one of those years.

She studied him. He was about thirty-five now, she reckoned, and the rounded contours of youth had completely vanished from his weathered face. He was dressed in leather and denim, as he'd always preferred. He was wearing cowboy boots that had seen better days. His face was tanned and thin in a hard I-can-handle-things sort of way. The dark hair needed a trim, but at least it was clean, what she could see of it beneath the hat. There were splashes of silver at his temples. But as always, it was the blue eyes that mesmerized, glinting impossibly clear and insolent against his dark skin.

He hadn't changed at all. He was still the same selfish, arrogant drifter who had destroyed her sister's life and left Kenny all these years. And now he wanted the boy back. He claimed he'd missed him. If that was true, why had he waited so long?

"Is he still living with your parents?" he asked.

She swallowed and prepared to tell a quick, defensive lie. "Yes. Only... only he's not there right now."

Jake's entire body seemed to harden, like a predator getting ready to strike. "What do you mean, not there?" he asked, his voice quiet but full of barely leashed intensity.

"He's gone. On a Boy Scout trip." Her words came fast, tripping over one another. "They're hiking in the Sierras somewhere. He's been excited about this trip all winter. It's... it's really too bad. I know he would have wanted to see you, but..."

"He'll be back for his birthday on Saturday," he said calmly, as though he knew it for a fact.

She hesitated, blinking at him. She'd been ready to tell him Kenny wouldn't be back for weeks, but she could see he would never believe it. Better to stick to something credible than to risk losing her nephew entirely.

"Yes," she admitted a little breathlessly. "He'll be back on Saturday."

"Good." He leaned against the wall. "I'll wait for him, then." His gaze locked with hers and he said slowly, deliberately, "I'm taking him with me when I go. You and your parents aren't going to give me any trouble about that, are you?"

She couldn't look away, and deep inside, she cursed him for still having that much power over her. "What makes you think he'll want to go?" she murmured.

His wide mouth suddenly twisted into something resembling a smile. "He'll want to come. He's my son, Paige," he said. "Nothing you and your parents have done to him will ever change that."

Anger got the better of her. "Done to him?" she repeated scathingly. "Done to him? How dare you! Who the hell do you think you are to come back here after four years and—"

"And save my son from your clutches?" He pushed away from the wall, grinning broadly now. "Come on, Paige. I know what you Kentons are like. Hell, I was married to one of you..."

Paige went cold as ice. "Don't you talk about Carol like that," she said with a quiet intensity that cut the air between them like a knife. The icy fury in her dark eyes pinned him to the wall.

He stared at her for a moment, then shrugged. "Okay. I'm sorry. I didn't come here to insult you, Paige. I just came to get my boy."

She turned away, picking up some papers Sara had left out and filing them mindlessly. She felt unable to look at him any longer without exploding.

It wasn't going to be as easy as he seemed to think. In fact, if she had her way, it wasn't going to be at all. How could he waltz in here with such a ridiculous demand? You would think the years would have brought some sort of maturity to the man. But no. He was just as unrealistic as ever.

Still, he was a rough one to go up against. She would have to watch her step. She couldn't outmuscle him, but she might be able to outsmart him if she kept her wits about her. She turned and looked at him narrowly.

"Where are you staying?" she asked.

"Nowhere. I wasn't planning on sticking around."

That was fine with her. She was sure he wouldn't stay if things got boring. That was just the way he was.

No, once he realized Kenny wasn't available for take-out, like a quick pizza, he would probably move on. In the meantime, it might be best to keep tabs on him. If she could prevent his finding out where his son was, she just might have a chance.

Steeling herself, she said what she knew she had to, despite the taste of bile that rose in her at the thought.

"You'd . . . you'd better come stay with me, then," she said as crisply as she could.

He grinned again, that know-it-all grin she hated. "Right. Good idea. Do you think I'll get through the night without your parents making attempts on my life?"

Hatred wasn't a strong enough word. There had to be something worse for what she felt for him. She fairly quivered with detestation. "I don't live with my parents any longer," she said curtly. "I have my own apartment here in town."

He cocked an eyebrow. "No kidding. So, little Paige finally cut the apron strings."

Her eyes flashed. "Are you going to come home with me or not?"

He shrugged again. "Might as well. Better your place than the Sleepy Pines Motel."

"Your graciousness is only exceeded by your impeccable manners," she snapped. Picking up her purse, she started for the door. "Come on. You have a car, don't you? You can follow me over."

He glanced at her as she passed him and something in the way she tossed her blond hair, something in the set of her mouth or the light scent of roses that filled the air as she went by him, opened a window to the past. Suddenly, he saw her sister, annoyed with him, whirling away, dissatisfied with something he had said or done, and that old feeling ripped through him, momentarily stopping the breath in his throat.

"Wait a minute, Carol," he said, frowning. "I'm not so sure I want to go stay in your—"

"What did you say?" she demanded, her face pale, her eyes huge as she turned and stared at him. "Don't call me that."

"What?" He had no idea what he'd done.

"Carol. You called me Carol."

"Oh." He felt a slight shiver down his spine and shook his head. "I didn't mean to. It was an honest mistake."

Their gazes locked for a long moment, then he shrugged. He almost changed his mind about staying with her. He certainly didn't want to be reminded of his wife every minute of the day. But that was nonsense, of course. Paige wasn't Carol. And he wasn't even the old Jake who had been married to Carol. So what did it matter, anyway?

"Well, lead on," he said impatiently. "I could use a hot shower."

She turned, but the sting of being called by her sister's name stayed with her.

"Damn you, Jake Winslow," she grumbled silently as she led the way to the street. "Damn you for always making me feel like an idiot."

The man had a knack. She only hoped she was going to be able to get beyond that and beat him at this game. Only time would tell.

CHAPTER TWO

"TOO MUCH BLUE," Jake said, surveying her living room, the navy chairs, the indigo couch. "Blue is a cold color." His own icy blue gaze flashed at her provocatively. "I always thought of you as more hot-blooded than that."

Paige swallowed the retort that sprang to her lips. She wasn't going to get into constant squabbling. She had to keep her focus tight on the mark. Still, she couldn't resist one tiny dig.

"When you get your own apartment," she said, forcing a light tone, "you can decorate it in your own colors."

He threw back his head and laughed softly. Paige was a smart girl. He'd always known that. Why use a sledgehammer when a hat pin would draw as much blood? But he didn't mind. The animosity between them was a good thing. It would keep them on their toes. He liked it, even if it did have roots in a past that was painful to dredge up.

"What makes you think I don't have a place of my own?" he asked, the humor draining from his expression.

Her smile was tight. "You never did before. When you were married to my sister, you dragged her from one mining town to another, living in rented rooms. Are you saying you've changed your ways?''

He stared at her for a long moment, then slowly shook his head. "No, Paige," he said softly. "I'm the same man I always was. I guess you've got me pegged, haven't you?'' Just like everyone else in this town, he added to himself. Just like always.

She was angry inside and she wasn't sure exactly why. The funny thing was, she could see the anger in him, too. She didn't want to see it. She didn't want to know anything about him or what he was thinking or feeling. She just wanted him gone. And without Kenny.

She had to get out of here before she said or did something stupid. Her date with Barry was an hour away, but if she left soon, she could catch him at the office and keep him from showing up here and finding out about Jake.

Yes, that would be for the best. The less contact Jake had with people who used to know him, the better. She wanted to keep him under wraps, and especially, away from anyone who might let slip where Kenny actually was.

"I'm going out," she said crisply, leading the way into the kitchen. "There are frozen dinners in the freezer. The microwave is on the counter. Go ahead and fix yourself something to eat."

"What? You're not going to cook for me?"

She looked at him, suddenly caught in his gaze. He was so male, so large. For some reason, she was finding it hard to breathe. Why? she wondered. Was she scared of him? Was that it?

If so, she had to get over it. Fighting him for Kenny was going to take every bit of her strength and moxie. She was going to have to toughen herself, guard against being influenced by Jake. She knew from having watched Carol how the man could hypnotize a woman. Forewarned was forearmed.

"Get take-out if warming up a frozen dinner is too much for you," she said shortly. "Have a pizza delivered. Whatever."

Turning, she gestured for him to follow her.

"You can use Kenny's room. It's through here."

She led the way down the hall, and Jake strolled behind her. "Here you go."

Pushing open the door to the boy's room, she looked inside. Kenny had left it a horrible mess, as usual, but she'd spent last Sunday tidying and dusting, and it actually looked pretty presentable now.

Jake entered slowly, looking at each object in turn. She watched him, trying to read some emotion in his cold eyes, but he kept every trace hidden. She had no idea what he was thinking. She knew he was affected by the room, though. She could see that in the long, slow time he took studying it.

"Kenny's room?" he asked at last, pinning her with his stare. "I thought I had your parents appointed as his guardians."

She'd known this was coming and she was prepared. "They are, of course," she said brightly. "But he comes to stay with me on weekends sometimes. I'm his aunt, after all. He likes to come into town and take in a movie or a game now and then. And when he does, he stays with me."

A complete lie, but a necessary one. Her parents were Kenny's guardians, but they were old and frail, and she'd brought Kenny with her when she'd moved into town. She was the one who was actually raising him. But she was afraid that Jake would take that as a chink in the armor of her case for keeping Kenny. And legally, it probably was. So it was best to keep up the pretence.

He looked at her intently. "Where is it you're going tonight?" he asked, his voice muffled as he faced away from her, looking over Kenny's collection of hockey cards. "Got a date, Little Sister?"

She froze. That was what he'd always called her. She'd forgotten—and forgotten how much she hated it.

"I've got some things I need to do," she said evasively, coloring slightly. It wasn't easy to continue the lies. In fact, it was darn exhausting. The sooner he left, the sooner she would be able to quit this deception.

"I've got an appointment." She glanced at her watch, then started to walk toward the door. She hadn't freshened up from work, but she didn't have time for that now. "I've got to get going. I'll be back about ten. Don't wait up."

She stopped and looked back when she reached the doorway. He had followed her into the living room. She couldn't imagine what he was going to do with himself in her boring little home.

"No wild parties while I'm gone," she said lightly, her hand on the knob.

"Damn," he drawled, watching her through narrowed eyes that sparked in the lamplight. "And here I was planning an orgy."

"You need written permission from the manager for orgies," she responded, almost smiling. "Plain old drunken brawls only need a verbal okay."

His mouth twisted slightly. "I'll keep that in mind," he said softly. He indicated the doorway with a nod of his dark head. "You watch yourself out there in the big bad world."

"What? Aberdeen?" She made a gesture of exasperation. "Nothing ever happens in Aberdeen. Isn't that why you left?"

"Small towns can be just as lethal as big cities, Paige. I remember what it's like to have everyone know what you're doing every minute of the day. And their feeling they had a right to comment."

And comment they did. She remembered it well, herself. But that was all a long time ago. The town had changed, grown bigger, more metropolitan. It was that old-time character and personality people were trying to revive with their emphasis on the Gold Rush Days festivities.

"That's how people act with those they care about," she retorted, noting the cynical twist to his mouth at her words. "But then, I suppose you wouldn't understand about that."

"I understand, all right."

Suddenly, he was there, right by the door. She wasn't sure how he'd moved across the room that quickly, and at the same time, managed to continue giving off that sense of slow-moving, casual unconcern.

"I cared about Carol, Paige," he said, his words crisp and hard. "I loved her. Why can't you and your family believe that?"

He was much too close, and bringing up things that were too hard to deal with. She stared at him, unable to think of anything to say in her own defense. And then she was out the door and walking quickly down the steps to the courtyard, going toward her car parked in the garage.

Loved Carol, she thought indignantly. How did he have the nerve to say something like that to her? If he'd loved Carol the way he should have, she would be alive today. Paige was sure of it.

JAKE MOVED restlessly through the apartment. Paige had been gone for over an hour. How long was this date going to last, anyway?

He tried to recall how long dates usually lasted, but it had been quite a while since he'd had a real date, so he couldn't remember.

He was sure it was a date. Though she'd denied it, she'd turned red at his words. Well, he supposed she wouldn't be bringing this one home for coffee afterward. He grinned to himself at the thought. Bringing your date home to find a strange man staying with you was not considered smart in most romantic circles.

Come to think of it, he wasn't sure what he was doing in her apartment, anyway. He hadn't been counting on a stay. He'd come to get his boy, nothing more, nothing less. The last thing in the world he wanted was another run-in with the Kenton family. He'd had too many of those in the past.

Turning, he looked down the hall at the room she was letting him use. Kenny's room. For some reason, he was reluctant to go in there again.

And perversely, as soon as he'd admitted that to himself, he had to go in immediately. There was no way he was letting some nebulous fear run his life. No way. Once you started doing that, you were done for.

He strode firmly down the hall and entered the room, going right to the center and standing there as though he'd conquered something. But he knew he hadn't. The worst part was just beginning.

And here it came as he began looking over his son's things again—the deep, suffocating, wave of emotion that surged inside him, a feeling filled with a sadness that squeezed his heart, an anger that cut like a knife. Suddenly, he felt his eyes sting with regret.

He took up the ragged baseball cap and held it in his hands, trying to imagine the size of Kenny's head, what color his hair was now, how it was cut. This cap was obviously a favorite, stained with sweat, torn in three places and hanging within reach, ready to be grabbed by the boy on the way out to meet his buddies.

Buddies. What kind of friends did he have? What did he like to do with them? Did they have fathers? Did Kenny find excuses to go to their houses and hang around the fathers, just watching, wondering—the way Jake had when he'd been a fatherless kid himself?

He put down the cap as though he couldn't stand to touch it any longer, but he didn't leave the room. Instead, he walked to the closet, opened the door and looked at the row of clothes hanging there, trying to gauge how tall Kenny was, how he was built.

His first impulse had been to see what types of clothes his son wore. It would help him to get a handle on what kind of kid he was. But hard on the heels of that thought came another. This closet was tightly stuffed with clothes. Way too many clothes for a casual visitor.

"He only comes here on weekends, huh?" Jake muttered to himself, frowning. "You're going to need a better one than that, Paige."

Evidence suggested that Kenny was living with her, and that seemed odd. Why would a young woman want a boy of that age around? How could she date or have any kind of privacy? And why had she lied to him?

She was hiding something. That much was obvious. And a moment later, he saw something that convinced him further.

There in the end of the closet, set toward the back, was a Boy Scout backpack, lantern and pup tent. Jake pulled some things out of the way and the whole collection was fully revealed.

So Kenny was off hiking with his troop, was he? Without any of his camping equipment? Fat chance.

Paige had lied again. Little Paige, Carol's baby sister who had always seemed more pest than adversary had grown up and was going to be a problem. He hadn't counted on that. He was going to have to readjust his thinking.

Turning, he closed the closet door, emotions damped down now. He had a goal, a purpose. He had something to look for. If Kenny wasn't on a scouting trip, where was he? He wanted his son and he wasn't leaving without him, no matter what Paige had up her sleeve.

"CALM DOWN, Paige. Don't get so excited. Everything in its own good time."

Paige took a deep breath and tried to pull herself together. Judge Randall was an old friend of the family, and probably in his seventies, but she wanted to shake him right now. Why couldn't he see how important this was?

"All right," she said slowly. "I'll take it easy. But you've got to tell me that you realize how serious this is. Something has to be done. I figure a court order is the only way."

"A court order to...?" Eyebrows raised, the elderly judge waited for her to fill in the blanks.

"A restraining order to keep Jake Winslow away from Kenny."

The judge smiled, his thin lips pressed together and his blue eyes bright. With his white hair and arched nose, he looked every bit the part he played in life, especially set against the beautifully bound books of his library.

"You require a restraining order to keep Jake away from his son," he said lightly. "On what grounds, my dear?"

"Grounds?" She repeated the word impatiently. Judge Randall had been her father's best friend since forever. If he couldn't find a loophole to justify this, who could? "On the grounds that he wants to take Kenny away from us."

The judge leaned back in his leather chair and gazed at her levelly. "But he's Kenny's father."

Paige twisted her hands together anxiously. "Judge Randall, you know the background of this situation. You know what it would do to my parents if we lost Kenny."

The judge raised one snow-white eyebrow. "What it would do to your parents is not the question here, Paige," he said gently. "Kenny's welfare is the issue the entire case will turn on."

She laughed bitterly, throwing up her arms in a gesture of frustration. "Well, there you go. You know what Jake's like. You can't think it would be better for Kenny to grow up being dragged around the countryside by Jake than to have a settled existence here, with my parents." She purposely didn't mention that Kenny's residence was actually with her. That was a problem they might have to deal with later. Right now, it could only cloud the real issue, which was to get Jake out of the picture for good.

The judge's smile was wan. "Of course I don't think that, on the face of it. But even if I do issue a restraining order, it will only be for a period of time leading up to a hearing. And at the hearing, I will have to consider all the evidence impartially. My friendship with your family can't enter into my decision."

"Of course not." But she didn't for a moment think that was going to be a problem. The judge had indulged her for years, from the special peppermints he used to carry around in his pocket for her and Carol when they were young, to the letters of recommendation he'd written to help her get into the exclusive Eastern college she'd wanted to attend. Besides, he knew how bad Jake would be for Kenny. He'd been there when Carol had died. He knew the hand Jake had had in that. She had every confidence he wouldn't desert her on this. "So you'll issue the order?"

"I'll consider it," he said slowly.

"Consider it!" She pressed her cool hand to her hot cheek. "But Jake's here now. What if he finds Kenny and takes him away?" Paige could hear the desperation in her voice.

"I don't think that's likely to happen," the judge said reassuringly. "Jake was once part of this community. I'm sure he'll stay at least long enough for you all to work things out to everyone's satisfaction. I don't think he'll run off with Kenny in the night, do you?"

Paige bit her tongue and remained silent, looking down at her hands, twisted in her lap. She wasn't convinced. She'd seen Jake do crazier things.

Judge Randall smiled again. "I'll consider the matter and let you know tomorrow afternoon."

Tomorrow afternoon. Could she wait that long? "All right," she said grudgingly, rising from the leather chair in which she'd been sitting. "But please—early in the afternoon."

"You know, Paige," the judge said, reaching out and holding her hand in his while he looked at her with concern. "Jake *is* Kenny's father. It is quite possible I might decide to let him take his son. The hearing—"

Paige squeezed his hand and shook her head. "Don't worry about that," she said breezily. Hearing, schmearing. Jake wasn't the sort of man to wait for hearings. He was a "to hell with the consequences, I want to do it this way" sort of man. He had no patience for laws and rules and the way things ought to be. That was what made him so dangerous. But it was also what made it impossible to think that he'd show up for any hearing.

"Schedule the hearing for as far away as you possibly can. He'll never last here long enough to appear, believe me." She grinned, happy at the thought. "I know this man. Only too well."

"You may be right, my dear," Judge Randall said, frowning. "But there are no guarantees, you know."

No guarantees. When had she ever asked for guarantees? This was only the first round of this fight. If things went badly for one reason or another, she was ready to make adjustments, define a new plan, try something else. She had to be. That was life—if you were handed lemons, you made lemonade. At least, that was the way it was if you were a survivor, which was exactly what Paige was determined to be.

Saying goodbye to the judge, she hurried out to the car where Barry was waiting.

"You're not going to tell me what that was all about, are you?" Barry noted as she slipped into the seat and sat back against the headrest in his long, low car.

She sighed wearily, and pushed away a pang of guilt. Barry and Jake had been good friends once, but that was long ago. She didn't want him to know Jake was in town.

"I can't, Barry. I'm sorry. This has to do with private business. You remember that the judge is an old friend of my father's."

"Yup, I remember." Barry grinned suddenly, shaking his handsome head. "I remember when Jake and

I were hauled in front of the judge one time when we were about thirteen. He scared the living daylights out of me, believe it."

She looked at him, trying to recall what he'd been like as a boy. Funny, she could remember Jake as though it were yesterday. But Barry was a hazier figure in her memories.

She knew his hair had been blond back then. It was light brown now, and cut close to his round head. Barry always had a pleasant expression on his face. It went well with his career in real estate. He was a salesman, born to the trade. Just as Jake was a drifter.

"What had the two of you done?" she asked curiously.

He chuckled, bringing up the memory. "Somebody caught us smoking in the old mill building by the river. They took it real seriously—it was fire season—and dragged us over to the hospital to the burn ward to show us what can happen if you fool around with fire. Then the doctor showed us pictures of smokers' lungs, and all." He shook his head, grinning. "It was not a happy day in my childhood, I'll tell you."

"I guess not." She looked at him thoughtfully. "Funny, though. Neither one of you ever became smokers."

"Nope. And neither one of us ever burned any buildings down, either."

She laughed. "Do you suppose that day had something to do with it?"

"It did for me. I don't know about Jake."

He moved uncomfortably and she realized that the subject of Jake was not one they discussed very often. There was too much baggage from the past to wade through when they did. In fact, not many people in town ever mentioned him. That was probably because mentioning Jake would bring up the topic of Carol, and everyone was a little squeamish about that, especially around her.

Barry turned the key and started the engine. "Well, it's too late for our dinner reservations. What do you want to do?"

She considered for a moment. Despite everything, she was as hungry as a horse. "I could go for a hamburger at the drive-in."

His eyes lit up. "Just like high school."

"Why not?"

But as he started the car in that direction, he made a face. "Some date," he said ruefully.

He was disappointed. It seemed she was always disappointing him for some reason. She regretted it. He was a good guy and deserved better than the casual way she was continually putting him off. Why did she do that, anyway? Why didn't she settle down and get serious? Somehow, there never seemed to be time for that, never a real reason to try it. Now here she was, heading for thirty, and no husband in her sights. Unless she decided on Barry.

That thought almost made her laugh. Her conscience pricked her. He was such a nice man, he didn't deserve her derision. Thoroughly ashamed of herself, she got defensive.

"This was never meant to be that kind of date, anyway," she reminded him. "We were getting together to go over plans for Gold Rush Days, remember?"

"I guess so." He grimaced at her. "Sometime I'd like to take you out somewhere really special, just the two of us. Would you like that?"

She hesitated. "Sure," she said at last, though she couldn't really muster much enthusiasm. "That would be nice."

"Nice," he repeated scornfully, but he seemed relatively satisfied with her answer.

He pulled the car into a space in the drive-in and began to order while Paige surveyed the cars lined up on either side of the island. This was the only drive-in left in the foothills that she was aware of. She hadn't been here in years. The same high school kids seemed to be hanging out of the same cars, calling to one another across the way. Everything she did, everything she thought about lately, seemed to be bringing back the past more and more strongly. She wished she could close a door on it, forget it. But Jake had made that impossible.

The hamburgers came, and they were just as greasy and delicious as ever. They laughed while they ate, teasing each other. Barry insisted on ordering hot fudge sundaes for dessert.

"Now, can we get down to business?" Paige said at last, spooning the last bit of thick brown chocolate onto her tongue and sighing with pleasure. "We're really running out of time on this. We've got to get things settled about the parade."

The parade. She was going to have to concentrate on it. Since the accident, her thoughts had been preoccupied with Kenny and his condition. And now, with Jake here, she was going to have trouble getting the parade back at the top of her list of priorities.

But she had to. A whole lot of people were counting on her. And she'd been bound and determined
from the time she'd accepted the assignment that she
wouldn't let the town down. Aberdeen needed to be
brought together, and the community leaders were
hoping that making the Gold Rush Days celebration
a bigger deal than usual would help provide a common goal they could all work toward. She'd bought
into the idea enthusiastically when it had first been
brought up at a chamber of commerce meeting, and
so had Barry. They'd decided to work on it together.

"You're right," Barry said, turning toward her.
"Okay, boss. What do we do?"

"Well, we agreed, I think, to divide things up.
You're going to handle the technical details and mechanical logistics of how the floats and cars are set up,
and you're going to check out methods of mobiliza-
tion and the timing of the events. I'll audition the entries."

Barry frowned, eyeing her worriedly. "Now, remember, it's a community parade, so don't be too
strict with the people who want to enter."

She looked at him, exasperated. Didn't he know her
better than that?

"I have no intention of being strict at all. I just want
to be sure there's nothing offensive or really rude, either intentionally or unintentionally. As long as things
are good-natured and well-meaning, I'm not going to
turn anybody away."

They talked a bit more, laying out the groundwork
for the plans they would have to put into writing soon.
Finally Barry reversed the car and they cruised out
onto the highway, heading toward her apartment.

"How's Kenny doing?" Barry asked as they drove along.

"Great." Paige smiled. She always smiled when she was thinking about Kenny. "I think he's going to be able to come home in a few days. His injuries have pretty much healed. The medical staff is just monitoring the concussion right now. He had some mood swings that worried them. They seem to be over, but the staff is still watching him."

Barry glanced over at her, a new sort of gleam in his eyes. "So you're all alone in that lonely apartment," he said, pretending a casualness that his fingers drumming on the steering wheel belied. "You could always come on home with me."

She looked up, startled. "Barry—"

He made a sudden move that startled her, pulling over to the side and turning to face her, his eyebrows drawn together.

"Come on, Paige. How long are you going to keep up this untouchable routine?" He reached out and rested a hand on her shoulder, letting it lie there tentatively, as though testing the waters. "We've been dating for a long, long time. We're both adults. Come on back to my place and I'll—"

"No." She pulled away, feeling annoyed with him, annoyed with herself at the same time. "I'm . . . I'm sorry, Barry, but the time just isn't right."

His hazel eyes were smoldering in the darkness. "I'm beginning to wonder if it's ever going to be," he said gruffly.

She swallowed and looked straight ahead. "I told you from the start that I couldn't promise you anything," she reminded him.

"I know. I know." He put the car back in gear and continued driving down the road. "It's hard, though," he went on, almost to himself. "I like you a lot, Paige. You know that. I've tried to be there for you ever since—"

"I know that, Barry," she broke in quickly, not wanting him to mention Carol's death. "And I appreciate it. Really, I do. But I don't want to get into any sort of... of binding relationship right now."

"You're getting a little old to keep on playing the field," he complained.

She froze, knowing what he said was right but resenting him for saying it. "If you want someone younger, why don't you find yourself another girl?" she snapped. "I never claimed to have any sort of hold on you."

He threw her a glare as he pulled the car up to the curb and watched, brooding, while she got out. But before she had taken more than two steps, he swore and turned off the engine, jumping out of the car and coming after her.

"Hey," he said, catching hold of her arm and swinging her around to face him. "You could at least kiss me good-night."

"Barry..."

"Just one kiss." He took hold of her shoulders.

Kissing Barry was the last thing she wanted to do at the moment, but she recognized a strange intensity in him that wasn't usually there, and she made a quick decision. A gentle kiss would be easier than arguing. Reluctantly, she lifted her face to his.

His lips touched hers, and then he tried to deepen the kiss. Ordinarily, she might not have minded, but tonight, something seemed very wrong about it and she reacted accordingly.

"Barry," she cried, jerking away. "Don't."

He pulled back, his face dark and angry. "Okay, Paige," he said evenly. "I won't. Not ever again." Turning on his heel, he strode back to the car.

She watched him go, her hand to her mouth. She hadn't meant to hurt him, but he kept pushing, and she'd warned him. Hadn't she?

A little worm of guilt still wiggled inside her. It would be better for both of them if she didn't go out with him, and she knew it.

But this was just a meeting, really, she protested silently. Still, she knew he'd taken it to be more, and she should have made sure he understood.

There wasn't going to be anything physical between them, not ever. Suddenly, she was very certain of that.

CHAPTER THREE

SHE STARTED TOWARD the entrance to her building, then stopped as a shadow disengaged itself from the others and moved toward her, just as Barry's car roared off into the night. She gasped. "Jake!" Warmth flooded her and she was glad for the darkness. He'd probably seen the whole idiotic scene.

He stopped in front of her, looking down. He had his hands jammed into the pockets of his jacket and a half smile on his hard face. "Quite a Romeo our Barry has turned into," he noted sardonically.

"You were eavesdropping," she accused, catching her breath.

He grinned, tilting his head to look her over. "It's a special talent of mine. You find out the most interesting and useful things that way."

"Oh, really?" She began to walk toward the courtyard of the apartment building, striding briskly.

"You're a despicable person," she fumed as she walked, knowing he was coming right along with her, though his long legs let him take one stride for every two of hers.

"Despicable?" he drawled, making her assessment sound outlandish. "Just because I watched Barry try to break through the ice you keep yourself encased in?"

She whirled, facing him, furious. "This is none of your business," she reminded him. "You stay out of my life."

He shook his head, his eyes narrowing. "Lay off, Paige. Don't overreact." He shrugged. "It was only a kiss."

She knew he was right, but she couldn't control the helpless anger she felt. "What were you doing out there, anyway?" she demanded.

"I was just coming home."

"Through the bushes?"

"I like to go incognito whenever possible." He grinned again. "And I thought I'd hang back and let you two play out your little love scene."

She wanted to throttle him. She was embarrassed he'd seen her, embarrassed it had been awkward. She should let it go, but she couldn't. "It *wasn't* a love scene," she noted icily.

"You're right. My point exactly. I guess Barry didn't think it was loving enough, did he?" He laughed shortly. "Did you two have a fight, or are you always that cold to your boyfriends?"

A nice tidy little murder—who would ever blame her? Why was it that, of all the people she knew, he was the only one who always brought out the extreme emotions in her? She forced herself to calm down as she took the stairs toward her apartment, two at a time.

"How I am with the men in my life has nothing to do with you," she muttered.

"You're absolutely right." He was right next to her, not missing a step. "It's fun to think about, though."

He stood watching her as she fumbled for her key. He had to stop teasing her. He was torturing her the way he used to when they were younger, when she was a teenager and he was courting Carol. Why did they fall into old patterns like this, anyway?

The scene with Barry had brought back certain memories. He couldn't help but wonder if Paige was like Carol in the romance department. No, there couldn't be two women in the world like that. Fate wouldn't be so cruel.

But then again, they were sisters.

She opened the door and switched on the light, wishing her place were the refuge it usually was. But how could it be, when Jake was sharing it with her?

Throwing her purse down on the couch, she shrugged out of her jacket and hung it on the hook in the entry closet, then turned and looked at him in the lamplight, realizing his trip into the town could mean trouble. She had to find out where he'd been and what he'd done.

"Where did you go?" she asked, trying to mask her anxiety and not succeeding awfully well. "Did you see anyone?"

His gaze shifted and she knew right away he wasn't going to tell her anything. Not anything substantive, anyway.

"There aren't many people from the old days still around," he said evasively. "Not any that don't hate me, anyway."

She sighed, sinking onto the couch. "I don't hate you, Jake," she said wearily, wondering if it was true. "Don't make more of the way I feel than it deserves."

He sat down beside her, a foot away, his shoulders back and his long legs stretched out before him. "Your parents hate me," he noted calmly. "Don't they?"

She hesitated, but what could she say? If she denied it, he would know she was lying. "Can you blame them?"

A darkness descended on his features, freezing them in a hard mold that chilled her. "Of course I blame them," he said coldly, his low, deep voice reverberating with power. "I blame everyone in this whole damn town."

She swallowed, shaken by his vehemence, needing to do or say something to counter it. "For what? For being here and bearing witness when you turned yourself into a jerk?"

He swiveled toward her and she shrank back. His eyes widened slightly as he noticed her reaction. It seemed to stun him that she might be wary of his physical presence. She saw emotion flicker in his eyes, then they glazed over with ice again.

"Jake the Jerk," he said, his voice carefully light. "That's me, huh?"

"That's not exactly what I meant."

"No? Then what did you mean, Paige?"

"I just meant that the way people feel about you has something to do with the way you acted toward them in the past. You haven't always been an angel, you know."

He didn't answer right away and she bit her lip and looked at the black pane of the uncurtained window. She didn't see the reflection of them sitting on the couch. She saw the picture of him as a young man, his face tough and cocky, his attitude insolent. He was the

town bad boy in those days, all right. And that was
what had drawn Carol to him.

She could remember the tears, the arguments, as her
parents had tried to get Carol to give him up and Carol
had insisted that she wanted Jake and only Jake in all
the world. Paige had been barely a teenager, and she'd
watched, wide-eyed, as Carol had chosen the dangerous unknown instead of the settled future her parents
had planned for her.

"College," she'd cried scornfully, throwing their
advice back in her parents' faces. "What can they
teach me that Jake can't? He's read everything worth
reading. He knows everything. He's going to take me
places I've never seen. We're going to strike it rich at
one of his claims and then we'll travel all over the
world. That'll be better than a college education. You
just wait and see."

They'd managed to get her to go to college for a
while, but it hadn't lasted. Jake had crooked his little
finger and she'd gone, like stepping off a cliff into the
void. Jake had ruined Carol. And so far, he hadn't
shown any sign of remorse.

No, he hadn't been an angel in the past. And as far
as she could see, he still didn't have a halo.

She glanced into his face and found him staring at
her, and for a second, she had the eerie feeling he
could read her mind. But only for a second. That, of
course, was impossible.

Still not speaking, he rose and began to pace the
room. Paige stayed where she was, her arms folded
across her chest, and wondered what he was up to. To
say she didn't trust him was an understatement.
Whenever she was with him, she was on her guard,

certain he was looking for a way to set her at a disadvantage. That, she was sure, was why her blood always tingled when he was near.

Jake shoved his hands into his pockets and continued pacing, silently going over his options. He knew she was hiding Kenny from him, but he couldn't figure out how she'd known ahead of time that he'd be in Aberdeen, and been so prepared. Of course, there was his promise. Maybe that was it.

"Where exactly was it that the Boy Scouts went on this hiking trip?" he asked casually, passing behind where she sat on the couch so that she had to turn to keep an eye on him.

Her heart jumped and she looked at him. "I told you—in the Sierras somewhere. Why?"

Stopping, he leaned over the back of the couch and looked into her eyes. "I'm sure you had to sign permission papers," he noted softly. "I'm sure there are emergency numbers to call. You wouldn't send a twelve-year-old boy off into the mountains without knowing where he was going. Would you, Paige?"

Her heart was thudding in her chest. This was it. He was going after the truth now.

"I . . . I don't have any of that information. It must be at my parents'."

"No." He shook his head, his eyes cold. "I stopped by at your parents' house. I couldn't find a thing."

That wasn't quite true. He'd found something, all right. He'd seen the bedroom set up for Kenny. It was obvious that the place where Kenny only visited was out there in the old farmhouse, not here in town. The bedroom of her parents' house was filled with things Kenny had probably played with at age nine or ten. All his current possessions were right here. Paige was who he was living with. There was no doubt about it.

But then, where the hell was he?

Terror froze Paige's heart. "What did you do to my parents?" she demanded, jumping up to face him. "What did you do? What did you say to them?"

He frowned, annoyed at her response. What did she think he was, anyway? "Don't get excited, Paige. They weren't there."

That only calmed her a little. Then she realized what his statement implied.

"You went in?" she demanded. "When they weren't home?"

"The kitchen door was unlocked. I'm still part of the family, aren't I?"

Her eyes flashed. "You didn't go in, did you?"

He stopped and grinned. "Gee, can't get a lie past you, can I, Paige?"

She glared at him, hands in fists at her sides. "You leave my parents alone."

His head went back and his eyes narrowed. "I have every intention of leaving them alone. As long as I get my boy."

"They... they have nothing to do with that. Deal with me on it. Okay?"

He watched her curiously, wondering. "Is something wrong with your parents?" he asked.

"Wrong?" That was a joke, wasn't it? Better to ask if anything was right. Jake had seen to it that their lives would never be the same again. "They're living quietly," she said, almost begrudging him the information. "They do a little gardening, a little traveling."

Jake raised one eyebrow. "Your father doesn't practice at all any longer?"

"No," she said shortly. "The government closed down his medical practice four years ago. You know that."

"Yes, but I thought by now—"

"No," she said quickly. "He hasn't had the heart to start over. He's just too old." She hesitated, then added, "Too old and too hurt by... everything."

"By me, you mean." He grimaced. "Are you trying to say that I'm the cause of all evil and pain in your family's life?"

Her chin rose. "That about covers it."

He shook his head slowly, staring at her. "If you only knew," he said softly.

But she wasn't really listening. Her mind was working feverishly, making plans. She felt as protective toward her parents as she felt toward Kenny. They'd been hurt enough. Besides, Jake might use them to get at the truth. How could she get them out of town before he went back there? Maybe she could talk them into taking a quick trip to the Coast—a condo at Cambria, or a hotel room in Santa Barbara. Anything to get them out of the way for a few days while she went through this fight to keep Kenny.

She should have thought of it before. Why hadn't she thought this through? It was too late to call them now. She would have to speak to them the first thing in the morning and try to find a way to convince them to go, without telling them Jake was here. Her mind raced. No, that wouldn't work. They'd sense something was wrong. She was going to have to tell them. Meanwhile, if she could just get through this, by tomorrow afternoon, it would all be over. Once she had that restraining order in hand, she would be able to breathe a little easier.

"Where is he, Paige?" Jake was asking quietly. "Where's Kenny?"

Fear shot through her like a flash of lightning. "I told you. He's backpacking with his Scout troop."

He studied her intently, knowing they both knew that wasn't where he was at all. What should he do about it? He knew it was no use trying to force the truth out of her. Once she got that chin up that way, wild horses wouldn't budge her.

"I don't suppose you're going to break under torture, are you?" he quipped, gazing at her with more bemusement than anger. "I could try to twist your arm, but all I would get would be your name, rank and serial number, right?"

The chin rose even higher. He could see the steel in her. She wasn't going to tell him a thing. Well, it was only a few days until Saturday, and she'd assured him Kenny would be back by then. He'd waited all these years, he supposed he could wait a little longer. And he was on his own in the meantime. There was no law against looking. He would do his best to find his son, just as he knew she would do her best to keep him from succeeding.

Turning, he smiled at her and sat down on the couch. "Tell me about him, Paige," he said softly. "Tell me what he likes, what he doesn't like, who he hangs around with, what sports he plays, what he watches on TV. Fill me in on some of the stuff I've missed."

She stared at him, thrown off balance by this sudden shift in mood. She tried to see into his eyes, tried to judge his sincerity, but it was hard to do. Still, she had a feeling that this wasn't manipulation. She sensed that he really wanted to hear these things.

Slowly, she sank onto the couch beside him. She had what he wanted, and despite how she felt about him, she wasn't going to keep it from him.

"He's a little young for his age," she began tentatively. "He... well, he likes all kinds of sports. He seems to be moving all the time. He's at that age—can't sit still."

As she always did when she spoke about Kenny, Paige smiled. She felt a wave of love whenever she let her mind dwell on him. A look of tenderness swept over her face.

Jake saw the look and distanced himself from her on the couch. She loved the boy. There was no hiding that. Which was good—and bad at the same time.

"What sports does he play?" Jake said, watching her face.

"He likes baseball and soccer. But his favorite right now is swimming. I've got him on—" She stopped herself and glanced quickly at Jake. "I mean, *my parents* have got him on the swim team at the YMCA, and he's doing really well. He wins local races all the time."

His mouth twisted in a slight smile. "I used to be a pretty good swimmer, myself," he murmured.

"Yes." She felt flustered, partly because of the mistake she'd made a moment ago, and partly for reasons she couldn't fathom. She went on. "His big obsession right now is the history of the gold rush in this area. He's been all wrapped up in getting ready for Gold Rush Days." She glanced at him. "That's become quite a major event for the town lately. We have a big parade and all the trimmings."

"Yes, I know, I've seen the billboards."

"Well, Kenny's been taking out books from the library and visiting old mines and everything, especially that old mine shaft on my parents' ranch. In fact, that's where he was when—"

She stopped cold, horrified. She'd almost told him about Kenny's injury, how he'd fallen down the mine shaft. It wouldn't have taken much more for Jake to realize Kenny was in the local hospital. What was the matter with her? Two mistakes in a row. She had to be more careful than this.

He had her rattled, that was all. She had to force herself to stay calmer and more detached.

She froze and her face became more remote. He was just too dangerous. She couldn't let down her guard for a moment.

He watched, fascinated, wondering what she'd been about to say. Something about Kenny and that old mine. It would be no use pressing her right now. But he would definitely keep it in mind.

Paige was rising, avoiding his gaze.

"I'm going to bed," she said firmly. "I assume you have everything you need. I put out fresh towels...."

"I'm fine." He rose, too, and pulled her back with a hand on her arm. "You don't have to run away from me, Paige," he said softly. "I'm not trying to trip you up or make you give anything away."

Oh, but you are, she thought silently, staring into his blue eyes. "I'm not afraid of you, Jake," she said. "Don't get the wrong idea."

He nodded slowly, his hand still holding her upper arm. "I don't want you to be afraid of me," he told her. "But I wouldn't mind seeing a little understanding in your eyes."

She couldn't answer that without insulting him, so she said nothing at all, and he grimaced, knowing why she was silent. Shaking his head, his eyes crinkled with humor and he said very softly, "I'm really tempted to kiss you."

Shock jolted through her. She tried to pull away from his grip, but his fingers tightened, holding her firmly in place.

"Why?" she asked defensively.

He shook his head again. "I don't know." His gaze slipped down to trace the line of her mouth and his lids drooped just a little. "Watching Barry try it was so painful, I sort of feel like someone ought to do it right, just to restore order in the universe, or something."

Her mouth was dry. He wasn't serious. Was he? Of course not. He was trying to make her squirm, and he was doing a darn good job of it. He didn't want to kiss her any more than she wanted him to.

"Listen, I've been kissed by better men than you," she said tartly. "I know how it should go. I don't need any lessons."

His free hand came up and took hold of her chin. "I don't know, Paige. I get this feeling that you haven't been kissed right for a long, long time. I almost feel as though it's my duty—"

"Duty!" Anger gave her a shot of strength and she managed to jerk herself out of his grasp. "I hate you, Jake Winslow," she cried. "Keep your hands off me and go to hell."

He threw back his head and laughed as she stormed off, but he caught up with her before she could slam her bedroom door.

"You know, Paige, sometimes when I look at you, I see Carol. And then I look again, and I realize you're not like her at all."

She glared at him. "I'm not."

"Of course you're not."

His eyes held hers for several seconds. She wanted to slam the door in his face, but something kept her staring at him. It was like looking into an ice cavern, full of jagged stalactites and mysterious passageways.

When he finally turned away and she closed the door, she was short of breath. Despite everything, he scared her. She had to admit it. She wasn't sure if she could win against this man. And yet, she had to.

She locked the bedroom door, then cringed when the sound of the lock turning echoed through the apartment. He'd heard that, she was sure of it. Well, so what? Let him know exactly how she felt. She slipped out of her clothes, put on the baggy sweatshirt that she wore as a nightgown and slid into bed, sighing with exhaustion. It had been a long day, and tomorrow was going to be another struggle of sorts. She needed her rest. But as she lay back, her eyes were wide open and she knew sleep was going to be long in coming.

JAKE LAY in his bed and laughed softly as he heard the sound from Paige's room. So she was locking her door against him. Just like Carol.

The laugh faded quickly. Carol. His heart twisted with bitterness when he thought of her. She'd gone off and left him alone with a son he didn't know what to do with. He'd made a mess of it so far. Was he really ready to take over now? It didn't matter. Ready or not, it had to be done. And he was going to do it.

CHAPTER FOUR

SHE GOT UP before dawn. She'd slept fitfully during the night and there didn't seem to be any point to lying there any longer, staring at the ceiling. Slipping out of bed, she dressed as quietly as she could, pulled her long blond hair into a twist at the back of her head, then slowly turned the lock on her door, holding her breath. She listened carefully. Not a sound.

That was a relief. She wanted to get out without having to face Jake again. The next time she saw him, she hoped to have a copy of the restraining order in her hand. A quick stop in the kitchen for a glass of orange juice, and she would be on her way. She rounded the corner into the kitchen and nearly jumped out of her skin when she found Jake there, standing over the stove with a spatula in his hand.

"Good morning," he said cheerfully, as though it were nine instead of five in the morning. "Did I wake you up, banging around out here?"

It took her a moment to regain her equilibrium, and while that was going on, she couldn't say a thing, she could only shake her head and lean on the back of a chair for support. He was always going to be one step ahead of her if she didn't watch out. Here he was right now, and the smirk on his face told her he knew exactly what he was doing.

"How about an omelet?" he offered, flourishing the spatula in the air as though it were a weapon. "You won't be sorry. I'm known for my delicate touch with eggs."

That made her look twice. "Delicate touch?" she echoed, still fighting for balance. There was nothing delicate about this man. His huge, strong hands were made for rock hammers, not whisks.

"No thanks," she said quickly, though she did cast a longing glance at the coffee he'd brewed as she got herself back to normal. "I've got to get going."

"Going?" He cracked an egg and threw the shell in the trash. "Where are you going so early in the morning?"

That was going to be a little difficult to explain. "Uh, I have things to do," she said evasively.

"Paige, unless you're planning to invade the state capital by dawn, there can't be any place you've got to be going to right now. It's too early. Come on. Sit down and try one of my omelets."

She hesitated, but she knew she couldn't— shouldn't—do it. Sitting down to eat with him would be letting him get under her skin. It would be giving him another opening to wiggle things out of her. And then she had a treasonous thought. Sitting down to eat with him could even be allowing herself to begin to like him. She couldn't afford to do that.

"I never eat in the morning," she said.

"Then sit down and have a cup of coffee. You can watch me eat."

She looked at the table and he reached to pull a chair out for her. "Go on. Sit down. I won't bite."

She supposed she might as well. To say no now would make it look as if she was afraid of him, and she didn't want him thinking that. Reluctantly, she sat, then started as he leaned in front of her, pouring a cup of coffee.

He was barefoot, wearing jeans that hung low on his hips, and his shirt was unbuttoned. Against her will, she noticed that his chest was as muscular as ever, though the hair seemed a little thicker, a little darker. On a purely physical level, he made her pulse race, as he always had. It was one of the things she hated about him.

"When Carol and I were married," he was saying as he walked to the stove and his egg concoction, "I used to make breakfast all the time."

She stiffened and stared down at her coffee cup.

"Why does that bother you so much?" he asked dryly, having noticed her discomfort.

She looked up at him, trying to keep her emotions in check, but determined to tell him the truth. "What bothers me is your talking about Carol so casually. I have a hard time dealing with that."

He stared back at her. "Carol was my wife."

She held his gaze. "She was my sister."

His mouth gave a quirk of exasperation. "True on both counts," he said, turning to the stove. "But let's face it, Paige. We both knew her about as well as anyone did, and she was what she was."

Her eyes widened and her chin rose. "What do you mean by that?"

"Paige," he said slowly, as though trying to figure out what she was thinking, "why can't we just remember the good parts?"

"Why do you pretend that things were good between you and Carol?" she said. "I was there, Jake. I know. It wasn't that good. Right there at the end, she was talking about..."

She bit her tongue. There, she'd almost done it again. She had better keep quiet, drink her coffee and get out of here. By afternoon she would have her restraining order, and then...

"She'd been talking about divorcing me?" Jake said calmly. "Is that what you were about to say?"

Yes, that was what she'd been about to say. But this wasn't right. She felt sick at heart. She wanted to fight him, but not like this, not with hurtful things that had no bearing on the real issue. She risked a glance at his face. His expression was hard, but she couldn't see any real pain there. Maybe he'd become inured to the pain by now.

"I know what Carol was saying when we came back here that last time," he said, his tone dark. "I know what she was upset about." He set down his plate. The omelet was golden and perfectly formed. He dropped into the chair and picked up a fork. "And I don't think you really do," he added quietly.

"Carol and I always talked," she said challengingly.

He nodded, cutting off a piece of the omelet and placing it carefully on his fork. "I know that. But Carol didn't always tell you everything. She didn't tell you things she knew you would disapprove of."

He was infuriating her again. She shouldn't let him have this effect on her, and yet, how was she going to stop it? There was something so fundamentally irritating about him. She had a feeling that once she put her finger on exactly what that something was, she would be able to get over this instant reaction she always had to everything he said and did.

"How do you know?" she demanded of this man who thought he knew her sister better than she did.

He shrugged. "I knew Carol, and I know how much she loved you and wanted your approval."

"Maybe you didn't know her so very well, Jake," she said, her voice low and angry. "Maybe you just thought you did. If you knew her so all-fired well, why didn't you stop her that day?"

His eyes were like stones in his face. "Maybe I didn't want to stop her," he said quietly. "Ever think of that?"

Rising abruptly, she made her way out of the kitchen and out of the apartment and got almost to her car before she stumbled. It was hard to see with tears in her eyes, but she could dry those once she was safely inside her car. She couldn't let him see her cry. Not ever.

SHE CALLED her parents from the store. She woke them, but she couldn't help that. "Where were you yesterday?" she asked, trying to keep the anxiety out of her voice as best she could.

"We went into town for some shopping, and then your mother decided she wanted to eat at Joe's Italian Restaurant. You remember how we used to take you girls there on special occasions?" Her father's words were unhurried, and she could tell he was ready to go on and on. "Well, the old place is still the same. Joe's still full of stories and the food . . ."

She waited impatiently for a break in his narrative before she jumped in. "Listen, Dad, was everything okay when you came home?"

His voice was suddenly alert. "Okay? What do you mean, okay?"

She grimaced to herself. She hated doing this. "No one had been there, or anything?"

"Not that I know of. Why?"

She sighed with relief. "I just thought I ought to tell you..." She paused, closed her eyes and said it. "Jake's in town."

"What?"

It was all there in his voice, the anguish, and anger, the bewilderment that seemed to come over him like a cloud at times. She hurried to reassure him.

"Now don't get upset. It's okay. He came to get Kenny, but I've got Judge Randall working on a restraining order to keep him from doing that."

"He can't take Kenny." Her father's voice was choked, strained. "We can't let him take our boy."

"Of course not, Dad." She spoke briskly, trying to convey confidence and efficiency at the same time. "Don't worry. I'm taking care of things."

But he hardly seemed to hear her words. "Why now?" he moaned. "Why did he come back now?"

"You remember he once promised Kenny he would come and get him when Kenny turned thirteen."

"That's right. I'd forgotten."

"Now, don't worry," Paige repeated urgently, her fingers tightening on the receiver. "Like I said, I'm taking care of everything. But I thought... Listen, Dad, I thought it might be best if you and Mother left town for a few days, until this all blows over."

"Don't be ridiculous," he said abruptly.

She licked her dry lips and tried to think of a way to convince him. "Dad, really. It would be so much easier if you two were out of the picture. Then he couldn't get to you."

"He's gotten to me enough, already, don't you think?"

She closed her eyes and shook her head. "Dad . . ."

"First he took our Carol away, dragging her down, making her live like a gypsy in those mining camps . . ."

"Dad . . ." She already knew all this. They all knew it. Why did he have to go over it again and again, like touching a wound that would be better off left to heal?

"Then, mired in his failure, he tried to drag me down, too, by reporting my office practices to the IRS. I haven't worked a day since those agents came bursting into my office and took my files. And that was all his doing. You know it was."

"Yes, Dad," she said dutifully. "I know." But she couldn't let him go on. She didn't want to relive that day, when Carol, seeing what her husband had done to her father, got into her car and sped off into the night, straight toward her own death.

"Dad, I've really got to get going here," she said hastily. "Believe me, I know how you feel about Jake. I feel the same way. That's why I'm determined to keep Kenny out of his clutches."

"Good. I'm with you there."

"But it would be so much easier for me if you and Mother—"

"I'm not leaving town," he said flatly. "You can forget about that."

She would keep trying, but she could hear the obstinacy in his tone. He wasn't going to budge. "Think about Mother," she urged. "Take her to Cambria, why don't you? Go walk on the beach."

"And let that jackal steal Kenny while I'm on vacation? Not on your life, girl. I can't leave my family unprotected. You should know better."

Yes, she should have known better. He wasn't going anywhere. She was going to have to figure her parents into any calculations she made. Sighing, she gave up.

"Okay, Dad. Whatever you say."

And while he went on talking, she tuned him out and went back to thinking and rethinking her options. If she was going to beat Jake at this game, she was going to have to be prepared for anything.

JAKE CLEANED the kitchen carefully, putting everything away. It was a habit he'd gotten into living alone these last few years. He'd quickly learned to do things on his own, and by now, he pretty much liked it that way.

He glanced at the clock. It was almost seven. Time to get going. The kids would begin arriving at the school very soon, and he wanted to be there when they did. Maybe he would see Kenny. Or maybe he would find someone who knew where Kenny was. Either way, it couldn't hurt.

"He's here somewhere," he muttered to himself. "All I have to do is keep my eyes open and I'm going to find him."

Shrugging into his jacket, he left the apartment, got into his truck and drove the short, familiar drive to the school.

The junior high didn't look much different than it had when he'd gone there. The name had changed, though. Lettering above the door read Aberdeen Middle School. As if changing the name, Jake mused silently, is going to improve the education.

He slid out of the bench seat of his truck and closed the door, but he didn't go up to the entrance. Instead, he leaned against the fender and watched the few kids who were beginning to straggle in. He was going over what he could say to boys Kenny's age that might help him find his son, when a long, low car slowed and someone hailed him.

"Jake Winslow, isn't it?" a voice said from inside the luxury sedan.

Jake leaned down and looked inside. It took him a minute to remember who the older man was, but he'd once known him well. "Hi there, Judge Randall," he said, grinning. "How you been?"

"Just fine, young man." The judge smiled at him. "You've been gone a long time."

"Too long," Jake said. "Much too long."

"Well, it's real lucky I found you this way. I was going to try to get in touch with you. I need to see you in my court this afternoon, if I may."

"This afternoon?" Jake's head went back. The reference to the court held too many bad memories for him. Surely there weren't warrants left over from four years before that still needed to be cleared up. "What for?"

The judge leaned farther to get a good look at Jake's face. "I'll tell you what for. There's been a restraining order requested against you."

Jake's eyes narrowed and he took a step back from the car. "A restraining order?"

"Yes. Paige Kenton has requested a restraining order to keep you away from your son for a time. I'd like you there when I deal with this. I think it only fair that we consider your side of the situation." He cocked a thick eyebrow. "You've got a pretty spotty record in this town. You've been in my courtroom before. I would hope you might have matured over the years...that your darker side might have been tamed. But Paige Kenton doesn't seem to think you've changed. And, while I might be tempted to give you the benefit of the doubt, don't forget, I know the Kentons well, and I know what happened four years ago. I watched you walk away from your responsibilities at that time."

Jake's face hardened. "That was a long time ago," he said levelly, his eyes burning.

The judge nodded, looking him over. "Maybe. We'll see. Be there at three o'clock, and we'll have this out."

Jake took a deep breath and kept his anger leashed as best he could. "Thank you, Judge." He managed to smile without revealing the turmoil the judge's words had just put him in.

With a wave, Judge Randall pulled away from the curb and continued on his way. Jake stared icily after him.

"Damn you, Paige," he muttered through clenched teeth. "You really are going to fight me tooth and nail on this, aren't you?"

And then, despite everything, he smiled. If Paige Kenton wanted to do battle with him, he'd be ready.

PAIGE WAS going nuts. The minutes seemed to crawl like earthworms in the rain, slowly sliding into oblivion, one after another. She couldn't keep her mind on the customers. She couldn't keep her mind on her work. All she could do was check the clock every thirty seconds and wish time would go faster.

She thought about calling Trent's sister, Sara, and asking her to come in and take over, but she knew that wouldn't work. She had no place else to go, except back to the apartment, and Jake might be there. Besides, Sara was coming in later so that Paige could go to the courthouse this afternoon.

"How's Kenny?" Mrs. Martinez asked when she dropped in to find a gift for her sister in Phoenix. "I heard about his accident. Is he still in the hospital?"

And Paige had to look over her shoulder before answering, just to make sure Jake wasn't lurking in the background, ready to pick up clues from something she said.

She kept looking over her shoulder at lunchtime, too, when she closed the shop and hopped into her car to run over to the hospital and visit her nephew. What if Jake was hiding somewhere? What if he knew she could lead him to where Kenny was and he was following her? She took obscure side streets and doubled back the way she'd come, but she didn't notice anything suspicious. Finally, she got to Kenny's room with barely enough time to kiss him on the forehead before she had to turn around and go back again.

When she reopened the shop, it was one o'clock. She had two more hours to go. Two long, agonizing hours. But at least, at the end, she'd have her restraining order.

And then what? She wasn't sure how Jake would be served with the papers. And once he was served, would he move out?

It wasn't going to be easy. He would be angry, of course. Who wouldn't be? She only hoped he would give up right then and there and head out of town.

But something told her she was dreaming. He wasn't going to give up that easily. In fact, her confident words of the night before were coming back to haunt her. He was still the unreliable drifter he'd always been, but there was a core of hardness and determination in him she'd forgotten about. He wasn't going to make it easy for her.

She was going through the mail when Barry came in.

"Hi, Paige," he said, sitting down on a bar stool in the corner near her desk.

Glancing up, she quickly tried to read the expression in his eyes. Last night was still vivid in her mind, and she was sure it was still pretty clear in his.

"Hi, yourself," she said lightly. "What are you up to today?"

"Thinking about you."

Guilt seemed to be a natural by-product of Barry's presence lately. She gave him a quick smile and busied herself slitting open another envelope.

"Dull day, huh?" she quipped.

"Thinking about how you're really not like Carol," he said softly.

Her gaze flew up to meet his. They had an unspoken rule—they didn't talk about Carol. And Barry was violating it.

"You're right. I'm not a bit like Carol," she said crisply, her dark eyes blazing. "How are plans for the parade?"

He ignored her attempt at changing the subject. "I used to think you were just a younger version of her," he said, his voice almost dreamy, his face strangely distant. "I used to think you'd grow into it. You know—get more like her as you matured."

She didn't like this at all, didn't like where his meandering speech was going, didn't like the mood in the room.

"Barry," she began warningly.

"But now I know," he went on, as though he hadn't heard her. "It's no use. You're not one bit like her."

Rising, he turned and left the shop without saying another word. Paige stared after him, bewildered. Carol had been gone for four years and suddenly she seemed to be very much alive in the minds of all who had known her. It was very odd. Very odd, and very unsettling.

Unwillingly, she pictured her beautiful sister. Paige had the same blond hair and dark eyes, but that was about as far as the resemblance between the two sisters went. Carol was light and laughing and carefree and naughty. She'd had men falling at her feet from the time she could stand on them. Everyone loved Carol. Everyone wanted to be wherever Carol was.

Paige thought of herself quite differently. She was the steady one, the boring one, the one who ended up doing the dishes while the Carols of the world went dancing. There had been a time when she'd resented it. But she'd grown up a lot since then. Carol couldn't help being who she was any more than Paige could change who she was.

The picture of Carol's car after the accident came into her mind and she cringed, pushing it away. It was true that Carol had raced off in the car as a result of what Jake had done—calling in the IRS to investigate his own father-in-law. And it was true that she'd died, her car crashing into the center divider of the highway when she missed a turn on a rain-slicked street. But did that make it Jake's fault?

Paige had always thought so. Why was she wavering now?

She shook herself mentally. She didn't have time to mull over this problem. She had to concentrate on getting things ready to hand over to Sara so she could get to the courthouse. It was almost time. And no matter what, whether he was guilty or innocent of the charge, she would never let him take Kenny.

TWO O'CLOCK. Jake stood in the kitchen, glaring at the hands on the dial. He still had an hour before his appointment with the judge. He should be looking for Kenny. But after a morning filled with fruitless searching, he was beginning to get discouraged. The visit to the junior high hadn't panned out. Neither had the stop by Daisy's Diner, his old hangout. He'd tried finding old friends, but everyone he'd known seemed to have disappeared. Not that he'd had many friends when he'd lived here. When you came right down to it, he'd probably had more enemies. And the few friends who still remained were either too close to the Kentons for comfort, or they'd moved away. After all, it had been almost seventeen years since he'd left town, and the place had changed a lot. It was no longer the sleepy little backwater it once had been. For the moment, he was stymied.

Moving restlessly, he paced the apartment, looking at everything, hoping to spark a clue. There was nothing in Kenny's bedroom to tell him anything. It looked as though he might be returning at any moment.

He surveyed Paige's room. Everything was neat and tidy. The huge comforter thrown over the bed had a white background to a riot of violet pansies. Sun streamed in the large window. A picture of Kenny sat on the chest of drawers. It was a warm, comforting room. Nothing out of the ordinary.

He wandered slowly back into the living room, looking at items on the bookcase, riffling through the books, glancing at the desk.

The desk. Something stopped him and he turned to look at it again. A telephone sat on the corner of the rosewood antique. Bills and notes were stuffed into cubbyholes at the back. And a pad of paper lay front and center—a pad of paper covered with characteristic doodlings and telephone numbers that had been scribbled there in haste.

A flicker of excitement lit in his chest. It stood to reason she would have jotted down the phone number where Kenny was staying. Didn't it?

There were four numbers written on the pad, two plainly, one entangled in a pen sketch of vines, one decorated with flowers. Hc sat at the desk and pulled the phone forward, punching in the first number with calm efficiency.

"Avalon Talent Agency," the female voice responded.

"Sorry," he murmured. "I must have the wrong number."

The next number turned out to belong to a furniture upholsterer who was annoyed at being interrupted in his work.

A child answered the third number.

"Victor Residence. Can I help you?" he chimed.

Jake hesitated. This could be it. "Can I talk to Kenny?" he asked tenscly.

"Kenny? My name's Bobby, not Kenny. We don't have a Kenny."

Jake sighed. "Sorry, Bobby," he said. Then he had an idea. "Say, maybe you can help me. Do you know Kenny Winslow?"

"Uh-uh. I know Kenny Barnes. He's in my grade at school. I have Mrs. Kirstner and I'm in third grade at Aberdeen Elementary."

That killed that.

"Okay, Jimmy. Thanks, anyway. Bye-bye."

There was only one numbor lcft. It was local, but there was another number written beside it—282— maybe a hotel room? He took a deep breath, then poked the longer number in.

"Aberdeen Community Hospital," trilled the switchboard operator. "May I help you?"

He opened his mouth but nothing would come out, and he slammed down the phone, staring at the wall. Aberdeen Hospital. Kenny was in the hospital.

A thousand possibilities swam through his head. Kenny sick with a life-threatening disease, Kenny torn and broken from a car accident, Kenny almost drowned or almost bleeding to death. Whatever it was, he had to find out, immediately.

But he had to think this through. How was he going to find out about Kenny without telling people who he was?

Wait a minute—this was still a small town. He'd grown up in this place when it was even smaller, but places like schools and libraries and hospitals didn't change all that much. A grim twist turned his wide mouth as he picked up the receiver and punched out the number again.

"Aberdeen Community Hospital."

"Hi," he said, putting on an exaggerated drawl. "Say, can y'all tell me how Kenny Winslow's doin'?"

He figured chances were nine out of ten that she would know who he was talking about, and he hit the jackpot.

"Kenny Winslow? Oh, Kenny, sure. He's in orthopedic. Do you want his room?"

"No, no." A flash of quick panic. He couldn't talk to his son yet. He had to lay the foundations first. "No, I just want to find out how he is."

"Oh, sure. I'll connect you with the nurse in his section. Just a moment, please."

He swallowed hard, waiting for the connection.

The nurse answered, and he went back into the drawl. "Hi, I'm Stu Kenton." He could pretend to be an uncle from Paige's side of the family, if need be. "I just wanted to check on how Kenny's doing."

"Kenny Winslow?"

"That's my boy."

The nurse laughed. "Cranky, but full of spunk. Doctor thinks he can probably go home before his birthday on Saturday."

"I see." He didn't see at all. What was he in for? He had to take a long shot. "So he's recuperating well?"

"Oh, sure. Most of his bruises have healed. It's just his head injury they're watching. He took a pretty bad hit. But things look good. Would you like to talk to his doctor? Dr. Holmes is here in the hospital and I can have him paged."

"Dr. Holmes? Trent Holmes?"

"Yes. If you'll hold on—"

"No, thanks just the same," he said hastily. "I'll come by later today and talk to him personally. Thanks." He hung up quickly and stared at his reflection in the glass of the window. So old Trent was the doctor on the case. He didn't know whether that was good or bad.

But at least there didn't seem to be anything seriously wrong with Kenny. Whatever had happened was righting itself. That was a relief.

Suddenly, he ached for his child. He'd stayed away much too long.

CHAPTER FIVE

PAIGE SAT nervously in the courtroom, watching people file in. She was a little miffed that Judge Randall hadn't called her into his office to do this privately. Well, no matter, as long as it got done. She glanced at the doorway, and then froze when a familiar form filled it.

"Jake." She rose, her hands clenching the back of her chair, her heart thumping dully. "What are you doing here?"

He came to a halt before her, his tall body dwarfing hers. "The same thing you're doing here, I guess. The judge called me in so we could settle this restraining-order lunacy."

He sank into a chair beside her and grinned. "You do fight tough, don't you, lady?"

"Judge Randall called you?" she asked, feeling betrayed.

He shrugged. "Well, not exactly. We sort of met on the street."

This did not bode well. She'd never imagined she would have to argue for her restraining order with Jake looking on. Turning when she heard her name called, she looked up anxiously as the bailiff approached.

"The judge would like to see the two of you in his chambers," the young man said. "Follow me, please."

The judge's official office was in some ways a replica of his den at home. Leather and polished wood set the overall tone. Books were housed behind glass from floor to ceiling. Thick carpeting muffled their steps as they entered the room. All in all, it was a setting meant to create a sense of awe, and it did its job.

Judge Randall came in, dressed in his robes, and greeted them both, offering them chairs and settling behind the massive desk. He didn't waste much time on pleasantries. Smiling at Paige, he turned from her to Jake, his expression hardening.

"Now, tell me, Mr. Winslow. What have you been doing these last few years?"

Jake's eyes were as expressionless as panes of glass. "Going to school," he said easily.

Paige looked at him, surprised. She hadn't known that. She'd thought he was off trying to find gold all this time. After all, that was what he'd done all the years he was married to Carol, dragging her from one goldfield to another. Why would he have changed once she was gone?

"Oh?" Judge Randall nodded, seemingly surprised, as well. "Would you care to elaborate?"

"Sure." Jake looked at ease, as though nothing the judge asked was going to throw him. "I was always interested in minerals and earth science. I'd taken a few courses at City College before I ever left home. So I got myself accepted at Placer State University, finished my bachelor's degree in geology and went on to complete my master's."

"I see. Are you currently employed?"

Jake nodded. "I've got a job with a development company."

"So you're probably in a rush to get back to it, I would think," the judge said.

"Not really. I'm on a sort of a leave of absence right now. I've been working for the company for the past three years, first as an intern, then part-time, now full-time. They trust me."

Trust him? *Trust him?* Paige felt outrage swelling in her chest. No one trusted Jake, not if they had any sense. He'd been bad news since he'd been old enough to throw rocks. And any company people who took a chance on him had to have rocks in their heads.

Paige had to work hard to stifle the urge to put in her two cents' worth. This was all crazy. He had to be making it up. And why wasn't Judge Randall asking for any proof of what Jake was saying?

In fact, Judge Randall seemed almost impressed by the man. She looked at Jake anxiously, wondering why he was having this effect. And suddenly she saw him with new eyes.

He didn't look like the town bad boy any longer. He was dressed in jeans and a leather vest, but they were clean and well-made. His hair was too long, but freshly washed and neatly combed. His face didn't have its old chip-on-the-shoulder look of a fight just waiting to happen. It was hard and determined, but there was no sense of barely leashed aggression. Despite everything she'd been telling herself, he had matured. She was going to have to face that fact.

And Judge Randall had noticed. He liked Jake. You could see it in the angle at which he held his head, the look on his face. Her hands went cold. What did this mean?

The judge was leaning back in his chair and asking, "Tell me why you left your boy behind after Carol's death, Jake. I'd like to hear your reasons."

Jake glanced at Paige before he began, and she took it as an admission that he was slightly embarrassed by the things he was about to say. They would have been quite touching—if only they were true, Paige thought.

"Carol's death sent me reeling. We'd been married for nine years. We had Kenny. I didn't know what I was going to do without her."

She couldn't believe it. Why, that was an outright lie. She remembered what it had been like, the screaming fights, the anger. How could he pretend they'd been the perfect couple? Once again, she clenched her hands together in her lap and held back the retort she wanted so badly to make.

Jake went on. "I didn't know what I was going to do, period. But I knew I couldn't go on the way I had, roaming from town to town, working the mines, following the latest rumors of a gold strike. That was no way to raise a boy. And yet, there wasn't really much else I was qualified to do. How was I going to make a living for us?"

He looked over at Paige again and she could hardly keep from rolling her eyes in derision.

"There was only one thing I could do, and at the time, it seemed the best for both of us. I knew I had to leave Kenny with his grandparents. He needed the stability of a home I couldn't give him."

"It's hard for a boy of that age to lose his father, no matter what the reason," Judge Randall said sternly.

"Of course." Jake looked pained. "And I'm not sure I did the best thing by completely shutting myself out of his life for so long. At the time, it seemed best." He grimaced. "I was really thrown off kilter by Carol's death. I could hardly take care of myself, much less Kenny. And as time went by, I concentrated on finishing my education so I could come back in a better position to rejoin his life."

Judge Randall stared at him for a moment, then nodded. "Carol's death affected us all, but I daresay it hurt you more than anyone else."

Paige bit her tongue. How could the judge say such a thing? He'd been around in those days. He'd seen what was going on. Had he forgotten it all?

"I think Kenny's been hurt the most," Jake said. "That's why I want to ease myself back into his frame of reference gradually. I want to make sure I don't disrupt his life again."

Paige gasped. Up to now he'd been shading the truth, but that was an outright falsehood. He'd come home to grab Kenny and go. He'd said so over and over again ever since he'd arrived.

"Judge Randall, that's not true," she protested.

The judge lifted a hand, stopping her before she could launch into an accusation. "Paige, my dear, I'm not interested in hearing what you think is true or not true about what Jake is telling me. What I want to hear from you is why you think Jake should be kept away from his son."

That was easy. Her eyes flashed. "Because he's no good, Judge," she said bluntly. "You've seen what he did to my sister. He was the reason Carol died. He was the reason my father lost his medical practice. You know that. You know he ruined all our lives. And now he's come to do the same to Kenny. Don't you understand? Kenny's had a good, stable life with us. He's a happy boy. What's his life going to be like if Jake takes him?''

Jake turned and smiled at her, his blue eyes sparkling as though he found this all very humorous. "Who said I was taking him?''

"But... but that's what you came for.'' She gaped at him. What was he doing now? Couldn't Judge Randall see through this?

"I came to see my son, Paige.'' Jake's face was serious and his voice took on a pious tone. "I came to see if he could accept me back into his life. I certainly didn't come to cause any more disruption than absolutely necessary.''

"What?'' She couldn't believe it. How could he say such a thing right to her face? "Jake, you liar!''

"Now, now, Paige,'' Judge Randall said reprovingly.

Desperately, she turned to the older man. "No, don't you see? He's not telling you what he's told me. He swore he'd take Kenny.''

The judge didn't believe her. She could see it in his eyes, and she began to panic. All rational thought seemed to be slipping away. "Judge Randall, you can't let him get away with this.''

The judge looked at her pityingly. "He came to see his boy as far as I can tell. And I'm sorry, Paige, but I just can't see the harm in that.''

He couldn't see the harm. Was this a case of blind justice? Someone was certainly blind, and she didn't think it was her. He wasn't going to give her the restraining order. The writing was on the wall. She pulled her arms close in and hugged herself, feeling strangely out of breath, as though she'd been running. He wasn't going to help her. She was on her own.

"You're both family," he was saying. "You belong to each other. In my opinion, this is something you should be able to work out together in a reasonable fashion. This situation shouldn't have to go to a court of law to be settled. Before going to that extreme, I'd like to see what the two of you can do on your own."

She wasn't going to beg. She would do it if she thought it would get her anywhere, but she could see that it was no use. There was a buzzing in her ears, a strange drone that added to the feeling of unreality. This couldn't be happening. She glanced at Jake. There was an unearthly gleam in his eyes. He was looking right at her, and yet she had a creepy feeling he was seeing something else.

"Where is Kenny right now?" the judge was asking.

Paige looked at him blankly, then realized he must not have heard about the accident, or if he'd heard, he'd forgotten. So she would have to tell him about the hospital. But how could she? Jake was sitting right there.

Words stuck in her throat. She couldn't lie to Judge Randall. She glanced at Jake, stricken, and found him smiling like the cat that ate the canary.

"Why, he's with his Scout troop on a hiking trip," Jake said smoothly. "Isn't that right, Paige?"

She nodded quickly, hating herself for lying, hating Jake even more for making her lie, unable to meet the judge's gaze.

The judge went on, saying something about coming together and working things out, but she wasn't paying any attention. There was going to be no restraining order. So what was she going to do now?

She walked out of the court building in a daze, only vaguely aware that Jake was beside her. She had to think of something, and she had to come up with it quickly. So far, Jake was turning out to be a stronger adversary than she'd expected. She was going to have to work harder at this.

"Where are you going?"

She turned, realizing it was Jake who had spoken. She blinked at him, half blinded by the low afternoon sunshine at his back.

"Back to the shop," she said dully.

He nodded, frowning slightly as he studied her. "I'll see you at home later."

At home? He couldn't mean her home. She stopped and looked at him intently, and darned if he didn't mean exactly that.

"You're still going to stay at my apartment?" she asked, puzzled.

He shrugged. "Where else have I got to go?"

Anywhere else. Just about anywhere. She shook her head as though trying to clear it. Then she frowned and fixed him with a steady stare.

"How could you lie like that?" she asked him. "Don't you have any conscience at all?"

"Of course I have a conscience," he said, leaning against a tree trunk and smiling at her. "But I also have a finely honed sense of self-preservation. My survival skills are up to speed, Paige. If I'd told him the truth, I'd be standing on the wrong side of a restraining order right now. And you know as well as I do, that wouldn't be fair."

"I only know one thing, Jake," she said softly, gazing into his eyes with fierce determination. "You can't do this. You can't just walk in and take Kenny. Not while there's a breath left in my body."

"We'll see about that, Paige," he murmured, his direct gaze unsettling her. "We'll just have to see."

Her shoulders sagged. His broad grin told her he had things up his sleeve and she was beginning to feel overwhelmed. She turned to go, but he caught hold of her arm and held her there.

"It's not true, you know," he told her, his blue eyes suddenly serious. "What you said in there to the judge. I didn't have anything to do with your father's losing his license." His eyes darkened. "And when you come right down to it, I wasn't responsible for your sister's death."

"What?" She glared at him, shocked by his gall. But then, why should she be surprised? He'd shown his true colors just moments ago in his bald-faced deceptions, which he'd admitted to her. "You're such a liar, Jake," she breathed. "How can you stand it?"

He grimaced, and for just a moment, she thought she might actually have hurt him. But then he was grinning again, shaking his head, dropping his hand from her arm and letting her go.

"Someday you're going to realize the truth, Paige," he told her. "I only hope it doesn't injure you too badly when it happens."

"Liar," she whispered hotly.

He shrugged. "See you tonight," he said, saluting her as he turned away. "We'll have to talk. We have things to settle, you and me." He laughed. "And now it's official. An officer of the court has ordered us to negotiate with each other. I guess we don't have any choice, do we?"

THE SHOP WAS EMPTY when she arrived. She was thankful for that. She was in no mood to deal with customers.

Sara looked up from a catalog as Paige entered, her pretty face lighting with welcome when she saw who it was.

"Hi! I didn't expect you back so soon." She smiled. "It's quiet as a church around here. I can handle things. Why don't you go see Kenny?"

"I'm too upset," Paige said, trying to keep the faint tremor out of her voice. "I'm going to have to get myself together before I can go out there."

She sank into a chair at the corner of the desk where Sara sat. The young woman reached out to her, concerned.

"Paige, what is it? What's happened?"

"Jake Winslow is back in town," Paige said, closing her eyes and letting her head fall back.

"Jake Winslow?" Sara obviously did not recognize the name.

"Kenny's father," Paige said wearily. "He's back, and he wants Kenny."

"Oh, *that* Jake Winslow. But I thought..." Sara shook her head, puzzled. "I thought you and your parents were Kenny's guardians."

"We are. Or they are, anyway. We've been raising him for the last four years." She sighed. It seemed longer. It seemed like forever. "But that all counts for nothing with Jake. He swore he'd come for Kenny when the boy was thirteen. And here he is." She drew her arms around herself. She was always feeling chilly lately.

"But, doesn't he have to go through some sort of legal formality to take his child back?" Sara asked curiously. "After all this time . . ."

"Jake Winslow is not a man to stand still for the niceties of life." She snorted. "And anyway, he's got the judge wrapped around his finger. So I'm going to have to think of something else," she added softly, frowning as she thought hard. "Some way to keep Kenny out of his clutches."

Sara hesitated. "Maybe you should talk to a lawyer," she suggested.

Paige smiled bitterly. "The only lawyer I know is Judge Randall. And he's no good now."

She'd been so sure he would be her salvation. She'd realized from the beginning that she had a very weak case legally, but her family's friendship with the judge and his firsthand knowledge of the background of it all should have carried the day. Without that, she was afraid she didn't have a leg to stand on. No lawyer would take a case like hers, especially in this day of protecting the rights of fathers.

She sighed and Sara squeezed her hand. "Let me know if I can do anything to help. Kenny is such a love. I can't stand to think of your having to give him up."

"Me, neither." She tried to smile back and failed. "Damn Jake," she whispered brokenly, her eyes filling with tears.

Sara reached out and gave her a hug and she collected herself quickly. She hated crying in front of people, but her emotions seemed to be on a roller coaster right now. Grabbing a handkerchief, she wiped her face and managed a watery smile.

"I'm okay," she said briskly. "I'm going to be fine."

"You know," Sara was saying, her eyebrows knotted together, "I think I do remember Jake Winslow. He was the one who took Trent out to some kind of party and got him drunk the night before his high school graduation. Mother was so angry. Trent wasn't the type to do something like that." She shook her head, biting her lower lip. "Trent was valedictorian. Boy, did he look funny giving that speech with a hangover." She giggled, remembering.

"That would have been Jake, all right," Paige responded with a humorless laugh. "He was a wild one in those days."

"Yes, that's the way I remember him, on that motorcycle, his hair falling over his forehead." Sara shook her head. "Does he still ride a motorcycle?"

"No, he's given that up, at least." She thought for a moment, then went on. "He's not really quite the immature kid he was in those days. He has grown up, I'll give him that."

And that was what made him so very dangerous, she realized. Because he was still the same basic wild man underneath, but he'd learned how to deal with the world. He'd figured out how to fool those who had to be fooled in order for Jake to get what he wanted.

No, it would be unwise to continue to think of him as some out-of-control, overage juvenile delinquent.

He knew exactly what he was doing. Look at the way
he'd manipulated the judge.

"Why do we women always fall for the wild ones?"
Sara was asking, shaking her head ruefully.

"We don't always," Paige retorted, offended by the
thought. "I've never fallen for a wild one in my life.
And I never will."

"Haven't you?" Sara asked laughing. "You're one
of the lucky ones, I guess."

"I guess." Jumping up, Paige grabbed her purse. "I
think I will run out and see Kenny," she said impulsively. "Since you're here to hold down the fort."

"Yes, go," Sara urged. "I'll take care of the shop."

And so Paige went, feeling calmer now that she'd
had a chance to settle down. Sara was right. Jake was
a wild one. But he wasn't invincible, and he was bound
to make a mistake sooner or later. It was only a matter of time. She wasn't going to let herself give up just
yet.

JAKE WALKED SOFTLY, trying to look as if he knew
exactly what he was doing and where he was going.
He'd learned long ago that people who acted confidently rarely aroused suspicion. That knowledge had
served Jake well in the past, and it seemed to be
working again, because no one had challenged his
right to walk the hospital corridors, and now he was
approaching the door to the room where Kenny was
supposed to be.

Suddenly, he hesitated and the mask of confidence
slipped a little. He was about to face his son for the
first time in four years. Those years stretched out like
a chasm at his feet, something so wide and so deep,

crossing it was no sure thing. How did you explain something like that to a twelve-year-old boy? He wasn't sure there was a way.

The door to the room was ajar and he pushed it quietly, following it into the room. The television was on and cartoons lit the screen. But the boy on the bed wasn't watching. He was sound asleep, his head back against the pillow, his mouth slightly open.

Jake stood rooted to the spot, hardly breathing. It was the same boy, all right, only so very, very different. He stared at Kenny, devouring the sight of him, the sense of him, much as a starving man might devour a plate of food. He wanted to touch the boy, to tousle his hair and feel the curve of his shoulder, but he didn't want to wake him. Not yet.

A feeling came over him, grew inside him like a summer storm, choking him and making his eyes sting, making him tremble inside. He tried to force it back, but it kept coming, strangling him, overwhelming him. The more he took in about his son, the more powerful the feeling became.

And suddenly, he knew what it was. And once he knew what it was, he stopped fighting it, and a sense of relief joined the other feelings, and tears blinded him. Love. He loved Kenny like he'd never loved anything else in his life. He loved him with a strength and a bond that would never be broken. The four years didn't mean a thing. This was his son.

He left without waking the child. He'd heard Trent's voice down the hall mentioning Paige's name, and he decided the timing wasn't right for a reunion. He made it out of the room without being seen, and no one stopped him as he walked easily toward the elevator.

As he went, he took note of the exits and estimated the safest way to leave without being seen. He'd done fine by himself, but soon he would have a young boy with him, and getting out of here without been seen might be a bit dicier.

Stepping out of the building, he lifted his head and took a deep breath of fresh mountain air. The day seemed brighter somehow. He was going to be whole again.

CHAPTER SIX

"WHERE DID you go when you left the courthouse?" was the first thing Paige asked Jake when she got to the apartment that evening.

He'd made dinner. The table was set and wonderful smells were emanating from the kitchen. She should have been relieved to have that responsibility taken care of, but instead it just annoyed her more. It was one of his most irritating traits, this uncharacteristic behavior that went directly against the image she had of him—the image she had too much invested in to give up.

"I went to the market and came back here," he said smoothly. "Why?"

She tried to read the truth in his crystal blue eyes, but he was much too good at hiding his feelings. She turned away, putting down her purse and shrugging out of her suede jacket. She felt slightly comforted. He actually hadn't had time to do much more than that, had he?

She'd come home from the hospital just this side of a panic. Kenny had been waking up from a nap when she'd gone into the room. He'd rubbed his eyes and frowned at her.

"Who was that man?" he'd asked.

"What man?" she'd responded. "You mean the doctor?"

"No, there was a man in my room just now. He was looking at me."

Icy fingers had gripped her heart. Could the man have been Jake?

But it couldn't have been him. He would have given himself away, somehow, said something, asked her something if he'd found out Kenny was in the hospital. Besides, if he'd been in Kenny's room, he surely would have woken the boy and talked to him.

She knew he didn't believe the hiking story, that much was obvious. Still, he couldn't know about the hospital unless someone had told him.

Paige picked up her purse and her jacket and headed for her bedroom. He stayed where he was, watching her as she walked down the hall. He knew why she'd asked, and it worried him. Had someone seen him and reported to Paige? Kenny couldn't have seen him. He'd been sound asleep.

And another thing—he still hadn't found out exactly what had landed Kenny in the hospital. He knew if he confronted Paige now, she would tell him everything.

But maybe she would do more than that. In her frame of mind, she might take the boy off somewhere and try to hide him. He couldn't risk that.

Besides, Kenny seemed to be doing all right from what the nurse had said. There was nothing Jake could do to speed the healing process.

No, he would just have to wait. Tomorrow he'd go back to the hospital and he'd find out everything he needed to know. And he would talk to Kenny. That was what he was most looking forward to.

He knew Paige was upset. He would be, too, in her position. But he couldn't help that. Kenny was his son. Seeing him there in that hospital bed had reaffirmed the bond he felt with the boy like nothing he'd ever dreamed possible. He was more determined than ever. He was going to take Kenny, come hell or high water. There was no alternative.

He began serving up the dinner, carrying the plates to the table. The steaks were just right, still sizzling under their glaze of mushroom-and-wine sauce, and the baked potatoes were steaming, white fluffy stuffing coming out of the dark skins like popcorn out of their kernels. Even the green beans looked perfect, their bright emerald color a contrast to the slivered almonds. He smiled to himself. He was getting damn good at this.

Turning as Paige entered the room, he couldn't help but give her an admiring look. She'd changed into slacks and a soft pink sweater and she'd taken her hair down. It was falling in waves around her face, making her look younger. For just a moment, he looked for the little spark that reminded him of Carol. Then he pushed that thought away. He didn't really want to be reminded of Carol.

"Dinner looks wonderful," she said faintly, not looking particularly pleased about it. "Thanks. I appreciate your doing this."

"My pleasure." With a dramatic flourish, he offered her a seat at the table. "Will you join me?"

"Thank you," she said again as she accepted the chair he held out for her, knowing she was being too stiff for the occasion, but unable to relax with the man who was planning to ruin her life.

But the food was marvelous. Surveying the spread set out before her, she could hardly believe it. She looked up at him questioningly as he poured her a glass of golden wine.

"What are you, some kind of master chef?" she asked.

He gave her a crooked grin as he settled the bottle into a bucket of ice. "I've done my fair share of cooking for men in mining camps. I've had a bit of practice." He sank into the seat across from her.

She took a bite of the steak and shook her head. It practically melted in her mouth. And the sauce was out of this world. "I'll bet you didn't cook them anything like this."

"No, nothing like this."

His eyes sparkled and for just a second, she couldn't look away. But she had to. She had to hold back this pleasure she felt in things he did. Because she couldn't allow him to get too close. She knew he was angling for an advantage. Everything he did was calculated for some gain. She couldn't allow herself to fall for it. Steeling herself, she took another bite and avoided his gaze.

"I took a chance that you weren't going out with Barry tonight," he said easily, taking a long sip of wine.

She threw him a dirty look. "Barry and I don't date all that often," she snapped.

"Yeah, I could see that." He chuckled as he cut into his own steak. "You two don't really have the hang of it yet, do you? It stands to reason, if you dated a lot, you'd be better at it by now."

She stared down at her plate, counting to ten. She wasn't going to let him draw her into a fight. Chewing methodically, she ignored him—or tried to, anyway.

He watched her, hiding his amusement as best he could. "There's been something I've been meaning to ask you, Miss Paige," he said teasingly a moment later. "What right did you have to go and get so pretty while I was gone?"

Her dark eyes flashed up and met his. "I haven't changed a bit," she said defensively. But she couldn't look away.

He smiled. "Oh, yes, you have. You are a good-looking woman."

It took effort, but she managed to pull her gaze away. She plunked down her fork and reached for her glass of water. "I've always been a good-looking woman, Jake. You just didn't notice. Something must have blinded you."

He stared at her. She meant Carol and he knew it.

"Something, huh?" He chuckled. "Oh, Paige, Paige, that's hitting below the belt."

Paige glared at him across the table. "Let's just eat," she suggested icily "Let's dispense with chatting, for once."

"Oh, no," he said calmly, passing her the sour cream for her potato. "Light conversation makes the meal. Didn't you know that? It helps the digestive process."

"Only if it's pleasant," she informed him, attacking her steak with an energy fueled by annoyance. "Bickering makes for stress."

"Who's bickering?" His wide eyes were all innocence. "I just want to talk."

She set her lips, refusing to meet his gaze, and chewed stonily.

He restrained a knowing grin and went on. "So, tell me, are you and Barry planning to get serious about each other?"

Her eyes flashed. "No. Not at all."

"Good." He gave her a wry look. "The chemistry really isn't right, you know. I just wanted to make sure you weren't making a mistake."

Her only mistake was inviting him to stay in her apartment with her. She was regretting it now. The food was wonderful, but the company stank.

"Barry's been a good friend to me," she said, doggedly cutting into her meat. She wasn't going to let him play games with her senses.

"Yeah, he was always a good friend of Carol's, too."

His voice was hard, more than ironic, when he made the statement. There was something bitter in it. She forgot her pledge and looked up, trying to divine the cause. "What do you mean by that?" she demanded.

He shook his head. "Nothing."

"I thought he was your friend."

"Sure. Growing up, we were inseparable. We did everything together. We got our mountain bikes at the same time, joined the baseball team together, shared a car when we first got our licenses."

"That's what I mean. You were best friends."

"Yes, we were." His eyes hardened. "Right up until when I started dating Carol." He gave her a long look. "You see, that was one thing I wasn't prepared to share with him."

She stared at him, her mouth open, and then she rejected his point. "Oh, come on. Barry had plenty of girlfriends of his own."

Jake studied her for a moment, then shrugged. "You're probably right."

"No, really. What are you trying to do? What do you have against Barry these days?"

"It doesn't matter, Paige. Drop it."

It was obvious he wasn't going to open up again, so she returned to her delicious food, and for a while, he honored her request for silence at the table. He was going to get the message soon. She didn't want to fight with him. She wouldn't fight with him. Unless forced to.

But he wasn't quite ready to give up, and pretty soon he was talking again. "So, let's discuss your love life," he said casually.

She turned on him. "Why are you so fascinated by my love life?" she demanded, incensed.

His face was open and innocent. "I don't know. I don't have one myself. I thought I might get some kicks listening to tales of yours."

She pressed her lips together and turned back to her food. "No way," she muttered darkly.

"You can't tell me you don't have one."

"I didn't say that."

"As I remember, you always had some poor slob hanging around."

"You are so observant."

He grinned. "Of course. Let's see. It seems to me you were going with Terry Shaw, last I heard."

"That's right."

"Whatever happened to good old Terry?"

"He's practicing corporate law in San Francisco. He's married and has twin boys."

"Oh. Well, before that, there was Johnny Cruz. Whatever happened to Johnny?"

"He's long gone. He's a structural engineer in San Diego."

"So that's what happened, is it? Everyone but Barry deserted town and you were stuck with him." He waited, but she didn't answer. "Are you and he the only younger people left?" he asked at last.

She turned and looked at him. Actually, he didn't seem to be teasing her any longer. And suddenly, she found herself answering quite naturally.

"Just about. It is hard in a town like this. There aren't that many men. At least not ones you'd want to date."

He nodded, looking at her. "I knew it had to be something," he said quietly. "Either that, or you'd just gotten real picky."

For some reason, that made her smile. "There's something of that in it, too. I am picky."

He smiled back and she looked away quickly.

"Why have you stayed?" he asked.

"Well, there are a lot of reasons. First, I didn't want to leave my parents alone after Carol's death. Then, I really do like this town. But third, and most important of all..."

The pause hung in the air. They both seemed to be holding their breaths, waiting. "Because of Kenny," Paige continued.

He nodded slowly. He'd known that was coming. Why had he bothered to ask?

She looked away, aware that she'd brought up the essence of their struggle and equally aware that he wouldn't want to deal with it right now. Neither did she, actually. Fortunately, the meal was over, and she could make a getaway.

"That was very good." She rose to clear the table.

He stood along with her, taking his own plate. "I'm glad you liked it. Sorry I didn't have time to make a dessert."

She couldn't help but smile. "What did you have in mind? Baked Alaska or cherries jubilee?"

He smiled back. "Neither. What would you have said to a macadamia nut fudge mousse?"

"Oh." She groaned. "I would have said, 'I surrender.' You wouldn't be so cruel."

"I can be just as cruel as I need to be."

He was still smiling, but his words chilled her. She knew he would do anything to get what he wanted. She suppressed a shiver.

It was a mistake, she decided as she ferried the dishes to the sink, to let him take the initiative all the time. She couldn't just hang back and wait to see what he had in mind for her. She still didn't know what she was going to do now that her plan for the restraining order had fallen through. But she had to do something. And in order to get a better grip on things, she was going to have to confront him more—let him know she wasn't fooled.

They finished clearing the dishes in silence, then all thoughts of a getaway gone from her mind, she turned and looked him squarely in the face.

"You said you wanted to talk something over," she said. "What is it you think we have to talk about?"

He gazed back, his eyes half closed, as though her spunk amused him. "You," he said softly. Turning, he flopped down on the couch and patted a place for her to join him. "You and me."

"You and me?" she echoed, hesitating before warily slipping down onto the couch beside him.

"Yes. We have to resolve how you feel about me."

"The way I feel about you?" That was easy. "I'm quite resolved, thank you. I know exactly how I feel about you. I've known you practically all my life."

"That's true." His blue eyes flickered with an emotion she couldn't identify, and that was surprising, because he was usually so good at hiding how he felt.

"But that doesn't mean you know the truth about me," he added.

Her mouth twisted with irony. "You mean there's more?"

He nodded, a slight smile on his lips at her sarcastic tone. "There's more. A lot more." His eyes darkened. "Tell me what you think you know about me."

What was he trying to do? She didn't have a clue, but she knew he was up to something, and she answered carefully.

"I know everything about you. You were my brother-in-law. You were married to my sister."

"That doesn't mean anything." He raised an eyebrow. "Do you think I know everything about you?"

She almost laughed out loud. "Of course not."

"But the same connections apply."

"Yes, but you never paid any attention to me," she reminded him. "I was always 'Little Sister' to you, just a brat, in the way."

"That's not true." His smile was suddenly slow and sensual in a way that disturbed her. "You'd be surprised."

She swallowed, not pleased with the way he could turn a mood on with just a twist of his mouth and a glint in his eye. "I doubt it."

He laughed, and something in the timbre of his voice sent a shiver down her spine.

"So go on," he said. "Tell me all about myself."

She licked her lips and settled as far away from him on the couch as she could without being obvious about it. Then she began, choosing her words with care, hoping not to fall into whatever trap he had set for her.

"I know that your father left when you were young. I know that your mother worked two jobs to support her family, worked her fingers to the bone..." She couldn't resist a little editorializing. "And you repaid her by becoming the wildest boy in school."

"Whoa. Wait just a minute." His head went back and his eyes narrowed. "What makes you say that?"

"It's true." How could he possibly deny it? "You were. You were always running around on that motorcycle, getting into trouble."

"Trouble?" He jabbed an accusing finger at her. "What do you mean by trouble?"

"I don't know." She shook her head. "Trouble. Bad-boy stuff."

He pinned her with his hard gaze. "Can you name one time I was arrested for something?"

"No. I didn't keep that close a watch."

His mouth twisted. "Can you name one time I hurt someone?"

She hesitated. Hurt feelings probably didn't count, did they? There was that one incident, the so-called "famous fight," where he beaten Ricky Samms to a pulp in front of the local teen hangout. But she didn't want to bring that up. As it turned out, he'd been the knight in shining armor there, once the facts were known. So it was probably best to ignore that memory.

"I was a lot younger," she said defensively. "You were gone by the time I got to high school."

He grinned, and though there was no humor in his eyes, there was a look of triumph in his expression. "You can't name one 'bad' thing I did. You just have this image of me being some kind of junior criminal, but you have no facts to back it up."

He was right. But she wasn't going to cave. "*Were* you ever arrested?" she asked.

His grin faded. "That's none of your business."

It was her turn for a triumph of sorts. "See?" she said saucily.

He grabbed her wrist, his hand loosely circling it. "Don't get smart with me, Paige," he said, smiling again. "I'm not a punching bag."

She looked down at his hand on her wrist and her heart beat quickly, scaring her. "Don't," she said, pulling away and rubbing where his touch had been.

"Okay," he said softly. "I won't." But his eyes were burning with some special knowledge, and when she met them, she winced. It was almost as though he knew something about her that she didn't know. She didn't like that at all.

They needed to get back to the subject at hand. Paige sat up straight and pushed what had just happened out of her mind.

"Okay, this is what else I know about you," she said as calmly as she was able. "You were not a model student."

"I graduated from high school."

"Okay, so you didn't drop out." She glared at him. "You got the valedictorian drunk the night before graduation." She was glad she'd remembered. "There! That's pretty bad, isn't it?"

"Who told you that?"

Hah! She'd finally stumped him. "Trent's sister, Sara, was reminiscing this afternoon," she told him smugly. "She gave me all the gory details."

He threw back his head and laughed. "Okay. I'm guilty on that one."

But she wasn't about to let it go that easily. "You'll admit that was bad?" she insisted.

He looked at her and smiled. "Sure. Though I hardly think it qualifies for capital punishment."

Maybe not. But it certainly was evidence that could be used in a court of opinion. She smiled back. "Okay. So you went to junior college for a while. I heard you got into some sort of trouble and had to leave."

He dismissed that with a wave of his hand. "No proof."

"Are you saying what I heard is wrong?"

"I'm saying it's half-right. I didn't get into any kind of trouble. I got bored, that was all."

She sniffed. "Well, what our mothers always tell us turns out to be right—get a bad reputation and people will always think the worst of you."

"You're probably right."

She nodded. "Back to the story of your life. You then went off to some mining camp north of Sacramento but you kept writing to Carol."

"Carol kept writing to me. I was responding."

"Which came first, the chicken or the egg?"

"Carol's letters to me came first." He saw the skepticism in her face and shook his head. "Believe me. I was there."

"All I know is that you became a sort of dream goal to Carol. I remember that really clearly. You were her beacon on the hill, her guiding light. She was always threatening to run off with you. That was what she would tell Mother whenever they got into a fight. 'I'm going with Jake,' she would say. 'I don't have to stay here and take this. I can go be free with Jake.'"

"Be free with Jake," he repeated softly. "What a joke."

He was mostly talking to himself and she ignored his comment.

"But then all that died down," she continued. "Carol had a pretty good senior year, as I remember. No more talk about running off with you. And then she went to the university at Santa Barbara. And the next thing we knew, she was marrying you."

He nodded. What could he say? It was true.

Paige stared at him, getting angry again, wanting to say something, not sure what. "She was much too young," she said at last.

He lifted his gaze to hers. "She was nineteen," he said, slightly defensive.

"You dragged her right out of school . . ."

He scoffed. "She hated college."

Outrage flashed through her. He couldn't do this, he couldn't rewrite her personal history this way. He had no right. "She loved it! She was having a wonderful time in Santa Barbara."

He straightened and looked her in the face. "No, Paige. I'm here to tell you. She was not having a wonderful time. She was flunking out."

Her heart was beating faster with fear now. She wasn't sure what she was afraid of, but she knew it had something to do with what he was saying. She didn't want to hear it. "I don't believe you."

"It's true," he insisted, all confidence. "She ran away from Santa Barbara and hitchhiked to Tailings where I was working in a mining camp."

Her hands gripped each other in her lap, her knuckles white. "What? I never heard that before."

"She never told you?"

"No." She looked at him suspiciously. "She never did."

"She wanted to stay with me, live with me. But that place was a little too rough for women. So I quit and we got married and came home to horrify you all with the news."

She didn't believe him. Why should she believe him? He was a liar. He would say anything to make up for what he'd done. And there was so much to make up for.

"You make it sound like she held a gun to your head."

His mouth twisted. "A shotgun wedding in reverse?" He moved uncomfortably. It wasn't easy looking back and analyzing what had actually happened, who said what, who did what. They'd married, but he couldn't remember now if he'd really wanted to. It had just seemed like something that had to be done at the time. His own sense of morality had demanded it. But that was something Paige wouldn't understand, feeling about him the way that she did. Still, that shouldn't keep him from telling her the truth of how it was.

"No, it wasn't anything like that," he said, shaking his head. "I'm the one who wanted to get married."

Her body jerked as though he'd hit her. She hated him more and more. She itched to throw something at his head. Did he have any idea how what he was saying was hurting her? "In other words, she would have been happy shacking up," she said evenly. "Is that what you're trying to tell me?"

"No." A look came over his face that told her he hadn't realized how his words might sound until now. "No, Paige, I didn't mean that."

"You meant exactly that." She had to stay calm, had to fight him, but her emotions were getting the best of her. Forcing back her anger, she added, "For some reason, you seem to think you can convince me that you are some sort of misunderstood saint and Carol was the wild one."

"Paige...." He should have known better than to bring this up.

"You don't fool me, Jake." For some reason, her eyes were full of tears and his image was swimming before her. "You can't make me turn on my sister. You might as well stop trying."

Was that what he'd been trying to do? He couldn't really deny it, not even to himself. He was tired of being considered the villain. He certainly wasn't perfect, but he wasn't evil, either, and he knew he needed to make that clear if he was going to get Kenny out of here without a fight. "Paige..."

She could hardly make him out through her tears, but suddenly his hands were on her shoulders, and she began to struggle, resisting his touch.

"Leave me alone," she said, but she was sobbing and he was pulling her close, and then she was pressed against his wide chest, letting loose all the emotions that had been building up inside her for days.

She had to cry. She knew this wasn't the time or the place, but it had to come out, and she let it go, clutching him, letting his warmth seep through her. His arms felt so good. His face was buried in her hair, and the sense of him sent a thrill searing deep into her soul. His hard, strong maleness with all its protective power was just what she needed right now, and she couldn't resist it. It enveloped her like a hot, comforting bath, washing over her, rendering her limp, turning her muscles to water.

He'd started out meaning to comfort her, to get her to stop thinking about Carol, to stop the flow of tears. But she'd melted so easily into his arms, and now that he had her there, she felt so right. The curve of her back, the slightly spicy scent of her hair, the way she clung to him, all the elements seemed to blend together into a package too warm and delicious to resist.

He forgot she was Carol's sister. He forgot he was in a struggle with her for the life and love of his son. He only felt her need as part of his own, and he responded without conscious thought or effort.

She wasn't sobbing any longer. The tears had stopped. But she couldn't pull herself out of the embrace. It was too good, too nourishing, and when his mouth found hers, she welcomed it without hesitation and felt his heat pour into her like hot brandy, like molten gold, gliding down her throat and into her body, changing her, leaving her breathless.

She took him in as though she'd been starved for what he was offering...and perhaps she had been. This was no casual kiss, no tentative exploration. He took her as though he had a right, and she responded as she'd never responded to a kiss before.

As he slowly drew away, her lips clung to his and she found herself yearning toward him without shame, still in his spell, caught in the enchantment of the moment.

He came back to reality before she did. Staring down at her, he was appalled by what he'd done. He hadn't meant to do it. And now he'd probably ruined everything. But she felt so good....

"Oh!" She was coming out of the fog and realizing what had just happened to her—to them. "Jake!" Suddenly, her muscles worked again and she leaped from the couch. Her hand went to her mouth. What had she done? "Oh, my God."

He stood, trying to stop her. "Paige, wait..."

But she couldn't wait. She had to get out of there. Without another glance his way, she raced for her bedroom, slamming the door, and leaning against it, trembling.

She'd kissed him—her sister's husband! She'd let herself feel things she'd been fighting for years. And that meant she had to face something she'd been avoiding. Her words to Sara earlier that day came back to haunt her. "I've never fallen for a wild one and I never will." Had she been fooling herself all this time?

No. Closing her eyes tightly, she refused to accept that. It couldn't be. It just flat couldn't be.

He'd caught her in a moment of weakness and she'd let physical attraction take over. That was all. It had to be all.

Opening her eyes, she made her way to the bed and sat down, not turning on the light. It was better in the dark. The demons didn't look so large.

She had to admit she'd always been attracted to Jake. She couldn't deny that any longer, much as she'd like to. She'd always felt guilty about it. He was her sister's husband, after all. But the attraction had always been there.

And that was what made him so dangerous. She had to be strong, that was all. She had to resist the feelings that seemed to overwhelm her from time to time. She could do it. She'd done it before.

But the memory of that kiss hadn't been with her before. It swept over her again, causing the tears to flow again.

"Damn you, Jake Winslow," she whispered. "Damn you to hell."

She'd opened Pandora's box. Would she ever be able to get it closed again?

CHAPTER SEVEN

THE NEXT MORNING, she was prepared. He wasn't going to tempt her again, not with his fluffy omelets, not with his provocative presence. She'd spent most of the night going over what she should do, and she was ready for anything.

Anything but meeting his gaze and keeping the memories of the night before from flooding her mind. She stood in the doorway of the kitchen and he stood in the hall. His eyes were still sleepy, his hair still mussed from the night, his gaze full of what had happened the last time they'd been together, and she found herself stuttering incoherently.

"I wanted to...uh...Jake, I..."

He stared at her for a moment, taking in her discomfort, and then he stuck out a hand. "I want to call a truce," he said firmly. "Let's shake on it."

She stared at his offered hand as though it might bite, not touching it. Why should she trust him? "I don't know what you're talking about," she said stiffly.

"Sure you do." He grabbed her hand, his fingers curling around it easily. "I'm...well, let's just say that kiss last night didn't mean a thing, okay?" he said, shaking her hand up and down as if it were a limp pump handle. "I mean, it just happened. We were both feeling a little sad and sorry and we just needed some comfort, that's all.'' He tried a smile, though he didn't get much of a response. "After all, we're practically family, like the judge says.''

She yanked her hand away and glared at him. She was in no mood to be charmed this morning. "That was no brotherly kiss, and you know it.''

He groaned, leaning his head back. She was right, but so what? Better they should both forget about it.

"Damn it, Paige, you're making it hard to put this thing behind us.''

She set her mouth with determined solemnity. "I don't believe in trying to live lies, Jake. It never works. Whenever you try to hide the truth, bad things happen.''

His face changed and his eyes hardened as he looked candidly into her eyes. She knew he was thinking about the big lie that stood between them, the lie about where Kenny actually was, and she flushed. She didn't like lying, didn't like having to stick to this one. But what else could she do? It was best to forget that and stick to the current problem. She was on firmer ground there.

"We can't just put what happened behind us,'' she said quickly, trying to get his mind back on another track. "We can't pretend it didn't happen. We can't undo it. We simply have to make sure it never happens again.''

He grimaced, shrugging and throwing his hands out, palms up. "Paige,'' he said softly, almost singing, "it was just one of those things.''

She shuddered. "If you break out into song about gossamer wings, I swear I'll . . .''

"You have no appreciation for the arts, is that it?"

She shook her head. He was trying to be charming again, and she couldn't get caught up in it. If she wasn't careful, he would make her forget all that her hard work had accomplished during the night. She was going to be strong, and she was going to resist him.

"Art has nothing to do with this, Jake," she snapped, turning and walking into the kitchen. "You're all craft, that's what you are."

"In other words, you don't trust me." The statement was made simply, without bitterness, but there was an underlying hardness to his tone that gave her chills.

And yet, what did he expect? What had he ever done to build confidence in his integrity?

Her answering laugh was hollow. "Surely this isn't a shock to you," she said as she reached out to pour herself a cup of coffee.

"No," he replied, sinking backward onto a kitchen chair and leaning on the backrest. "But I had hoped you might give me a chance this time."

She turned and looked down at him. "A chance?" He was dreaming. Or amazingly arrogant. "A chance?" she repeated incredulously.

He looked up at her from beneath his mussed hair, his eyes clear and frank. "Yeah, Paige. A chance."

He really meant it. She hesitated, taking a sip of the steaming coffee, wondering why he cared what she thought of him. "What sort of chance?" she asked suspiciously.

"A chance to prove to you that I'm not such a bad guy."

She rolled her eyes. "Oh, please."

He shrugged. "You've never given me that chance, Paige. When I first started coming to your house to take Carol out, you lurked around corners and gave me the evil eye every time. You hated me from the first time you saw me."

"No," she said softly, her hands wrapped around the hot coffee mug, remembering, too. "No. I saw you many times before you ever started coming to the house."

He looked up blankly. "You did?"

She nodded, gazing at him speculatively, recalling the past like an old faded film. She'd always known who he was, always seen him around town. But there had been a time when she'd been obsessed with him. Would he remember? "That summer when you worked as a lifeguard at the park pool."

His eyes narrowed, recalling the time with pleasure. "Ah, yes."

She noted his look and her jaw firmed. "When all the little girls in town sat around the deck and giggled about you."

He grinned, enchanted by the memory. "You were one of those little girls?"

She nodded again, but she didn't smile. "We watched you a lot that summer. We watched every move you made. You were our hero. We made up stories about you, lovely, romantic stories, and giggled about them while we watched you flex your muscles."

"Jeez, Paige."

He looked embarrassed and she was surprised at that, but somehow pleased. It was nice to think he might have a bit of a conscience, after all.

"Then, in August, the older girls came back from cheerleading camp and took over the pool. We watched them come on to you. And then we watched you make out with—" she began to tick them off on the fingers of one hand "—Debbie Clinger and Sharon Cruz and Midge Fontana and Carly Parks..."

He sighed with happy recollection. "Yeah, those were the days, all right."

"You broke our hearts," she said calmly.

He laughed, looking at her as though she should be in on the joke. "You all were a little young to have your hearts broken just because I didn't pay that much attention once the older girls arrived."

"No." She shook her head. "That wasn't it. You broke our hearts when we realized you didn't care what girl you were with, as long as you were with a girl."

He blinked at her. "What?"

"That's when you lost all your chances with me, Jake Winslow," she said coolly. "That's when I realized what a rat you really were."

He gaped at her. "Paige, I was sixteen. I was just learning how to kiss. A sixteen-year-old boy needs a lot of practice. And when there are older girls around, willing to give lessons . . ."

"So when you showed up a year or two later," she went on, ignoring his rebuttal, "saying you were crazy about my sister, you can hardly blame me for taking it all with a grain of salt."

He shook his head, looking at her, his silver-blue eyes glittering. "You do hold a grudge, don't you, lady?" he said softly, impressed and just a bit unsettled by her determination. She was just as complex as Carol had been, and that surprised him. And spooked him. Beware of complex women—that was what he always said.

"I do," she responded, putting down the mug and preparing to leave. "So don't go asking for chances, Jake. You used them all up years ago."

He watched her, fascinated, watched the morning sunlight streaming in the kitchen window illuminate her hair, watched the way she moved, the jerky movements that belied her calm facade. She was nervous. Why?

Because of him. He knew it in a flash. His presence affected her. Was she scared of him?

No, he didn't think that was it. She was confident enough, strong enough to face him.

Was she angry at him? Yes, in a way. But it was more than that. There was something else, something that was telegraphed by the look in her eyes, something he could sense in her voice, feel in her movements.

She was attracted to him. And she hated herself for it.

He wanted to touch her, to reach out and run his hand along the length of her arm. But he wouldn't do it. They weren't meant to be lovers, no matter how much fire flared between them.

"No more chances, huh?" he said lazily. "You're a hard woman, Paige. Can't you see I've reformed?"

She gave him a look and started for the door, then turned back. "By the way, we can't have a repeat of what happened last night. So, just to make sure it doesn't happen, I think one of us should go. And since you don't seem to have anyplace to go to, I'm thinking of sleeping on the sofa in the back office at the store until you leave town. That way—"

He rose from the chair with a movement that almost sent it flying across the room. Dark anger filled his face and he stood before her with both hands balled into fists. But his voice, when he spoke, was soft and persuasive.

"Don't be ridiculous, Paige," he said, his eyes burning. "You don't have to be scared of me. I promise I won't kiss you again."

She studied him intently. He looked sincere. He wouldn't try to kiss her again. But could she promise she wouldn't kiss him? She steeled herself to resist his influence. She could never let him know how close she came to needing his touch, his affection. Knowledge was power, and letting him know that would give him something to hold over her she couldn't afford to let him have.

"I'd rather not risk it, Jake," she replied crisply. "You should be just as happy to have me out of your hair, anyway."

"Paige, don't." He stood before her, an odd combination of aggression and vulnerability. "Don't do this." He shrugged, his eyes darkening. "I didn't come back here to seduce you, or to mess up anybody's life. I just came to... to get my boy."

She heard the pain in his voice, the yearning, and for a moment, something choked in her throat. But she couldn't weaken. Not now.

"And that is the one thing I can't let you do," she said softly. "Don't you see? Kenny belongs here, with his family. It's not fair for you to try to take him away. It's not fair to us, it's not fair to Kenny."

The vulnerability faded from his eyes and only aggression was left behind. "He's my son, Paige," he said firmly. "I have a right to take him, and that is what I'm going to do."

She leaned against the wall, despair sweeping over her. When was she going to learn? Every time he tried to charm her, she fell for it, and every time, it was an act. He was fighting her just as hard as she was fighting him, and there was no room for mercy. If she wanted to keep Kenny, she was going to have to use everything in her arsenal. She couldn't let pity or compassion or anything else stand in her way. She had to be strong, just as strong as he was.

Straightening, she glared at him. "You may have the right," she said, "but you don't deserve it. As far as I'm concerned, you forfeited your rights years ago."

He was smoldering, but her words gave him pause. "What are you talking about?" he asked.

"You did a terrible thing to Kenny, Jake," she said, anger hardening her resolve and helping toughen her stance. "You went off and left him when he needed you most. He'd just lost his mother, and you took away his father, too."

Jake's head went back as though she'd slapped him, but his jaw jutted out. "I left him with people he loved, people who loved him," he responded dismissively.

"Yes. But that doesn't make up for it." She took a deep breath and forced herself to go on, making the speech she'd been planning all night. "You walked away when he needed you, and now you expect him to welcome you back with open arms? I mean, what are you thinking? Kenny isn't some pet who can be left in a kennel while you go on an extended vacation. That's the way you left him, as though he meant no more than that. And you expect no repercussions? What you did will affect Kenny for the rest of his life. There are no second chances for that. It's over. It's done."

There. She'd said all the horrible things she'd wanted to say ever since he'd returned, and her heart was beating so fast, she was afraid she was going to black out.

"There's some truth in what you say," Jake said coldly. "But that's just it. If I leave, if I don't take him with me, I'll just be making things worse, won't I? I'll just be compounding the damage I've done."

A flicker of panic raced through her. "Worse?" she responded quickly. "How can you say that? He's happy here. He's settled. He has a full and happy life. And you want to rip that away from him, turn his life upside down again. He doesn't know you, Jake. You're a stranger to him. How can you think of taking him away from everything he loves?" She stopped for breath, then added the crowning blow. "And anyway, what makes you think he wants you back?"

He didn't answer, and she put a hand against the wall to steady herself. "Leave us alone, Jake. Please, go back where you came from. Leave us alone."

She could see the turmoil in his face. Had she gotten through to him? She waited for his response. Would he demand to know where Kenny was right now?

But he didn't say a word. She frowned as he turned away and walked down the hall and out of sight.

There was no way of knowing what he was thinking. She'd taken her best shots, said things she'd never thought she'd say to another human being. And now she had to fight remorse, fight the urge to go after him, to comfort him, for God's sake. What was the matter with her? How was she going to be able to fight him effectively if she had this emotional response to him?

Turning, she went blindly for the door. She had to get away... and keep away from Jake. He was getting more dangerous all the time. And she had a last, desperate plan to put into action. If only she could manage the nerve to do it.

But her plan was going to have to wait a while. She needed to see Kenny. There was a hunger inside her to see him, touch him, make sure he was still there in that hospital room.

"I WANT TO GO HOME," was the first thing he wailed when she arrived by his bedside. "I'm so bored!"

She tousled his hair, her heart full at the sight of him. "You'll go home when the doctor says so," she told him. "I brought you some books. And a fancy new solitaire game."

Kenny sighed and looked at his presents without much enthusiasm. "Thanks," he said sadly. "But I just want to go play baseball."

She laughed and sat beside him. "You'll get to play plenty once you get back home." She grinned at him. "I have one more thing for you. A surprise."

"What?" Suddenly, he sniffed the air, and his eyes widened. "Did you...did you really?"

"Yup." Reaching into the depths of her purse, she pulled out a cheeseburger, still warm in its waxed paper. "Hurry. Don't let the nurses catch us."

Kenny crowed with delight, but he didn't need the warning. The burger was gone in seconds, devoured with a sigh and a small burp of pleasure. "Man, that was great," he said, stretching back as though sated with sensual delight. "When I get my own apartment, that's all I'll ever eat."

"That and hot fudge sundaes. I know." She smiled, remembering her own vows along those lines when she was his age. Then the smile faded, and she looked at him speculatively. Should she say something about Jake? Should she warn him? Or would that just set him off? She wasn't sure what to do, and before she could decide, familiar voices could be heard calling out from down the hall.

"It's your grandparents," she said, reaching out to take the burger wrappers. "I'll hide the evidence."

The papers had barely cleared the wastebasket rim, when her parents stepped into the room.

"Hello, darling," her mother cried, going straight for Kenny.

"Hey, sport," said her father. "Look what we brought you."

He held up a bag from the same fast-food restaurant Paige had raided.

"A cheeseburger. Bet you haven't seen good food like this for a while, have you?"

Kenny laughed and looked at Paige. She grinned back at him and gave her head a slight shake.

"Gee, Grandpa, that's great," Kenny said happily. "I was dying for one of those. You're the greatest."

"I'm the greatest," Dr. Kenton repeated, giving his daughter a jab in the ribs with his elbow. "See there? Kenny says so."

"And Kenny never lies," Paige responded smoothly. "Do you, Ken?"

"Nope." He began unwrapping the cheeseburger with a gleam in his eye. "Anyone else coming to see me today?" he asked hopefully as he prepared to take his first big bite.

"Not that I know of," she said quickly. "And if anyone does show up, we're going to frisk them for contraband food at the door."

"Let the boy eat," her father said, gazing at his grandson affectionately. "It's good for him." He turned to Paige with a smug smile. "See how much he looks like Carol already?" he said softly. "Just like your sister. He's going to be a good-looking man, this one. Just wait and see."

It was the sort of thing he always said, the sort of thing she expected from him, but for some reason, this time it cut into her like the thrust of a very sharp knife. She didn't want to hear comparisons to Carol. Why was everyone and everything in this family always compared to Carol? Why couldn't they let her go?

Everything Kenny did, from his athletic ability to the cartoons he'd taken to drawing lately, was attributed to Carol—her genes, her influence. That was natural, she supposed. After all, Carol was his mother. But—darn it all, Paige had been raising him for four years. She was pretty sure she'd had her own effect on him. She was the one who'd taught him how to draw those cartoons. She was the one who'd taught him how to toss a fastball. She was the one who'd taught him table manners and how to write thank-you notes and how to play the harmonica. And yet, at one time or another, she'd heard every one of those things credited to Carol.

She turned away, out of the room, so that they wouldn't see her annoyance, but her father followed her. A tall, distinguished-looking man, he walked with a slight stoop, as though there were a weight on his shoulders. But his face was still handsome, his eyes still blue, his hair full and white.

"What's going on with this Jake business?" he asked her sternly. "Has Kenny seen him yet?"

She shook her head. "No. Kenny doesn't even know he's in town. Don't tell him, okay? I'd rather he didn't know just yet."

Her father shrugged. "Don't worry about that. I sure won't tell him. But listen, how's it going with that restraining order? I tried to get a call in to Randall, but he was in a meeting."

She took his hand in hers. She could see the worry in his eyes. He'd never been like this in the old days. She'd always thought he was the strongest man she knew. Now, his eyes seemed watery and his step unsteady. She ached with the need to protect him and her mother from pain. They'd had enough of that.

"Don't worry, Dad. I'm taking care of it," she assured him again, wishing she knew it were true.

"You're sure?"

She nodded. She wasn't sure at all, but she had a plan. All she needed now was the courage to carry it out. "I'll do the best I can, Dad. You can count on me."

She only hoped she would be able to keep her promise. It would kill them to lose Kenny. They'd lost so much over the years. No, she couldn't let it happen. She would do anything... anything... to keep away any further loss.

THE HOSPITAL CORRIDORS were white, cold and antiseptic—definitely unwelcoming as Jake walked down them an hour or so later. His steps slowed as Kenny's room loomed ahead. This was it. He was going to talk to him this time. He was going to find out whether there was any chance of establishing a relationship with his son.

The things Paige had said to him that morning were still resonating in his head and cutting into his heart. His first reaction had been stone-cold anger, but after giving her words more thought, he had to admit she made a lot of sense. There was no reason to think Kenny was going to welcome him back. There was no reason to think his son was going to want to go with him.

That didn't mean he was going to give in and let Paige have her way. Not by any means. But at the same time, he knew it wasn't going to be as easy as he had hoped it would be.

He almost longed for the innocence of his feelings just days before, when he'd imagined racing back to find his son. He hadn't doubted that Kenny would be pleased to see him. In his mind, Kenny had still been the eight-year-old boy who'd held on to his hand so tightly whenever he'd walked alongside him, the kid he'd taught to throw a ball, the child who'd fallen asleep against his shoulder on long drives.

To him, the four years had flown by, barely a blip on the screen of life. But now he realized that to Kenny, those years were huge, practically forever. Why had he been so sure Kenny would want to be with him? Maybe because he'd wanted it so strongly himself.

Now here he was, at the door. He reached out to open it, and to his shock, his fingers were trembling. Swearing softly, he pushed his way into the room and found himself looking into the wide, gray eyes of his towheaded son. The boy stared, and he stared right back.

The face was perfect—a little boy's freckled innocence just beginning to hint at taking on the lean, tough lines of a man. The choking wave of love came over him again. He would do anything for this boy. He would endure anything from him. But he would never leave him again.

"Hi," he ventured at last.

"Hi," Kenny said, his eyes luminous. "Are you my dad?"

Jake nodded, and waited, almost holding his breath.

A huge grin broke over the boy's face. "See?" he crowed, delighted. "I told them you would come. You came for my thirteenth birthday, right? Just like you promised."

Jake blinked. "Of course," he said simply. "I promised."

"Right." Kenny nodded happily, leaning forward with pure eagerness. "This is great. When can we go? Can we go now? Are you going to take me to the mines? Are you going to teach me all about gold?"

He was almost bouncing out of the bed in his excitement, and Jake grew a little alarmed.

"Hey, take it easy," he told him, stepping forward and putting a hand on the child's shoulder. "You don't want to pull out any stitches, or whatever."

"I don't have any stitches," Kenny said, but he did lie back again. "It's my ribs. And my legs. And my head. But I'm okay, really I am. I'll stay quiet in the car. When can we go?"

Jake wanted to feel joy at this open acceptance, but something didn't feel quite right about it. After what Paige had said to him, he couldn't quite believe it could be genuine.

"Listen, Kenny," he said, sinking to sit on the edge of the bed. "Do you remember me?"

Kenny nodded, looking at him solemnly. "I always read your letters at night," he said, and Jake felt a stab of remorse that there hadn't been more of them. "And I always have your picture," Kenny added, gesturing toward the bedside table.

Jake turned and saw a younger version of himself, his hair longer, his face rounder and softer.

"I knew you would come for me," the boy said serenely. "I was just waiting."

There was a lump in Jake's chest and it was affecting his throat. He had to cough before he could speak again, and in the meantime, he silently cursed himself for his heartless actions of the last four years. How could he have done so little for this boy? How could he have forgotten him?

"I did come for you, Kenny," he said when he could speak clearly. "But we're not going anywhere until the doctor says you're ready."

Kenny's face fell. "Dr. Holmes won't ever say I'm ready," he cried. "He already made me stay here over a week."

"And you'll stay until you're well."

"I'm already well." His frown was close to a pout, but his smile was back almost immediately. "Will you take me to the mining camps? Paige says that's where we lived when I was little."

His head came up at that. "What else did Paige tell you?"

"That you and my mom used to have fun looking for gold. That you went all over the West looking for it, camping out and stuff. That you're like this expert miner."

"She said that?" he asked, surprised.

"Uh-huh. I'm ready to go, honest." His face took on an earnest look. "I've been practicing up. I keep trying to find caves and old mines to explore. That's how come I got hurt. I was in the old mine on Grandpa's ranch and I fell down the shaft."

So that was it. Jake's gaze traveled quickly over the boy, looking for damage. "You're sure you're okay?" he asked.

Kenny nodded. "Just my head hurts sometimes. And my ribs are still sore. But they won't let me do anything, and I'm so sick of lying here. It's so boring."

Jake took him all in, his handsome young face, his spirit, his awkward young body, and felt a connection like none he'd ever felt before. This was his son. He could see it in him. He could hear it, feel it. Finally, joy broke through. This was for real. This was his.

"Hey." He grinned at the boy. "We'll get you out of here as quickly as we can." Another thought came to him. "But in the meantime...listen, don't tell Paige about this, okay? That I came to see you. I want to surprise her on your birthday."

"Okay." He agreed, but gave Jake a penetrating look that worried him.

"Paige and I have talked," he said quickly, wanting to explain, yet knowing he couldn't really do that fully. "Don't worry about that. But I don't want her to know we've been talking, you and I. Not yet. We've got to cook up something special for your birthday, you and me."

"Okay." He still didn't look convinced. "But I want to get out of here before that."

"I know you do." Jake was about to say more, but a sound at the doorway drew his attention. Turning, he found Trent standing at the entrance to the room, his arms folded around the chart he held.

"So," he said, looking at Jake expectantly but not smiling. "You did come back, after all."

"Of course I came back." Jake hesitated, then stuck out his hand. "How are you, Trent?"

"Just fine." Trent's normal smile was back as he shook hands vigorously. "How about you?"

"I'm great, now that I'm back with Kenny."

Trent's gaze went from Jake to Kenny's sunny face and his own smile disappeared. "Uh, listen, why don't you come on out into the hall. I'll fill you in on Kenny's condition."

Kenny frowned fretfully. "I don't know what the big secret is," he grumbled, smashing a fist into his pillow to fluff it up. "It's *my* condition."

"And you'll get to take it home with you when you go," Trent agreed with a grin at the boy. "But right now, I want to talk to your father about it without your butting in."

Kenny's eyes lit up at the word *father* and he didn't make another protest. Jake followed Trent into the hall, looking at him anxiously.

"What is it?" he asked. "What's the problem?"

"No problem." Trent put a hand up to reassure him. "Really, Kenny's doing fine. He had a pretty bad fall and there have been some complications." He quickly went over all Kenny's injuries, documenting them one by one and giving Jake the status of each, flipping pages, showing him information on the chart. "The only thing we're still worried about is his head. He had a pretty bad concussion. We want to keep him quiet to make absolutely sure—"

"That there's no brain damage?"

Trent hesitated, then nodded. "That's right. So far, so good. But there have been a couple of episodes of fluctuating emotional states that have concerned us. So we'd like another twenty-four hours or so..."

"Tell me what you think, Trent." Jake said, handing back the chart. "What your gut instinct tells you."

Trent shook his head and answered honestly. "I think he's fine, like I said. But you learn to be extra careful in this business. What you don't prepare for will come up and bite you in the backside every time."

Jake looked toward the room. "He's such a great kid," he murmured.

"Yes." Trent smiled, looking more relaxed. "I'm really glad you made it back. He was so sure you would, and we've all been trying to hold back his expectations, just in case."

Jake looked at him, surprised. "I promised I'd come get him on his thirteenth birthday."

"I know. But—"

"But Paige thought I wouldn't come," Jake finished, looking annoyed.

"Listen, Paige has been doing a wonderful job with Kenny," Trent insisted.

"Has she?" Jake's eyes narrowed as he tried to read Trent's expression.

"Yes." Trent was completely sincere and it showed. "She's devoted herself to raising him. You won't find anything to complain about there."

"Okay," Jake agreed reluctantly, his face hard. "But she's not supposed to be his guardian. Do you want to explain to me what exactly is going on there?"

Trent swallowed hard and didn't seem to have anything to add.

"That's what I thought," Jake said with grim satisfaction. "She doesn't have a legal leg to stand on, you know. Once I start going through channels, getting my ducks in a row, and all, her claim is going to crumble. She's not his legal guardian. He's not living with his legal guardians. He's not being raised by the people I said could raise him. I'm home-free when it comes to getting back custody.''

"You're not going to take her to court over this, are you?''

Jake's smile was cold and humorless. "We've already been to court. Haven't you heard? Paige tried to get a restraining order to keep me away from Kenny.''

Trent's face fell. "Oh, Paige.''

"So what do you think I ought to do, Trent? Like they say, you gotta fight fire with fire.''

"No. Jake, I can understand that you want to be with Kenny. And you should be. But I don't think you ought to be thinking about what *you* want and how you're going to get back at Paige. You ought to focus on what's best for Kenny.'' He looked almost angry for a moment. "It's about time you did.''

"What's best for Kenny is to be with me,'' Jake said firmly, hooking his thumbs into the pockets of his jeans. "You should hear him. He can hardly wait to get out of here and go with me.''

Trent sighed. "Of course, that's what he says now. He's finally got his father back, and he's thrilled.''

Trent put a hand on Jake's arm and tried to make him understand. "But he's only twelve, Jake. He doesn't realize having you means giving up Paige and his grandparents and his friends and everything else about his life. Don't you see that?''

Jake didn't want to see it. His expression darkened and he turned, itching to get back to his son. "Listen, Trent,'' he said before leaving him. "Paige doesn't know that I know where Kenny is, and I wish you wouldn't tell her."

"Why not?" Trent asked, clearly surprised.

He hesitated, looking at Trent speculatively. "To be honest, I don't know what she'd do if she knew. She might just grab the kid and run."

"Paige wouldn't do that," he insisted.

Jake gave him a hard look. "Wouldn't she?" he said skeptically. And then he turned and went back into the hospital room, back to the boy he was never going to let go again.

CHAPTER EIGHT

PAIGE WAITED until the secretary got up from her desk and left the room, before she entered the lobby and headed straight for Judge Randall's office. She didn't want to deal with another brush-off. That's all she'd been getting all morning. If he really wasn't in, she wanted to see for herself.

She pushed open the door to his office, and there he was, engrossed in a thick book.

"Hi," she said coolly, stepping in and making her way quickly to the desk. "So I've caught you in at last."

"Ah, Paige." He had the grace to look guilty, at least. Closing his book, he rose to greet her.

"I'll only keep you a moment," Paige said evenly. "But you've got to listen to me. There has to be something I can do to keep Jake from taking Kenny."

The judge sank back into his chair with a sigh. "Paige, my dear, I think you're overreacting."

"No, Judge Randall, I'm not." Instead of sitting, she leaned on his desk and stared into his eyes, forcing him to give heed to what she was saying. "Jake has come to take Kenny away. He's told me so over and over. He told you differently because he knew that was what you wanted to hear."

The judge shrugged, looking slightly impatient. "Well, Paige, he is the boy's father."

Her heart sank. If this was his attitude, she was in more trouble than ever. "Is that all that counts?"

"No. But it goes a long way."

Quickly, she recounted all the reasons she didn't agree, repeating pretty much what she'd said to Jake that morning. She emphasized the bad, played down the good. It wasn't exactly fair, but it was something that had to be done. And when she was finished, she sat back and waited for the judge's response.

It was slow in coming, and when he finally did face her and begin to speak, his look of pity told her as much as his words did.

There wasn't much hope of help from this quarter. Jake was Kenny's father, and that was what counted. She was going to have to fight a little harder. She was going to have to fight a little dirty.

"The only cases I've seen where the rights of the father were set aside," the judge said at one point, "were ones in which actual criminal convictions could be held against him. Then there was one case where the child was adamantly opposed to going with the father. Threw a tantrum every time he looked at the man. That, against a background of suspicious behavior on the part of the father, was enough to persuade a jury that the child should be left with the guardian."

Paige sat with her arms folded tightly across her chest. What was he saying here—that she had no grounds for keeping Kenny? Maybe she should try framing Jake for a crime. Or turning his own son against him. *Thanks for nothing,* she thought desolately. *But here goes.*

She took a deep breath. She felt like a rat, but she was going to do it.

"What about...what about a history of violence?" she asked shakily.

"What?" The judge frowned at her. "What are you talking about?"

"Don't you remember the famous fight in front of the DeliDelight?"

He gazed at her blankly for a moment, then his eyes cleared. "Oh. That's right. I'd forgotten all about that." He frowned again. "Yes, I remember now. Jake beat that poor boy pretty badly, didn't he? As I recall, I encouraged the family to press charges, but for some reason they declined." He shook his head. "Yes, I'll admit, I felt Jake deserved more punishment at the time."

She swallowed, avoiding his gaze, hating herself for doing this. Jake hadn't deserved punishment for beating Ricky Samms the way he had. He'd deserved a medal. Ricky had sweet-talked Jenny Reed, gotten her pregnant, and been prepared to walk off, laughing, leaving Jenny to deal with the consequences. Jake had confronted him about it. Ricky had waited a day or two and had jumped Jake from behind.

But not many knew that, and the judge could be made to think the incident evidence of Jake's bad character if she played it right.

"I...I really don't think someone who explodes in anger like that should be put in sole charge of a child. Do you?"

Judge Randall considered, his head to the side. "That was an awful long time ago," he reminded her. "People change."

"Yes, but..." Okay, here it was, time to go into action. She had her story ready, had gone over it a thousand times in the last few hours. "What if a father had a history of aggressive behavior? Of settling arguments with his fists? Wouldn't that preclude his gaining custody of a minor child?"

Her voice sounded like glass on pavement, harsh and ugly. The words were ugly. The implications were even worse.

"What are you trying to say, Paige?" Judge Randall said slowly, searching her face. "Are you accusing Jake of being violent?"

This was it, time to take that final step. To say something that would make the judge refuse to give Jake custody.

Her mouth felt as though it were full of cotton. She opened it, trying to give her prepared speech, but nothing came out. She tried again. Nothing. She couldn't do it. Not even to keep Kenny. She couldn't lie about Jake.

"No," she said softly at last. "No, I'm not accusing Jake of anything." And she closed her eyes, reaching for control.

"My advice," the judge said at last, looking at her with a great deal of sympathy, "is to work something out with Jake. Talk to him. We all know what sort of man he is, how hard it is for him to stay in one place. Maybe visitation periods would be enough for him, once the original bloom is off the rose, so to speak."

So to speak. Paige didn't have a lot of hope in that direction. Jake seemed to her to be a pretty determined man right now.

But it was all she had to cling to, wasn't it?

"At any rate, my dear, I'm sure the two of you can come up with a plan that will work for you both." He patted her hand and looked into her face. "You look so much like Carol nowadays," he mused out loud. "I would think the resemblance would be very gratifying to Jake."

Going cold all over, she rose unsteadily and turned away, hating him for saying that. Carol's face seemed to be laughing at her at every turn lately. She could hardly stand it. She left the building as quickly as she could and sat for a long time in her car, calming herself down, making herself relax.

Her great plan had fallen through because she hadn't had the stomach to pull it off. So—now what? She had no idea what she was going to do. But she had to do something. She couldn't let him win.

All that would have to wait for later, though. Right now she had appointments with some backers of the Gold Rush Days celebration she had to meet with. Glancing at her watch, she started up her car.

PAIGE SAW HIM coming and she didn't know whether to make a run for it or stay and take her chances. After all, she hadn't been gentle with him that morning. She wouldn't have been at all surprised if he'd been one angry man.

But she couldn't tell by looking at his face. He had dark glasses covering his eyes. She was standing in front of the chamber of commerce office, waiting for a businessman who'd promised to listen to her pitch for a donation to the parade effort. And instead of the businessman, she got Jake. And maybe, trouble.

"I'm waiting for someone," she warned him as he approached her. "He'll be here any minute."

He stared at her, wondering why he'd felt such a compulsion to find her. He'd seen Kenny, been overwhelmed with the experience and then he'd wanted to share it with Paige. But that was crazy. He couldn't do that. So what was he doing here?

Well, he'd wanted to see Paige, and here she was.

Stopping in front of her, he smiled. "I just wanted you to know, Paige," he drawled. "I've thought over all that stuff you threw at me this morning. I've really taken it to heart. And you know what?"

Without warning, he took her face between his hands, holding it in place before him. "It's all a bunch of garbage. Nice try. But no cigar." He dropped a kiss on her mouth.

"Sorry, kid," he said, drawing back. "You lose this round. Better luck next time."

And he turned, striding off, before she could even catch her breath.

She tottered on her heels, stunned. But strangely enough, she wasn't angry. She wiped her mouth with the back of her hand, and then she smiled. "Jake, you're nuts," she whispered, glancing at the interested bystanders who had seen it all. "Absolutely nuts."

But a part of her was relieved that he'd weathered her tirade. And all of a sudden, she couldn't hate him.

HE WENT BACK to the hospital. He couldn't stay away, he had to see Kenny. The look on his son's face when he walked in was all the reward he needed. He helped Kenny finish the green jelly from his lunch, then they sat and talked for a while. Jake couldn't get enough of him, couldn't stop examining him, marveling at what a great kid he was.

"Tell me about the accident," he suggested when the topics of baseball and swim team had been exhausted. "What happened?"

"I goofed," Kenny said, shrugging. "That's all. It was stupid."

"Tell me about it."

"Okay."

He settled back against his pillows and began. "Me and Jimmy Callister, we'd been planning this for a long time," he said in his young-boy voice. "We wanted to go down and explore that old mine on Grandpa's ranch."

Jake frowned. "You know you've been told never to go near that mine. At least, that's what you were told in the old days, and I'm sure nobody changed that order."

"I know. It's dangerous. But I had this great idea." His eyes brightened and he sat up straighter. "See, I was going to find gold to surprise you with when you came back. So you could see I could be a miner, too."

"Kenny...." Jake wanted to take him in his arms, but his young masculine shoulders were set in a way that let his father know that wasn't to be allowed just now.

"Anyway, me and Jimmy, we went in, and it was so dark."

"You didn't have lamps?"

He nodded eagerly. "Oh, yeah. I found one old helmet in the garage with a carbide lamp on it. We had to share. And it went out after a few minutes."

Jake groaned.

"Then I just started sliding, and once I started, I couldn't stop. Next thing I knew, I was at the bottom and Jimmy was looking down at me and yelling. I hurt pretty bad. So I said, 'Jimmy, go on and get help.' So he ran off."

"And you were all alone in the dark."

"My eyes got used to it a little. I could see some things. And I could hear voices."

"Voices?"

"Yeah." He looked a bit sheepish. "Everybody thinks I'm nuts, but I could swear a coyote came and looked down at me."

"Maybe one did." Jake grinned at him. "What did he say?"

Kenny looked surprised. "How did you know?"

Jake blinked. "Know what?"

"That he said something to me. Everybody else thinks I was halluci . . . whatever."

Jake frowned, unsure how to handle this. "Kenny . . ."

"He did. Really. I looked up and he said, 'Hey, kid, how you doin'?' And I didn't say anything back. Then he said, 'You'd better get out of here, kid. If you're still here at midnight, you're dead meat.' "

"Kenny . . . ."

"Dad, I swear, that's what he said." He looked a bit deflated that his father didn't believe him. "I don't know, maybe it was like a dream, or something. But it seemed real."

Jake shook his head. "Then it was real to you," he said simply. "What happened next?"

His eyes got big. "Then . . . bats."

"Bats?"

"Yeah. Bloodsucking bats." He looked very pleased with himself and the drama of his story. "They buzzed around me like bees. It was horrible." He smiled. "Paige was really scared when I told her about the bats."

"Bloodsucking bats," Jake scoffed, grinning. "There are no bloodsucking bats in the Sierra Nevada."

"Well, maybe they weren't sucking blood, but they were mean, all right." He punched up his pillow and sat up higher. "They got tired of flying around my head after a while, and they flew off. Then an owl swooped down."

"An owl, huh?" Jake's eyes crinkled.

"Yeah," said Kenny, sailing right along. "Boy, that was the scariest sound in the world. I didn't know what it was at first. There was a long, low hoot, like a ghost call or something, and then the wings flapping." He shook his head, obviously enjoying himself to the hilt. "I thought maybe the devil had come to get me."

Jake nodded, swallowing a grin. "No mountain lions?" he asked. "No floods? No earthquakes?"

Kenny frowned, thinking. "I think I felt an earthquake."

"Right." Jake laughed.

Kenny looked at him, indignant. "I did. I swear it. All the little rocks started rolling past my head."

"But you were brave, anyway."

"Yes, I was. I didn't cry when they pulled me out in that sling thing. And it hurt like h—"

A stern look from Jake stopped him cold.

"It hurt like crazy," he amended quickly, and Jake smiled.

"Do you remember when you were a kid and I used to take you rock hunting with me?" he asked.

Kenny nodded, his eyes big. "Yeah. I remember."

"I used to swing you up on my back and carry you up the mountainside." Jake looked out the window and focused on the distant peaks of the Sierra Nevada. "Right up the mountainside," he repeated softly, remembering.

Kenny watched him for a moment, then tugged on his sleeve. "And remember when you took me to that cave and you showed me the stalactites and stalagmites? And the waterfall?"

Jake smiled at him. "You remember that?"

"Sure."

He went on chattering, but Jake hardly heard him. He was swept up in a wave of emotion that was going to bring him to tears if he didn't watch it. This boy, this part of himself and Carol, this piece of his soul... they were tied together by more than blood, more than convention. They were tied together by the past, as well. And by love.

"Thank God for that," he whispered to himself.

PAIGE TAPPED her foot impatiently and tried to wish her headache away. Things were not going well. The auditions were a joke. She'd had tap-dancing frogs, synchronized kazoo players, a barbershop quartet whose members sang their notes in burps, a group of ladies in their seventies who wanted to drape themselves around a float in miniskirts, and some teenage girls who thought a strip routine would be fun.

"They had, like, prostitutes and stuff at the mines in the olden days," one young gum-cracker insisted. "We'd be, like, right on historically, and like that, you know? So what's wrong with it?"

With a little slick talk and fancy footwork she got them to tone it down to cancan dancing, but they weren't happy. They were milling around now, throwing dirty looks her way, causing her to wonder why she'd taken on this thankless job.

She'd auditioned eight acts and though she didn't actually turn anyone down, she did have to have long talks with each entrant, trying to make them understand that their piece of the action had to relate somehow to the theme. It didn't help that Barry showed up, gloomier than ever, to hang around in the background and make disparaging comments.

"You can't dictate what everyone does, you know," he told her in an aside that was just loud enough to be heard by the teenage girls, who giggled appreciatively. "I think strippers would be a real hit. I know I'd like them." And he threw the girls a wide grin, just to prove it.

Paige turned and glared at him. "Thank you so much for your support, Barry," she grumbled. "I'm not trying to dictate to the entrants. But I do think it is my job to make sure we have a bottom line in the taste department. I know standards are uncool these days." She gave the girls, who were still hanging around making eyes at Barry, a sweeping glance. "But that's just too bad. I'm in charge. And standards we will have."

Barry shrugged. "Sorry, ladies," he told the disappointed teenagers. "I did what I could." And he sighed with regret as they sashayed out of the auditorium.

"A little young for you," Paige noted without much interest, gathering up papers.

He looked at her sideways. "I don't know. I seem to be striking out in the older age groups these days."

She glanced at him, then away, not wanting to get into that. But before she could think of another topic he changed the subject himself. She immediately realized that this must have been the reason he had shown up here this afternoon.

"I heard something rather disturbing this morning, Paige." He moved closer, as though it were a tale he wouldn't want spread around. "Did you know Jake Winslow is back in town?"

She froze, not meeting his eyes. "Yes," she said simply.

"You knew?" His tone was incredulous.

"Yes," she repeated, shuffling papers into a folder.

He moved around to where she had to face him. "Why didn't you tell me?"

Paige hesitated, feeling guilty and resenting it. "It didn't come up," she said weakly.

He swung away from her. "Oh, right."

She deserved the sarcasm, but that didn't make it any easier to take.

Barry turned back, searching her face for clues. "What did he come for? Do you know?"

She didn't answer, and he didn't seem to notice, going right on to the next question.

"Do you know where he's staying?"

She glanced at him, then away. "Yes."

He waited another beat, then said impatiently. "Well? Where?"

Still she didn't answer, though she knew she was going to have to eventually.

"Are you going to tell me?"

Turning, she looked him full in the face. "Why do you want to know? What do you want with him?"

Barry was taken aback. "I didn't say I wanted anything with him. I just want to know."

She took a deep breath and let it out. "He's staying with me."

"He's what?" Barry's face flushed and he stared at her. "You're not serious."

"I'm very serious, Barry. He's staying with me. After all, he is Kenny's father."

Barry laughed without humor. "That's not all he is. He's also the reason your father lost his practice, and the reason Carol is dead."

Yes, that was the litany. She'd said those same words herself, over and over again. But for some reason, she felt defensive this time. She wanted to challenge Barry, contradict him.

And defend Jake?

She held back a quick flash of vertigo. No. This wasn't right. This couldn't be. She refused to be one of those silly women who fell for the bad guy.

The auditorium was empty now, except for the two of them. She sank into a padded audience seat and closed her eyes, trying to calm herself. Barry sat down beside her, but he didn't seem to notice her inner turmoil. He went on, bringing back memories.

"You remember what it was like, don't you?" he said, his voice soft, but not pleasant. "Remember that last time Jake and Carol came home? There was so much anger between the two of them, sparks flew when their eyes met. I thought Carol would go for his throat a couple of times that last night." He shook his head. "I tell you, that was one case where love had really turned to hatred."

Still staring into the distance, Paige shook her head slowly, denying his view of things. "No," she whispered. "No. They didn't hate each other." She frowned, remembering. "But they were going through a bad period. I think Carol was sick of being dragged from one mining town to another."

He snorted. "You can say that again. But it was more than that. She was sick of him, too. She wanted out."

Paige frowned at him. "I don't remember it quite that way," she said icily.

He shrugged, looking a little uncomfortable. "Well, you wouldn't, would you? She told me things she didn't tell other people."

"You?" Barry had always been around, hovering in the background. But she'd never thought of him as a real player in the drama that was life for the Kentons and the Winslows in those days.

"Yes," he said coldly. "Me."

She looked at him curiously, struck by his intensity, but still not convinced. "What did she tell you, then?"

"That she was tired of being poor and living in rented rooms. She'd had it. She wanted a change of scene, and if Jake wouldn't give it to her, she was going to get it some other way."

Paige wanted to find a way to refute Barry's words. But something was holding her back. Over the last few years, she'd been careful to recall only one side of Carol, the good side—the one she wanted to remember. Now she was being forced to let the dark side in.

In other words, there were really two Carols. There was the Carol who'd lied to their mother about staying overnight with a girlfriend, when Paige knew her sister was going out with a sailor she'd met at the county fair. There was the Carol who regularly swiped Paige's best sweaters and turned up wearing her new pearls. There was the Carol who stole her best friend's boyfriend on a whim.

And then there was the sweet, lovely young woman who'd come home with baby Kenny in a yellow blanket and cried when his finger got pinched in the door—the Carol who had sat up all night listening to Kenny's breathing when he had a cold, just to be sure.

This was the side of her sister she wanted to remember. And she didn't appreciate Barry's forcing her to remember the other Carol.

"She told me all about her plan," Barry reminisced. "She was going to confront your parents and demand they help her out. She figured your father had enough money, and he could afford to finance her for a while—either with Jake or without him. She wanted something better. Who could blame her?''

Who, indeed? Paige frowned, not liking what she was hearing. Bits and pieces of that weekend began to flow back, joining to form a picture she'd forgotten—or suppressed. But now that Barry had triggered the memories, she couldn't stop them, and once they started, she sat riveted, as though watching an episode of "This Is Your Life."

Carol and Jake and Kenny had come home for Paige's birthday, arriving in an old rattletrap of a car. Jake and Carol were sniping at each other, and Kenny was ignoring it, as children of that sort of relationship often did. Paige had taken Carol's side in an argument with Jake. She couldn't remember what it had been about, but she'd said something cutting and Jake had glared at her. And she'd stuck her tongue out at him in a childish gesture.

She flushed, remembering, regretting. What a foolish thing to do. She hoped Jake didn't remember it.

But he hardly could have forgotten what had happened later that evening. Friends of Paige's had been invited for dessert, to celebrate her birthday. Among the small crowd were certain friends of Carol's and Jake's. Barry was there, and so was Trent. Carol had been out of the room, talking to her mother, and Paige thought now she must have been presenting her plan, the plan Barry was talking about. And getting it rejected. That would explain why she'd been so furious when she'd come back into the room, why she'd said something to their father that had angered him.

It was all coming back now. Dr. Kenton had muttered something about Carol's having made her bed and being stuck with it. Jake had gotten involved somehow, saying something that caused Dr. Kenton to call him a drifter and a loser, saying it loud and clear.

That statement had shocked the crowd. Everything had gone dead silent for a moment. Paige remembered the surprise on all the faces, the anger in Jake's. And then her father had started out of the room, brushing past her, and Jake had followed, stopping him in the hall. More ugly words were exchanged, and then the fateful ones.

"I may not be the success you are," Jake had said bitterly. "But at least I'm honest."

"What do you mean by that?" Dr. Kenton had demanded, his face reddening.

"I think you know," Jake had said, starting to turn away.

But Dr. Kenton had grabbed his arm, pulling him back. "You make an insinuation like that, a worthless bum like you, you'd better make it stick."

Jake had looked at him in complete disgust. "Forget it," he'd said.

"No. Spit it out. You come into my family and ruin my daughter's life and make accusations against me. You'd better come up with the details, right here and now."

It was the charge of his ruining Carol's life that seemed to have sparked the rage in Jake's eyes. He had turned back, glaring at his father-in-law.

"Okay. You asked for it. What I'm saying is, you're a cheat. Everyone knows you pay half your office staff off the books to keep from having to pay their taxes and benefits."

Paige had gasped, turning to look at her father, who'd appeared to be on the verge of a heart attack. "Are you going to turn me in to the IRS?" the older man had shouted, shaking his fist in Jake's face. "Are you?"

"Why not?" Jake had said coldly, his arms folded across his chest. "After all, when you cheat on taxes, you're cheating all of us, aren't you?"

Her father had lurched toward Jake, as though he was going to attack him. Someone had grabbed Jake at that point, and Paige remembered she herself had gone to her father and pushed him away, coaxing him to go to his bedroom to calm down. That had been a struggle. He'd been so angry.

By the time she'd gone back to the living room, Jake and Carol had gone out dancing somewhere with a group of their friends, and only a few of Paige's were left. She'd been relieved to discover that most people hadn't witnessed the altercation in the hallway. But the incident rankled, nonetheless. And the consequences were fatal.

Her mind flashed again to Carol's car, crushed against rocks off the mountain road. The rain was falling. The lights of the emergency vehicles were whirling around and around. Men were shouting. And horror was enveloping her family, a horror that would never really leave them.

She blinked hard, pushing the vision away. "Oh, Carol," she thought silently. "My darling sister, Carol."

"She should never have married him," Barry was saying, still sitting beside her in the darkened auditorium. "She'd still be alive today if she hadn't married him."

"And who do you think she would have married, instead?"

They both jumped and turned to find that Jake had come up behind them, looming large and dangerous in the gloom of the auditorium.

"It wouldn't be you, Barry," Jake said with a crooked grin. "So you can kiss that dream goodbye."

Barry rose and turned to face him. "Hey, Jake," he said nervously. "This is a surprise."

Jake faced him without smiling. Both men were about the same size, but something about Jake made him appear larger, more solid.

"Hey yourself, Barry," he said dryly, without a hint of friendly greeting in his eyes. "How have you been?"

"Fine. Just fine." Barry glanced at Paige, then back at Jake again, smiling tensely. "It's...it's been a long time since I've seen you."

"That may be true for you." Jake's grin didn't quite reach his eyes. "But I saw you just the other night."

"No, Jake," Paige said softly, shaking her head. "Don't."

But he didn't pay any attention, and when Barry asked, "Where?" he answered.

"Over in front of Paige's apartment building. You were trying to kiss her, as I recall, and doing a lousy job of it."

Barry's face reddened and his friendly facade fell away. "Shut up, Jake," he muttered, his gaze shifting.

"Barry, I came back to town to get my boy," Jake said firmly. "I didn't mean to stay this long, and I certainly don't mean to get involved in anything going on here."

He glanced at Paige, but his expression didn't change. "But I've just got to give you one bit of advice. After all, we've known each other for a long, long time, and I think we can be straight with each other, don't you?"

"I don't know what kind of advice you could give me."

Jake's jaw tightened. "Here it is. Stay away from the Kentons. Carol wasn't right for you and neither is Paige. Leave her alone. Go find yourself someone else to prop up your life."

Barry's hands balled into fists. "Go to hell, Jake," he said, anger suffusing his face.

Jake laughed softly. "I must admit, that's a distinct possibility," he said.

Barry whirled and looked at Paige, glared at Jake one last time and stomped off, heading out of the auditorium.

And Paige finally reacted, rising from her seat, furious. "How dare you?"

He shrugged. "It's in my nature," he told her simply, and his eyes crinkled around the edges.

But she wasn't going to be charmed so easily this time.

"Who do you think you are?" she demanded, glaring at him as though she were about to attack him where he stood. "What gives you the right...?"

"I have every right," he said easily. "Hell, Paige, we're family. Remember?"

"I...I..." She wanted to tell him that she hated him, but the words wouldn't come out. He was doing it again. Somehow, he cast a spell over her, left her incapable of normal thought and movement.

He reached out and grasped her shoulders. "Calm down," he said softly. His hands worked like magic, relaxing her where she stood, and her knees were turning to jelly. To her chagrin, she was doing a fair representation of being knocked off her feet.

"That's it," he murmured, his fingers pressing into her flesh. And then slowly, very, very slowly, his hands slid down her arms until he had hold of her elbows.

She couldn't move. She looked up at him, her eyes wide with shock. She watched his gaze explore her face.

The moment lasted much too long. Paige couldn't breathe, and Jake continued to fix her with his stare. He seemed to be as mesmerized as she was. Time seemed to stand still, as though even the air were holding its breath.

Jake finally ripped free of the spell. Swearing softly to himself, he dropped one hand and turned toward the seats.

"Come on back over here and sit down with me," he told her gruffly, leading her by the hand. "We need to have a rational talk."

She went along as though she'd been hypnotized, hoping desperately that he hadn't sensed how badly she wanted him to kiss her. She had to get control of herself. Snatching her hand away from his, she sank into the plush chair and scrunched down, wishing she could hide underneath it.

He sat beside her, facing forward, trying to ignore the powerful effect her presence was having on him. He could still smell her hair, still feel her softness beneath his touch, and it was going to drive him crazy if he didn't shove it out of his head and get on with things. So he stared at the stage and forced himself to concentrate.

"I've been all over town today," he said at last, "and everywhere I go, everyone's telling me I should get out of here and leave Kenny with you."

He glanced at her. She turned in her seat, her mind taken up with what he'd just said. The provocative tension between them was forgotten.

"That it would be a crime," he added, "to take him away."

Hope sprang in Paige's chest. What was he saying? Were others getting through to him? "They're right." She smiled, happiness flowing through her. "Oh, Jake, they're right."

But things hadn't changed all that radically, not quite yet. Jake shook his head, watching her reaction.

"I don't think so," he said quietly. "And I'm going to tell you why."

She sank back, disappointed, but still hopeful.

"Okay," she said coolly, her fingers nervously threading the fringe on her leather jacket. "Make your case."

He half turned to face her. "You've been great with Kenny. Everyone says so. And I appreciate what you've done. But, Paige...a boy needs a father."

She nodded stiffly. "He's got my father." She knew she had a weak case there, though. Her father was not exactly Jake's favorite person. "They're together all the time," she added lamely.

Jake looked away. "Your father is old and he's tired. He doesn't have what Kenny needs."

She frowned, not willing to lose this argument so easily. "And you do?" she retorted resentfully.

His head swung around and he glared at her arrogantly. "Damn right I do."

Their eyes met and she knew he was right. He was large and strong and male and good at things, a father any boy would die for. All her doubts, all those thoughts that Kenny might not want to go with him crumbled into dust as she sat there and looked at this handsome, compelling man. Who wouldn't want to go with him?

But she wasn't ready to give up. Not by a long shot.

"So, that's your entire case?" she challenged, lifting her chin. "A boy needs a father, and you're a handy male, therefore, problem solved?"

He gazed at her with steady confidence. "I'm not just a handy male, Paige. I'm the handy father of this boy. There is a difference."

She swallowed and nodded. "Okay, I'll give you that. You're his father, and every boy does better with a father around."

"But... what?" he asked warily.

She smiled. "But... he needs a mother, too. I've been a mother to him for four years. Don't you think ripping him away from that would be as harmful as depriving him of a father?"

He shrugged. "Okay. So marry me."

The words were obviously spoken in jest but just the same, the idea sizzled between them for a moment, putting a slight buzz in the air, leaving them both tingling.

Her laugh came a beat too late and was a shade too forced. "I'd do just about anything to keep Kenny. But that may be going a little too far."

"I didn't really think you'd be tempted."

"No, I'm not." She blinked, trying to sound sincere. "But the problem still stands. Kenny needs a mother as much as he needs a father."

He shrugged as though he were tired of this train of thought. "So I'll marry somebody else."

Something flashed like a bolt of painful lightning through her chest and she wasn't sure what it was. "Don't be ridiculous," she said sharply, wincing. "You can't just hire a wife."

He gazed at her levelly. "What makes you so sure I don't have someone waiting in the wings? It's been four years, you know. And I've had my chances."

Her smile was stiff. Did he really think any casual date would do? "I'm sure you have," she told him crisply. "But I don't need to hear about all your conquests. We're not talking about a Saturday-night bed warmer here. We're talking about a mother."

He grimaced. "He's had four years of mothering. Now he needs some fathering to make up for it."

She could have risen to the bait and started in on him, but she held back a retort. There was no point in going on with the bickering. It was getting them nowhere. So far today, she'd made him face a lot of unhappy truths about what he'd done to Kenny. She'd had to face some painful facts given to her by Judge Randall. It was looking more and more as though she didn't have a legal leg to stand on in trying to keep

Kenny. That meant she had only one option left. She had to get through to Jake somehow. She had to appeal to him on an intellectual and emotional basis. There was no point fighting him. It was time to play this a little smarter.

She looked at him earnestly. "Jake."

"What?" he asked, looking at the sparkle in her dark eyes and wanting to touch her cheek.

She took his hand in hers. "Give me until Saturday."

His fingers curled around hers. She was so warm. "Saturday?" he asked, and his voice just missed cracking.

She nodded. "Kenny's birthday."

His hand tightened on hers. "To do what?"

"To convince you." She bit her lip and shook her head. "I can, you know," she said eagerly. "Let me just show you. Give me time."

He raised her hand, looking at the fingers laced with his, and then brought it slowly to his lips, turning it and opening it so that he could drop a kiss on her palm.

Her breath caught in her throat, but she didn't pull away, and he looked up at her. He wanted to be alone with her. He wanted to be with her, to have her calming influence, to watch her move. He longed to watch her hair settle against her shoulders whenever she turned her head, to watch her lips turn up at the corners when something amused her.

"Let's go out to dinner," he suggested suddenly, impulsively. "We'll talk about it."

She was taken aback. "It's early," she muttered.

"So we'll have an early dinner." He dropped her hand so that he could look at his watch, and she began to breathe again. "If we go right now, we'll still have an hour or so of daylight after we eat. That would suit me fine. I've got some things to do."

She hesitated, but after all, what was the harm? "All right," she said at last.

And they left the auditorium together. But there was a new tension between them, and it had nothing to do with Kenny.

CHAPTER NINE

THE RESTAURANT WAS SMALL and dark. They sat at a table with a lace cloth and a flickering candle and ordered things with French names that made them laugh.

But everything was delicious and the wine made them both feel at ease. It was early and there weren't many others in the restaurant. There in the darkened room, the world seemed to constrict into their small circle of light, and they leaned closer and closer together as they talked.

Paige was surprised that they had so much to talk about, even when they left topics like Kenny and Carol and her parents out of the conversation. There was more to Jake than she'd realized. Sitting there with him, making small talk, she could see what an attractive man he was, and why any woman might be tempted to make his capture a full-time occupation.

But not her. No, sir. She was too smart for that.

They finished dessert and sat back in their chairs, relaxed and pleasantly satiated. Jake told a joke and she laughed, enjoying its witty punch line. Then he turned to her and spoke seriously, though there was still a twinkle in his crystal blue eyes.

"Now, explain to me how you're going to do this convincing," he said.

"Convincing?"

"About Kenny."

"Oh." She collected herself up and thought for a few seconds. Obviously they were getting back to the important stuff.

"I guess what I meant is that I'm going to show you what kind of person I am," she said, not able to think of anything else at the moment.

He smiled. "I already know that."

"No, you don't." She shook her head. "You only know what kind of little sister I was to Carol. That is the only way you've ever known me."

He looked as if he was going to contradict her, but then he shook his head. "That's true," he said, smiling again, one eyebrow raised provocatively. "And I must admit, there are aspects of you I'd like to explore more fully."

She flushed. "Don't tease me," she said softly.

His smile evaporated and he touched her hand where it lay on the table. "I'm not teasing. I'm telling the absolute truth." His hand covered hers. "That's something I do a lot of. Haven't you learned that yet?"

She stared at his hand on hers. She had to erect defenses again, but it was getting harder and harder to do that. "Learned what?" she said coolly. "That you only lie when you need to?"

There was a moment of ominous silence, and then he laughed. "Paige, have you ever heard of little white lies? Have you ever heard of—if you can't say something nice, don't say anything at all?"

"That's not what I'm talking about."

"I know that." He sighed, withdrawing his hand and leaning back in his chair. "Okay, I'll admit I have lied. I lied to the judge. We both know that." He gazed at her solemnly. "But I'm not really a chronic liar, Paige. I think you know that. I've only lied when I've had no choice."

She smiled. "Spoken like a professional prevaricator." She reached out a hand to stop him when indignation flared in his gaze.

"I do know what you mean, Jake. And believe it or not, I trust you."

A flash of surprise thrilled through her when she realized she really meant it. "And I'll go on trusting you. Just as long as you never lie to me."

He grabbed her hand and held it. "And how about you, Paige," he said softly. "Will you promise not to lie to me?"

How could she promise that when she was living a huge lie, as it was? She stared at him for a long moment, heart beating hard in her chest. What could she say?

And then it came to her. She had to tell him the truth. There was no other way, not for her.

"I...I can't promise that right now, Jake," she said, her mouth dry as cotton. "I...well, the truth is, I have lied to you in the past. And I'm not ready to mend that just yet. I...I can't."

To her surprise, he didn't press.

"But you will soon?" he asked her, still holding her hand in his.

She nodded. "I will. I promise you that."

"Okay, then," he said quietly. "I'll be waiting."

She gave him a puzzled look, suddenly not at all sure who he was. This wasn't the monster she'd steeled herself against all these years.

"Have the last four years changed you?" she asked softly, looking at him intently. "Or did I just not know you very well?"

He thought for a moment, then gave her a wan smile. "Both," he said. "But isn't that the way it always is?" His gaze flickered over her face. "I feel the same way about you. You're not the 'Little Sister' I thought I knew."

She nodded slowly. "But you know all about me and what I've been doing for the last four years. I don't think I have those years filled in for you yet. You said you were going to school?"

He nodded. "I've got a B.S. in geology, an M.S. in geochemistry." He gave her a half grin. "Shall I have the university send over my transcripts, or will you take my word for it?"

She made a face at him and went on. "And you're working for some big company?"

He nodded again. "United Techno Associates. They're involved in mining operations, as well as development of some major investment co-ops." He hesitated, then went on. "In fact, I'm here partly on business. I'm making some preliminary reports on prospective sites for a major theme park Techno is considering in the area."

"Theme park?"

"Sure. And I think Gold Rush Days could be a winner as a concept for them. I plan to suggest it."

"Oh." It was odd to think of Jake in this context, as the sort of man who might be making suggestions at board meetings of major corporations. She could hardly imagine it. But she believed him. Every word he said.

Still, there were other things that bothered her.

"Jake," she said hesitantly. "Why did you say those things to Barry?"

He drew back from her, his face hardening. "Because they're the truth."

She paused, knowing she was treading on the privacy of others, but needing answers, anyway. He'd said ugly, hurtful things to Barry, and Barry hadn't seemed shocked. He had, in fact, reacted more like a guilty man.

Taking a deep breath, she ventured, "You acted as though he was some sort of rival for Carol."

His face didn't change. "He was," he said simply.

That surprised her, but she managed to hold on to a modicum of control. "In . . . in what way?"

"In a lot of ways." He gazed at her, putting distance between them with the coolness in his eyes. "Barry used to call Carol. And he would drop in from time to time."

"After the two of you were married?"

He nodded. "He came to visit us when we were living outside of Elko, Nevada." He laughed softly, remembering. "He stayed for three weeks. He stayed, in fact, until I kicked him out."

She swallowed, not liking the picture that evoked. "Carol never told me that," she said.

"That's what I've been trying to convince you of, Paige." He moved restlessly in his chair. "There are a lot of things Carol never told you."

She didn't want to ask, but something inside compelled her to. "Barry and Carol...they weren't...oh, Jake, tell me they weren't..."

He grabbed her hand and squeezed it tightly. "They weren't. Don't worry. If they had been, the way I was then, I probably would have killed him."

She breathed a deep sigh of relief, then hated herself for even thinking it. "Oh, I'm so glad," she murmured involuntarily.

He threw her a penetrating look. "You don't really care for him, do you?" he asked bluntly.

She looked up quickly, realizing he meant Barry. "Only as a friend," she answered truthfully, shaking her head emphatically.

He studied her face for a moment, then his slow grin resurfaced. "The kiss of death," he remarked.

"Not necessarily," she said defensively. "A lot of people can develop love out of friendship."

"Not you." He shook his head, gazing at her with a half smile, leaving no room for doubt.

"Not me?"

"No."

"Why not?"

He didn't touch her, but she felt as though he had reached out and stroked his hand down her arm. Every hair stood on end, every nerve tingled.

"I can see the fire burning behind those eyes," he told her softly, leaning close. "You've got a passion inside, a passion that's going to be unleashed some day." His slow smile deepened. "And when it is, Paige, a storm is going to come roaring through town."

She shivered and tried to laugh. "Oh, that's ridiculous," she said, but she was pleased just the same. Ridiculously pleased. She *had* to get hold of herself.

"That's quite a line you've developed, Jake," she added, trying to be smooth about it. "I'll bet you have them begging for more all over gold country."

He stared at her, and she waited for him to deny what she'd said, to tell her she was the only one he'd ever spoken to so provocatively. But he didn't. Instead, he laughed as though she'd caught him out and glanced at his watch.

She noticed the gesture. "I suppose it is time to get going, isn't it?" she said, gathering her things. "I've got an errand to run before I go back to the apartment."

Jake turned and looked at her. He guessed where she was going, and for just a moment, he hesitated. The way they were getting along right now, he had the urge to tell her he knew all about Kenny and to suggest they go to the hospital together.

But, no. That would be indiscreet. Letting her know now would probably destroy everything. This was just a tender little sprout of a relationship that they had growing here, and in order for it to flourish, it was going to need very careful cultivating. Too much, too soon, would wipe it out.

"Okay," he said grudgingly. "I have a couple of places I need to go, too."

"Where?" she asked quickly, her eyes anxious.

He smiled at her reaction. "I do have a private life, you know."

She looked away, knowing she'd had no right to ask in the first place. "Okay. Fine. Keep your secrets if you must."

"I will," he noted dryly.

They left the restaurant and he drove her back to pick up her car at the auditorium. They didn't speak along the way, and Paige was glad, because her mind was absorbed with the things he had told her this evening.

Carol and Barry. How could that have been going on all that time and she be so unaware of it? She and Carol had had their differences, but they had been close in many ways. Carol had made occasional phone calls to Aberdeen when she was bored, calls that lasted for hours, with Paige the sounding board for all her crazy thoughts and elaborate plans for the future. She'd often complained about Jake, but only in the random way that any young bride might complain about life without the fun she'd had as a single. Carol had never taken it seriously. And she was sure Carol had never told her about Barry.

Barry. What was he thinking? How could he even begin to think he could win any woman away from Jake?

She glanced at Jake's handsome profile and had to hide a smile, because she realized she was becoming biased in his favor. What a change that was. Still, she knew Carol could never have preferred Barry. So why did she let him hang around that way? Was she using him as a foil so that she could get her own way with Jake? Or was she just amusing herself with the two of them? Paige supposed she would never know the truth now. And it had all been so long ago, there didn't seem to be much point in obsessing on it.

"Here we are," Jake said, and she looked up to find they were back at the auditorium parking lot. Her little car was the only one left.

"See you later?" she asked, looking at him searchingly.

He nodded. "I have a few people to see and a few errands to run. Then I'll be back." A slow smile curled the corners of his mouth. "You're not going to move to the shop for the night, are you?"

She'd forgotten all about her threat of the morning. Reddening slightly, she hesitated. "I guess not," she said archly. "Not unless I have to."

"Don't worry," he said. "I'll be on my best behavior. I swear."

She slipped out of the car and looked at him over her shoulder. He gave her a wink as he drove off. She watched him go, shaking her head, and suddenly what Sara had said about the "wild ones" came back into her mind.

"Not me," she repeated stubbornly. "Not me."

THE DRIVE TO the hospital was short and fast. She was later than usual and she knew Kenny would be wondering where she was. It was so boring for him to stay cooped up like this all day. But for now, it was for the best.

Trent was in the hall as she got off the elevator.

"How's he doing?" she asked as she came striding toward him.

"Fine." Trent gave her a searching look that surprised her. "And how are you doing?"

"I'm all right. Why wouldn't I be all right?" She looked anxiously toward Kenny's room. "Is something wrong? Can I go in to see him?"

Trent seemed odd, not his usual friendly self. "Uh...yeah," he said reluctantly. "He's okay. I ran some simple tests on him and he passed with flying colors. In fact...Paige, I think he can go home tomorrow."

"Oh, no," she said quickly. "Not yet."

"What do you mean, not yet?" Trent frowned at her suspiciously.

She had to think of something, fast. She couldn't take him home. Jake was there.

"I...I don't think that would be a good idea," she said lamely, unable to find any compelling reason to back up her case.

"What is it, Paige?" he asked, gazing at her with real concern. "What's the matter?"

She didn't want to tell him. More and more people were finding out about Jake, but she wanted to hold off as many as she could for as long as she could, and she especially wanted to keep it away from the hospital.

"Never mind, Trent," she said. "We'll talk about it later. Just take my word for it. He really needs to stay another day at least." She glanced around nervously. "Right now, I want to get in to see him, because I'm really late and I know he'll be annoyed."

Trent started to say something else, but she ignored him and hurried away. There was no way to fight this logically. But maybe, just maybe, Trent would take her word for it and let things ride for another day.

Kenny looked up hopefully as she walked in, shutting off the sound on his television. "Hi. Guess what? Dr. Holmes says I can go home in the morning. Cool, huh?"

She smiled and dropped a kiss on the top of his head. "Well, I just talked to Dr. Holmes, and you know what?" She tousled his hair. "We're not sure if you're ready yet."

His face fell. "No! I don't want to stay here anymore. I'm sick of this bed and I'm sick of the nurses and I'm sick of—"

"Kenny," she said warningly.

"I want to go home. I wanna..." His voice faded and he bit his lip, his gaze shifting strangely.

She frowned. "What? What do you want?" she asked him.

He looked away rebelliously and didn't answer. She sank into the chair next to his bed and reached out to take his hand in hers.

"Kenny, we've got to be careful. When you do come home, I want you to be able to run and play like you're used to doing. I would hate to have to keep you in your bed..."

"That's all I'm doing here. I could do the same thing at home."

"But if something goes wrong here, the doctors are ready to make sure you're okay."

He looked at her and then looked away, his face stormy.

"Hey, Mr. Grouch," she coaxed. He certainly wasn't himself, and for just a moment, she wondered. But there was no reason to think he knew his father was in town. None at all.

She stayed only about fifteen minutes. Unable to cajole him into good humor, she left, feeling guilty about making him remain an extra day.

But what else could she do? She desperately needed that day to work on Jake, and if Kenny came home, she knew he would be all wrapped up in his son and completely oblivious to anything she was trying to do. Before he got his hands on her boy, she had to convince him she was a better parent for Kenny than he was. And right now, she thought there might be some hope. She didn't think he'd thought through what things would be like with a teenage boy in his life. She had to make him do that, make him face facts.

Kenny belonged with her and Jake was going to have to learn that.

JAKE REACHED the top of the hill and slowly turned, taking a moment to catch his breath. The sun was sinking behind the mountain range that hid the sea. The jagged Sierras towered behind him, still snow-covered in late spring. Below, he could see the tailings from some old mines, like bleeding eruptions in the earth. But otherwise, the land was much the same as it must have appeared to the inhabitants who walked here five hundred years ago, to the Spanish conquerors who rode in almost three hundred years ago and the forty-niners from the last century who had come looking for gold and, for the most part, found nothing but heartbreak.

"Just like me," he said aloud, but the wind snatched his words from his mouth and flung them against the purple evening sky. He laughed abruptly. No self-pity. That would be the last thing he would allow himself. If he fell into that trap, he would be no good to anyone, especially Kenny.

But the view was too magnificent to waste. It was a beautiful sight—a perfect site. One of many in this area. Pulling his flip-top notebook out of his back pocket, he jotted down coordinates and an evaluation of the area, then stuck it back and looked out at the view again.

And the troubling thoughts returned. Funny, but it was only out here in the big-sky countryside that he could ask himself the questions that he normally kept suppressed.

Had he failed Carol?

"No," he said aloud. Their marriage had been good and bad, all at once, and it wasn't anything he would ever want to repeat. But he'd tried damn hard to please her. And to provide for her. And to a large extent, he'd done it. It was a tragedy she'd died that day on the rain-slicked highway, but he hadn't put the keys in her hand. He hadn't told her to run off into the storm.

So the answer, firmly, was, "No."

Was he going to take Kenny with him when he went?

"Yes," he said just as uncompromisingly. That was what he'd come for, and that was what he was going to do. There was no ambiguity in his mind over that one.

And now for the biggie, the one that had his thoughts and emotions in a tangle. Was he going to let himself fall for Paige?

Slowly, he shook his head. "No," he whispered. "Can't do it. Won't do it."

There was no denying that she bothered him, tantalized him, conjured up a physical allure that had him aching at times.

He wasn't holding back because of Carol. Even if she was Carol's sister, Carol had been gone for four years. It was time for him to get on with his life.

The problem was, he liked Paige, liked her more than he ever thought he would. He wanted things to go well for her, didn't want her getting all messed up over him. It wouldn't be fair. After all she'd done for Kenny, she deserved the best.

Actually, what she deserved was some nice clean-cut young guy with his own business somewhere. She deserved babies and a house with a white picket fence, if that was what she wanted. She deserved more than someone who's always had trouble putting down roots.

Okay, that was settled. No lovemaking.

But they could still be friends, couldn't they?

And he did want to take her a present. Looking around, he began picking wildflowers—California poppies, wild larkspur, lupine, wild sweet pea, columbine—until he had a huge bouquet. Wildflowers. That suited Paige somehow. Smiling, he started down the hill.

CHAPTER TEN

PAIGE WAS DISAPPOINTED when she let herself into her apartment and he wasn't there. She scolded herself severely, then tried to convince herself that she just wanted another chance to woo him over to her side. But deep inside, she knew it was much more than that.

The place seemed cold and empty. She made herself a pot of tea and turned on the television. But in moments, she'd turned it off. She couldn't concentrate on television. She couldn't think about anything but Jake and Kenny. They filled her mind, filled her consciousness. What was she going to do?

Suddenly she lifted her head. There was a new scent in the room. Frowning, she turned slowly and found the source—a huge bouquet of wildflowers shoved into a glass vase and put on her dining-room table. Jake must have picked them off some nearby mountainside meadow.

They were lovely. Wildflowers—brilliant colors. Reaching out, she touched a brilliant orange blossom, and suddenly she wondered whether Jake's gift was symbolic. "Put a little of the wild in your life," the flowers seemed to say. "Here, see? It's not so scary. Give it a try."

Or was she making things up? She didn't know. She seemed to be reading things into every situation these days. And she was getting so jumpy, she was a wreck.

She took a long, cold drink of water and tried to calm her nerves. The minutes were crawling by. It was late, time to go to bed, and Jake wasn't back yet. Where could he be? What could he be doing?

All sorts of possibilities flowed through her head. What if he'd found some old friends who had told him about Kenny's accident? What if he'd gone to talk to Judge Randall? What if he'd met up with an old girl-friend? What if he'd gone to see Barry again?

It was ridiculous to let his absence get to her this way. There was no way of knowing what he was up to. And even if she did know, there was very little chance anything she did about it would matter.

That settled in her mind, she went into her bed-room to prepare for bed. But for some reason, in-stead of reaching for the old worn sweatshirt she usually donned for the occasion, her hand slipped back farther in the drawer and came up with the white, lacy nightgown she'd been given one Christmas two years ago and never worn.

She rationalized, telling herself she wanted to talk to Jake when he came in and this would be what she would wear to greet any visitor. And besides, she'd be wearing her robe. But she avoided looking in the mir-ror, knowing she was kidding herself.

Another hour dragged by. She curled up in her bed and dozed. It seemed as though she'd only just shut her eyes, when a sound popped them open again. Jumping up, she listened intently. It sounded like the front door.

She grabbed her robe, threw it around her shoulders and made her way out into the hall. "Jake?"

There was no answer. She ventured into the living room without hesitation.

He was sitting on the couch, looking disturbed.

"Jake, what is it?" She went to him quickly, alarmed. "What's happened?"

"Nothing. I... I'm just tired." He smiled at her quickly, then looked away again. "You shouldn't have waited up."

"I didn't. I was asleep." She slipped down beside him on the couch. "What is the matter? Where have you been?"

He stirred uncomfortably at her question. He didn't want to have this discussion right now. He'd been all over town. But the last place had been Carol's grave. That was something Paige probably wouldn't want to hear about.

"It seems like I've been just about everywhere," he told her vaguely. "I visited some places from the old days. Saw some people."

Her heart skipped a beat and she waited to hear what he'd learned, but he didn't go on, and finally, she had to prompt him. "What has made you so unhappy?" she asked softly.

His smile twisted his face but didn't light his eyes. "I'm not unhappy, Paige. I'm just... tired. And in a bad mood."

She wanted to help him. She ached to help him. But he was making it quite clear he didn't want her help, so she bit her tongue.

"Thank you for the flowers," she said, instead.

His face did light up at that. "The wildflowers. Do you like them?"

"They're beautiful."

He looked over at the vase. "A lot of them are already wilting," he noted.

"They do that," she agreed. "Some thrive in captivity and some don't."

"Yeah," he said cynically. "Just like hopes."

"Jake, what is it?" She was unsettled by his mood. She'd never seen him like this before. She moved closer to him on the couch, her hand touching his arm. "What have you done? What have you heard?"

He stared at her for a long moment, then, with a soft groan, he reached out and pulled her to him, holding her gently in his arms, stroking her hair.

"Paige, Paige," he murmured softly. "Stay safe, will you? Will you do that for me?"

Her heart was pounding. He felt so good, so right, his strong arms so protective, his hand so gentle in her hair. And his intentions were clearly pure affection.

Affection! They had come a long way since that night he'd appeared in her shop and scared her so. But something was bothering him right now, and suddenly she had to know what that something was.

Lifting her face, she gazed into his. "Is this about Carol?" she asked him, her voice trembling.

He looked into her eyes, and then he nodded slightly. "I've been gone for four years," he said, his voice low and husky. "I hadn't been to her grave since the funeral."

"Oh, Jake." She leaned back so she could see his face more clearly.

"I thought I ought to go and settle things between us," he said quietly. "Carol and me, I mean."

Paige was shaking. Something was touching her deeply, reaching far down into the depths of her soul.

"And did you settle things?" she asked, trying to control the shaking by pulling her arms in tightly around her, hoping he wouldn't notice even though he was still holding her.

And just as she thought the words, he released her, distancing himself away from her on the couch, looking away, his face troubled once again.

"I don't know yet, Paige," he said. "I just don't know." He ran a hand through his dark hair, leaving it disheveled. "You know, there are too many things that we do too young, before we really understand the significance of them."

She nodded. "Like?"

"Like falling in love." He stretched back against the pillow. "Getting married. Having children. We tend to do all those things before we've grown up enough to handle them."

"Yes, but maybe we wouldn't grow up at all if we didn't do them," she suggested wisely.

He turned to look at her and half smiled. "So you're saying it's a Catch-22?"

"Maybe." He looked away again, and she asked softly, "Do you wish you'd waited?"

He stared into space for a moment, then said in a dull voice, "I loved Carol."

Her breath caught in her throat. "So did I."

He turned and met her gaze defiantly. "So did we all," he said, his voice as bitter as his eyes. "And all for what?"

Paige shook her head. She couldn't help but think it would be best if he talked his problem out. But how could she tell him that, knowing the sort of thing he might reveal? In truth, she was afraid of finding out too much.

Still, she found herself pushing on, unable to stop. "You said you visited her grave. Is that right?"

He nodded slowly, turning away, his eyes haunted.

She said suddenly, irrationally, regretting it the moment the words were out of her mouth, "Did you take her some wildflowers, too?"

He looked up, surprised. "No. Carol would have scorned wildflowers. You know that." He shrugged. "I stopped and bought some roses at a flower market."

Paige held herself even closer.

"I'm sure she would have liked the roses," she said simply.

He grimaced. "What the hell?" he snapped. "She's dead. Taking flowers to the cemetery comforts the living. It doesn't do a damn thing for the dead."

She shrank back against the corner of the couch. "Don't talk like that," she said softly. "You don't know that for sure. You don't know—"

"I know she's dead. I know she's gone. I know my son doesn't have his mother." His face twisted. "And I know I could have prevented it all."

She couldn't meet his eyes. "Jake..."

"The funny thing is, Barry was right. I never should have married her, Paige. And once we realized we wanted different things out of life, we should have separated right away, before she got pregnant."

Paige looked up, shocked. "But then there would be no Kenny."

His eyes finally met hers. He stared at her long and hard, but he didn't say a word.

She was confused. Did this mean he would be ready to accept the thought of giving up his son? She couldn't let the opportunity to advance her cause pass her by. Licking her dry lips, she said hoarsely, "Let him stay with me, Jake. Please. If you can say something like what you just said—"

He reached out and grabbed her forearm in his strong hand and pulled her closer.

"Don't you ever, ever get the idea that I don't love my boy, Paige," he said harshly, his eyes as fierce as a winter ice storm. "I'd give up everything for him. The only thing I regret right now is that I was stupid enough to stay away from him this long. Believe it. Kenny is going with me."

Her heart sank. There was no mistaking the intensity in his voice and his face.

"I'm sorry," he added, his fingers loosening on her arm. "But this is the way it has to be."

She stared at him, trying not to lose hope. After all, he hadn't seen Kenny yet. Maybe that would be enough for him. Once he saw what Kenny was like, how happy and well-adjusted the child was, he would change his mind. Not that he wouldn't just love him all the more. Of course he would. How could he help it? But once he'd come face-to-face with the fact that Kenny had a life here, he would begin to see things more realistically. He might reevaluate his options. She couldn't lose faith at this point. If she gave up, there would be nothing left.

Slipping away from him, she rose from the couch. "How about a cup of tea?" she suggested cheerily, hoping to lighten the mood in the room. "I'll go fix us both some, okay? Be back in a minute."

He didn't respond. Sinking back into the pillows on the couch, he didn't watch her leave the room. He hardly noticed that she'd left.

His mind was on Kenny. Jake had stopped by the hospital before he'd gone to the cemetery. Kenny had told him all about how Paige was not letting him go home the next morning, even though the doctor said he could. He'd thought that over before he'd responded to the boy's concerns.

"You know, she's probably right," he'd said, glad to think that at least he wouldn't have to worry about her running off with Kenny if the boy was safely in his hospital bed. "I don't think it'll hurt you to stay another day."

Kenny was shocked and Jake could see the beginnings of a feeling of betrayal growing in his eyes. His father had deserted him before. Would he do it again?

Jake winced. This was what he had done to his own boy. For this he would never forgive himself.

"Listen," he said quickly, trying to forestall the fear. "What you ought to be doing during this last day here is making lists and getting ready."

"Getting ready?"

"For the things we're going to be doing once we're together."

"Oh."

He smiled at the boy. "Okay? I want you to think of good ideas, because it's been a long time since I've been a kid, and I don't even know what kids like."

Kenny shook his head, his eyes strangely haunted. "I just want to be with you," he said in a voice that was trying hard to be strong.

Jake reached out and put a firm hand on his son's shoulder, emotion choking his throat. "Believe me, Kenny," he said gruffly. "You will be."

And he would be. He would be.

There were problems to overcome, and it wasn't going to be easy. He was beginning to realize how hard this would be on Paige. At first, he'd assumed this was only a power struggle between the two of them, that she would be against anything he was for, ready to fight him just for the hell of it. But now he knew that wasn't right. She cared for Kenny. She wanted what was best for him. What she hadn't yet faced was the fact that the best thing for him was to have his father back in his life.

The sound of Paige coming back with the tea roused him from his musings. He found he felt more relaxed as he watched her walk in, carefully balancing two porcelain cups full of steaming liquid.

"Thanks," he said, taking the tea from her. "I'll drink this and go right to bed."

Paige didn't answer. She slipped down beside him and settled her robe modestly around her knees, then adjusted the neckline, before glancing at him. He was concentrating on his teacup and hadn't noticed a thing.

A flash of annoyance shot through her, but she stifled it. What did she want, anyway? Nothing consistent, that was for sure. She scolded herself again, sighed and got back to business.

"Do you remember that last night years ago, Jake?" she asked softly. "My birthday dinner?"

His dark head rose and he nodded. "Yes, I remember. Some birthday for you, wasn't it?"

She moved forward until she was sitting on the edge of the couch. "Do you remember the confrontation you had with my father in the hallway?"

His eyebrows drew together and he set down his cup carefully on the table. "Of course I remember. Everything else hinges on that."

"Yes, it does."

His face was hardening and she knew he wasn't going to like her drawing him out about that night. But she had to. Just as he had to settle things between himself and Carol, Paige had to settle things between herself and him. She had to know he remembered and regretted. His feelings of guilt would go a long way toward freeing her from her own.

"Do you regret it?" she asked.

His frown was deepening. "Of course."

Her heart was beating so hard she could hardly stand it. Her hand was shaking and she had to put down the teacup to avoid its rattling. The next question was the hardest she'd ever had to ask anyone. She got the words out, but they sounded stiff and shaky.

"Why... why did you call them?"

He glanced at her almost casually. "Who?"

She took a deep breath. "The government. The IRS. The police. Whoever those agents were."

She found herself gasping slightly, felt her hands trembling. "Why did you do it, Jake?" she went on when he didn't answer.

It was awful, horrifying, to bring up that night and the day that followed. And yet, if she didn't, the incident would hang between them forever, and she couldn't stand that.

"If you hadn't called them... If they hadn't shown up the next day to padlock my father's office and carry off all his files, Carol wouldn't have driven off the way she did... none of that would have happened."

She shook her head, fighting tears. She didn't want to cry. She wasn't looking for sympathy. She was only looking for truth. "How could you have done it? You know my father didn't deserve it. Sure, he paid some of his office workers under the table. And that wasn't right. But maybe if you'd talked to him you'd have understood why he did what he did."

She stared at him, going from anguish to anger, wanting to shake him. Why didn't he respond?

"Jake, did you ever know how much pro bono work he did for the community? Did anyone ever tell you how many women he helped in his New Mother and Prenatal Care Clinic for absolutely no pay? Did you know that he spent every Thursday doing charity work at the hospital?" Her voice was rising. She couldn't help it. "The problem began when he lost a malpractice settlement. Unfairly, I may add. But nonetheless his insurance premiums shot up to where he couldn't afford to keep his office operating. So he began to pay some workers off the books. He didn't deserve to be stabbed in the back the way you did it. One call to the government, and it was all over. He lost everything. And all those people he used to help lost a lot, too."

She stared at Jake in frustration. He stared back, looking for all the world as though he hadn't heard a thing she'd said. "Well, say something," she demanded at last. "How could you have done it, just because he hurt your feelings when he called you—"

"Paige." He reached across and grabbed her hand. "Paige, you have to understand something. I didn't call them."

She blinked. It was as though he'd said there would be no midnight tonight. That was just plain wrong. "Of course you called them." Everyone knew it, had known it for four years.

"No."

There was no hesitation in his response. He didn't even try to convince her. He just stated it as fact. For the first time, she began to doubt.

"But...you were the one who threatened to."

He shook his head. "I know I said a lot of angry things that night, a lot of things I've regretted ever since, and will suffer for the rest of my life. But I never called the IRS. Paige...I never did."

She gazed at him dumbly. How could she believe that? What could she say?

"Think a minute," he went on. "Does it sound like something I would do? Have you ever known me to be a snitch?" He waited a moment for an answer, but she just stared at him and he frowned impatiently.

"Oh, hell, Paige, everyone knew your father had been treated unfairly and that he padded his payroll to survive. Nobody really cared, least of all me. I know all that stuff about his pro bono work. Your father did more good for this community than a few dollars extra to the government bureaucracy could ever pay for.

I never did blame him for that." He hesitated, then charged on. "He hurt me that night, insulted me. If he'd been a younger man, I could have hit him and gotten even that way."

He threw out his arms in a gesture of indignation. "But I couldn't hit him. And the frustration of the years, of everyone thinking I was such a rotter when I was actually trying hard to live my life right. It all suddenly came down on me when he said I'd ruined Carol's life. I had to hit back. And since I couldn't do it with my fist, I did it with words." He shook his head, his blue eyes haunted by a distant misery. "And ended up," he added quietly, "causing more damage than my fist could ever have done."

She shook her head slowly, still trying to take it all in. He was right. He'd never been the sort to snitch before. But this had been different. This had been revenge, hadn't it?

Still, when had she ever known him to take revenge? Could he be telling the truth? Could he be?

"Paige, I didn't do it." His face was sincere, his eyes were solemn.

She tried to think of a rebuttal, and all she could come up with was, "But, why didn't you deny it at the time?"

He groaned, throwing his head back. "I did deny it. I denied it all over the place. But no one was listening to me. No one believed me. Each one of you was very busy blaming me. And then the news came about Carol."

She put her fingertips to her temple, trying to remember how it had been, but all she could recall was the turmoil, the anger, and then the shocked horror, the despair.

He touched her, let his hand sift tenderly through her hair, and looked at her honestly. "I didn't do it," he said again. "I would never have done such a thing."

"But then why...? Why didn't you come back for the hearing, or even for the trial?"

"When your father faced the charges against him?" Jake threw his head back and closed his eyes for a moment, then looked at her again and shrugged. "He didn't want me there. And there didn't seem to be any point in it. He had Judge Randall and the rest of the community rallying behind him."

"He still lost everything," she said bitterly.

"I know. And I'm really sorry that happened. But my being here wouldn't have changed anything." He shifted uncomfortably. "Okay, the truth is, I wanted to blot all of you out of my mind. I wanted to leave you all behind, start a new life and forget all about you."

"Even Kenny?" she asked softly.

Slowly, he nodded, his eyes tortured. "Even Kenny," he admitted. "I was a fool, I wasn't thinking straight. I can't deny it."

"But you think you can return now and—"

"And get it all back?" He nodded, staring at her hard. "Yes. That may not be fair, but it's what I want."

He amazed her. The insolence, the selfishness, the careless arrogance of the man. She didn't know whether to laugh or cry.

"But, back to the subject," he said crisply. "I didn't call the IRS. I didn't do it."

Despite everything, the logic and the utter sincerity with which he spoke completely bowled her over. "I think I believe you," she said.

He stared at her. She believed him. Oh, God. No one had believed him for so long. A feeling welled up inside him, part relief, part gratitude. He took her face in his hands, framing it, looking down at her lips, wanting to kiss her. He stopped himself. He couldn't do this. He shouldn't do it. Starting a physical relationship would involve too much, risk too much, ruin too much. He had to resist.

His gaze was drawn lower. Her robe had fallen open. He could see the full swell of her breasts, see the dusky nipples beneath the lacy white fabric, and something deep inside him fell away, making him feel as though he'd taken a steep drop on a roller-coaster ride. He'd never seen anything so beautiful, never seen anything he wanted more to touch, take possession of.

She knew her robe was open. She knew what he was looking at. And for once, she didn't move to avoid what she knew she was risking.

She wanted him. She'd never felt quite this way before. It was as if a very different woman had taken over her soul—a woman who was bold and aggressive in love, someone who reached out and took what she wanted from life. Instead of drawing back, of covering up, Paige moved so that her robe opened even wider, and then she watched, trembling, holding her breath, as he reached for her slowly, drawn in by her obvious invitation, his fingers barely grazing the cloth before coming together to take hold of her nipple as it hardened, tugging slightly, sending a shock wave of erotic sensation through her, turning her flesh to molten gold. She gasped aloud, her eyes wide as they stared into his.

But she didn't pull away. He looked at her, his fingers holding her, rubbing lightly, and he slowly sank toward her, until his mouth covered hers, taking hard and total control, filling her with a need that was as much hers as it was his.

She melted against him, every nerve, every muscle turning to liquid, every sense attuned only to his touch. She ached for him, longed for his body, needed his soul. At this moment, she was ready to live only for him. For the moment.

But he was pulling back, shaking his head as though to clear it, as though he was trying to figure out where he was, and then his hand drew away from her breast as though it were suddenly scorching him.

"Paige," he said softly, "I promised you I wouldn't do this."

"That's okay," she murmured, deep in her throat. "I promised myself, too." And she reached for him, sliding her hand down the side of his cheek. "So we're even."

He shook his head, but she ignored the gesture. The emotions inside her were overpowering and she couldn't deny them. She was caught up in a feeling of fatalism, as though destiny were finally taking a hand and deciding the outcome.

She wanted him. There were a lot of things she'd wanted in the past, things she'd wanted and been denied. But she wasn't going to let this pass her by. Reaching out, she slipped her hand inside his shirt, flattening the palm on his hot skin, cupping his pectoral muscle, digging her fingers gently into his hard flesh, reveling in his strength.

"Turnabout is fair play," she whispered, and then she leaned forward and pressed her lips to the skin above his collarbone.

He groaned, writhing beneath her touch, and then he pulled her back into his arms, taking in her scent, her warmth, burying his face in her hair. She felt so good...so good...

"Paige." His speech was slurred, almost as though he'd been drinking, and he felt that way, lethargic, as though his body had turned on him. It would be easy to let go, let it happen. But he couldn't let that be. There was too much at stake here. "No. No, Paige..."

Pulling away from her was like fighting his way up through quicksand. For a moment, he thought he might not be able to do it. But then she was cooperating, leaning back, searching his face for answers.

"What?" she was asking breathlessly. "What is it?"

"We can't," he told her, touching her cheek and trying to convey the tenderness he felt with his fingertips. "You know we can't. Not with all there is between us."

"You mean...Carol?" she said, sounding slightly puzzled.

"No. Yes." He shook his head. It was more than that—it was Carol and Kenny and the past they all shared. It was the wrenching thing he was going to do to Paige and her family when he took Kenny away. It was his own fear of falling too hard for another Kenton woman. It was all of that rolled into a vague, sinister fear that held him back. He didn't want to screw things up again. He didn't want to ruin any more lives.

She swallowed and looked away, hurt and confused. He didn't want her, after all. She'd thought for just a moment there... But what did it matter? He'd never wanted her. He'd always wanted Carol.

She moved away from him on the couch, distancing herself with her cool glance, as well, pulling together her disheveled clothing. She felt humiliated. She'd thrown herself at him the first chance she'd had. He'd told her he was innocent of what she'd always hated him for, and she'd gone giddy in the head, going from hating him to jumping into his lap in one giant leap. The only problem was, he hadn't been there to catch her.

"Hey thanks," she said crisply. "I needed a nice slap in the face to put me back on track."

He winced and shook his head, not sure how to tell her she was entirely too desirable without confusing her even further. The funny thing was, if he hadn't cared about her at all, he probably could have made love to her without a second thought.

"I'm sorry, Paige," he began, but she jumped off the couch and gave him a brittle smile.

"Think nothing of it," she said lightly, tightening the belt of her robe with a vicious snap. "It's all just part of the hospitality."

"Paige, don't." He rose and went after her, but she was too fast for him.

"Good night, Jake," she said, standing at her bedroom door, peering at him through her tangled hair. "I guess I don't have to lock my door, anyway." She smiled at him again, a smile less angry than bittersweet. "No need to fear you'll come knocking in the night, is there?"

"Paige," he groaned, shaking his head. "Don't do this. You know damn well I'm attracted to you. It's just that—"

"You've got a headache, I know." She shrugged, pushing the heavy hair away from her face. "Them's the breaks."

Throwing him one last regretful glance, she whirled into her room, closing the door with a firm shove and then listening to his footsteps leading away.

He was gone. And she was... what was she? Embarrassed? Humiliated? Relieved?

She didn't know which. Her mind was cluttered up with too many emotions going in too many different directions. But she did know one thing. She'd made a play for the man, and he'd gently held her off.

She groaned, throwing herself down on the bed. Why had she done it? Was she trying to buy her way to Kenny by selling her soul? Was she trying to make up for something, change something? Or was it purely a sexual attraction like no other she'd ever felt— something overpoweringly provocative, tempting her, leading her on? Whatever it was, whichever it was meant to be, she had to fight against it.

Because it was obvious Jake didn't share the feeling. Jake had loved Carol. Jake had married Carol. Jake had lost Carol through an ugly twist of fate. And that loss had hurt him so much, he'd gone off and left his son behind.

She had to face it. No matter what he said, he'd still been in love with Carol when she died. And he mourned her, even now. The only thing about Paige that might even slightly attract him was her resemblance to her sister.

She stared into the night, a pain too deep for tears pressing on her heart. Why did it always have to be this way?

Why was Carol always in the way?

CHAPTER ELEVEN

"DID IT EVER occur to you," Paige asked herself the next morning as she combed her hair before the bathroom mirror, "that every single man in your life was involved with Carol before he had a relationship with you?"

It was true, and a chill ran down her spine just thinking of it. Every single man, including Kenny, including her father.

"Oh, this is really childish," she went on, scolding herself as she threw her brush down. "Next I'll be comparing the vowels in our names to read the future, or something equally nutty."

But she couldn't stop thinking about it. What was wrong with her? Was there lingering resentment she hadn't let surface? Was she trying to relive Carol's life? What exactly was going on here?

Whatever it was, it was time to put a stop to it. She could break the chain all on her own. She could easily rid her life of Barry. That wouldn't bother her at all. Jake was another story, but she ought to be able to send him packing. As long as he left Kenny behind.

"That's it. I'll wash that man right out of my hair and never think about him again."

But that would be a little difficult if he had Kenny with him. Kenny was the one male she could not lose, although it was getting harder and harder to see how she was going to convince Jake to leave him with her.

She walked through the silent apartment, passed the wildflowers and noted that very few looked fresh and vibrant. Most of them had crumbled and fallen apart.

"Wild things should be left to the wild," she whispered to herself, looking back at them. "That's where they belong."

She glanced toward the hallway. Jake hadn't appeared this morning, and she was just as glad. She still wasn't sure if she was embarrassed by what had happened the night before, or merely tired of thinking about it. She'd thrown herself at Jake and she knew it. She also knew why, and it wasn't because she was trying to jockey for position, or trying to bribe him into rethinking the Kenny situation.

The trouble was he probably thought it was for all those reasons. Well, maybe it was just as well that he think that. Better that than the truth. Better that than he realize she was very much afraid she was falling head over heels in love with him.

What a laugh. Carol would have roared. Little Paige, the careful one, the cool one, the one who never seemed to need constant male companionship or hoards of admirers like Carol did—Paige, in love with the man who had caused more misery for her family than anyone else.

But had he really? That was the question, and she didn't have an answer. She'd told him the night before that she believed him when he said he hadn't been the one to call the government agents on her father. But if not Jake, who? Who else had the motivation?

She thought it over as she drove toward the hospital. If not Jake, who? Barry, who was so jealous of Jake's life with Carol? Could he have thought that doing it in Jake's name would ruin the relationship and give him a chance with Carol? He'd been in the hallway that night. He'd heard Jake's threat. But would he really have done such a thing?

How about Dr. Trent Holmes? He was also in the hallway. And he was the one who actually gained the most from what happened, taking over the practice Dr. Kenton had to abandon. Could anyone believe that dear, kind Trent would pick up a phone and call the IRS to turn in another doctor? She didn't think either one could have done such a thing, but if not them, who?

It was a question she hadn't had to deal with before, and it stumped her now. But there was a new determination growing in her—a need to prove one way or another what had happened. And secretly, she hoped Jake was telling the truth, that he wasn't the one who had called the authorities and set the chain of events in motion that sent Carol running off in anguish that day.

She called her father from a pay phone as soon as she got to the hospital. After all, he had to know that Jake hadn't betrayed him.

His voice, when he answered, was a little groggy, and she frowned, worried about him, as always.

"Are you okay?" she asked.

"I'm fine, just fine." He coughed. "Now, what is it you want? Anything wrong with Kenny?"

"No. No, he's fine."

"Good. I've got plans for that boy." His voice quickly became more lively as he got into his subject. "Remember when we used to take that cottage on the beach in Carmel every summer when you and Carol were little? I got in touch with the owner. I'm going to rent the place for the month of July and take Kenny up there. What do you think?"

"Oh." She closed her eyes, holding back the apprehension. July wasn't very far off, but things might be very different by the time they all got there. If Jake had his way, Kenny would be gone. "Uh, I think he would love it, but—"

"Sure he would love it. Your mother says we ought to let him bring along a friend. How about that Ryan kid, the one on his swim team?"

"He's a very nice boy and Kenny likes him a lot."

"Great. We'll do it." Pure joy filled his voice. "It's a wonderful idea. You know, Paige, it gives me hope to have something like that in front of me. There are some days when life hardly seems worth the effort. But then I look at that boy's face and I know I have to go on. He makes it all worthwhile."

Paige felt a burning in her eyes. "I . . . I know what you mean, Dad," she said softly.

"Now, what was it you called to tell me?"

She took a deep breath. "Nothing. I just wanted to say hi. Give Mother a hug, okay? I've got to get going."

She hung up quickly, before he could ask about Jake. That would have to wait for later. Much, much later.

She steadied herself and then took the elevator to Kenny's floor to pay the usual morning visit. For once he greeted her with a smile and a kiss, his bad mood of late seemingly forgotten. He threw his arms around her neck and hugged her closely, making her laugh.

"Tell me about my dad," he said eagerly, his eyes bright and clear. "Tell me all about him."

Paige hesitated. "Well..."

In the past, when he'd asked, she'd tried to be as general as possible. She'd never, ever let him hear the anger that had lived inside her. And now she was glad she hadn't. She could hardly claim to hate him any longer, especially after what had happened the night before. She knew now he was definitely not the monster she'd once thought he was—that she'd fooled herself into thinking he was.

"Your father is a big, strong, handsome man," she said. "He's a man who knows how to get things done."

"Yeah?" Kenny's face shone.

"Yeah. And...he loves you very much." She smiled at him affectionately.

His young face was so eager. "Can I go with him?"

Her knuckles whitened as her hands clutched the edge of her chair. "What do you mean?" she asked.

"When he comes on Saturday. Can I go with him?"

She swallowed hard. "He is going to be here for your birthday." Wasn't that enough? No, of course it wasn't.

Kenny persisted. "But when he goes, I'm going with him. Right?"

She shook her head, her throat tightening with trepidation. This was just what she'd been dreading. "Oh, Kenny, no. How could I do without you?"

His face clouded. "What do you mean, no?"

She hesitated, unsure. How to convince a twelve-year-old boy?

"Kenny, listen. A boy needs a settled life, with a place to call home and people to take care of him and his friends and his school..."

"My dad could give me that." His lower lip was protruding stubbornly and there was a storm brewing in his eyes.

"Kenny..." There wasn't really anything she could say. She didn't know what was going to happen. It wouldn't be fair to try to set Kenny against his father at this point. She wouldn't have done it even if she had thought she could. Kenny needed a strong, loving father as much as he needed anything. But he also needed just what she'd said, a stable, supportive environment. How was she going to explain this to him? How did you make a kid understand?

She didn't know. She couldn't find the words. And in her frustration she panicked.

Turning, she rose from her seat, reaching out a hand to steady herself against the railing at the foot of his bed. "Kenny, we'll talk about this later. I've got to get to the store and...and take care of things."

Once outside his room, she slumped against the wall. What was she going to do? It was quite evident that Kenny was going to demand he be allowed to go with Jake. And why should that surprise her? She was about ready to go with him herself. Straightening, she walked quickly to the nurses' station.

"Is Dr. Holmes in this morning?" she asked the nurse on duty.

"No, he has office hours right now. Would you like me to call him there?"

"No. No, thank you. I'll contact him later."

But not too much later. Trent was going to have to help her. Something had to be done.

She gathered together the shattered shreds of her composure and left the building, striding toward her car. She had work to do. She would worry about everything else later.

JAKE SAT on Kenny's bed and stared at the poster of Wayne Gretzky on the wall. Funny. Over the last four years he thought he'd managed to turn his life around. He'd taken control, matured, became a contributing member of society instead of a scavenger. He'd finished his formal education, done well at it and found himself a darn good job. He'd squared away his emotions and decided the time was right to bring his son back into his life. He'd shown up here full of confidence, sure of himself, sure of what he wanted.

Where had it all gone? The longer he stayed, the more he seemed to revert to his old self—the rebel, the outsider, the misunderstood and the misunderstanding one. What the hell had gone wrong?

"Nothing."

He said it aloud, said it vehemently. Rising from the bed, he began to pace the room, stopping to touch Kenny's things—his bat, his dirty old baseball cap, his swim trophy. No, he wasn't going to let himself fall into that old way of thinking. He was here to get his boy and that was all he was going to do.

All things being equal, he should have come and gone by now. He should have been able to grab Kenny and make a run for it. It was only bad luck that had

Kenny in the hospital and him cooling his heels here, waiting.

Stopping in front of the mirror, he stared at his reflection. Yes, it was the waiting that had done the most harm. But he would get over it. The only thing he really worried about was Paige.

He'd never dreamed they would turn their antagonism into the kind of red-hot attraction that had flared between them the night before. If he'd known, if he'd had any idea, he would have stayed as far away as possible. Because it couldn't be. It just couldn't be. And it wasn't fair to Paige to let her think it might happen.

Paige. She had grown to look so much like Carol, with her long blond hair and her dark eyes. She was a little taller, a little more serious. She didn't have the same devil-may-care glint to her smile, the same way of sticking it to you when you were most vulnerable, as Carol had had. But she had the same sweet scent to her, the same way of tossing her hair back, the same way of raising one eyebrow when she was surprised. It would be easy to pretend that she could take Carol's place—if he actually wanted that place taken.

No. Carol was gone, and in a lot of ways, he was better for it. She'd swept into his life like a hot desert wind, encircling him in her spiral of needs and demands and expectations. Carol wanted a lot—a hell of a lot more than he had been able to give her, both materially and emotionally. He'd never made her happy. He didn't know if anyone ever would have been able to.

He'd felt trapped, married to her. He was never going to let himself get into a situation like that again.

But then there was Paige, beautiful Paige—what was he going to do about her?

"ALL WORK and no play will probably make you rich," Sara said breezily as she came into the shop and found Paige on her hands and knees, scrubbing a stubborn area of the tiled floor. "But when will you have any fun?"

"Fun is for kids," Paige retorted, getting up with a sigh. "Hasn't anyone told you life is a constantly evolving spiral of misery?"

"Ouch," Sara said with a laugh. "Go back home and back to sleep and get up again. Only this time, try the other side of the bed."

"Sorry," Paige said, laughing ruefully as she wiped her hands dry. "Let's start over." She put on a bright smile. "Hi, Sara. Thanks for coming in to help me with this inventory."

"No problem. I was glad to get out of the house." Sara put down her things and rolled up her sleeves. "Where do I start?"

They worked together well, chatting and working silently by turns, with Paige stopping to help customers as they entered. Noon was rolling around when Sara looked up with a smile and asked, "Is Jake going to be coming by today?"

Paige turned around and looked at her in surprise. "Jake?"

"Yes." She pulled off the gloves she was wearing and jotted down numbers on her form. "Didn't he tell you? He came by yesterday when you were gone. We had a talk."

Paige stared at her. "You like him," she said softly.

Sara grinned. "I think he's adorable. I think that man you've been so dead set against all this time must be Jake's evil twin, or something." She shook her head. "It sure can't be the man I talked to yesterday."

Paige felt a twinge of jealousy and forced it back, turning away quickly before Sara could see any signs of it. She was not going to be jealous over this man. No way. Especially not with someone she liked as much as Sara.

"He can be a charmer," she agreed, turning back with a forced smile.

The doorbell rang out its warning. An elderly couple had entered. They'd been in the shop before, studying an expensive antique lamp they were interested in.

"The Jordans," Paige said, jumping up. "Maybe they're finally ready to buy."

She'd only been out on the floor with them a moment when the bell was ringing again, and this time it was Jake who entered the shop.

His gaze met Paige's immediately, but she looked away quickly, talking to her customers. Her face reddened slightly, and he groaned, but too softly for her to hear. It was obvious that she was embarrassed by what had happened the night before. He was going to have to do something about that.

Turning, he caught sight of Sara waving to him from the back room, and he made his way toward her.

"Hi, Sara," he said with a smile. "How's it going?"

"Just fine, Jake. How are you?" She made room for him at the table where she was working, and he plunked down the two paper bags he'd brought along.

"Passable," he responded to her question. "I brought cheeseburgers for all."

She took in the aroma and sighed happily. "Is this a peace offering of some kind, or just bribery?" she teased.

He grinned. "You *are* perceptive." Then his face sobered. "Paige didn't tell you about what happened last night, did she?"

Sara looked back blankly. "Nope. Not a word."

He looked relieved. "Good."

And she leaned forward, eyes sparkling. "But you can tell me right now. I'm all ears."

He chuckled. "Not on your life."

She watched as he began pulling items out of the bags.

"Are you going to take Kenny away from her?" she asked softly.

He looked up quickly, startled. "He's my son," he said simply.

She nodded. "But he's Paige's, too."

"How do you figure that?"

"That boy has four years of her love in him," she said convincingly. "I think that counts, don't you?"

Of course it counted. He sank back into his chair and stared at the young woman, sick at heart. "If you mean, it's not fair, of course, you're right," he said. "Life isn't fair. Life is just what it is."

"Life just is," she agreed. "But you don't have to let it run you over."

Everyone was a philosopher these days. As if he didn't already feel guilty enough about what he had to do. Very deliberately, he opened a container of french fries and put them in the middle of the table. "Have something to eat," he told her grumpily. "It'll give you something to do besides delivering lectures."

She laughed, but before she could say anything else, Paige reappeared in the doorway.

"Did the Jordans come through for you?" Sara asked her.

Paige glanced at her, distracted. "Uh...no. They'll be back later this afternoon, after they've thought it over."

Sara laughed softly. "You'd think it was a gold mine, wouldn't you? All this hullabaloo for a lamp, for heaven's sake."

"Well, it's a very pretty lamp," Paige answered lamely, for her mind wasn't really on that topic. She looked at Jake, searching his face.

"Cheeseburger?" he offered, gesturing toward the sack. "There's one left for you."

She hesitated. "No, thanks," she said. Her gaze flickered over him again. "We need to talk," she told him firmly.

Sara began to rise from her seat. "I'll just go and—"

"No, Sara," Paige said quickly. "You stay right here. Jake and I will go for a walk."

"A walk?" He cocked an eyebrow, but he kicked back his chair and joined her. "Why not?"

She pushed her blond hair back nervously, smiling a quick farewell to Sara, and led the way out of the shop with Jake right behind her. As soon as they left the building, she turned and looked at him. "Let's just go down to the park and back," she suggested.

"Ah," he said, glancing up and down the street, lined with small businesses and shops. "So that's your plan."

She looked at him, not sure whether to be alarmed at his choice of words or not. "What plan?"

"To keep marching up and down the street." He grinned at her teasingly. "It's a nice public place. We'll both be safe. I can't threaten you, and you can't seduce me..."

"Seduce you!" She swung around and glared at him, her face raised toward his in indignant challenge. "What are you talking about?"

"Exactly what you're thinking about." He brushed back a strand of her hair and smiled at her. "Come on, Paige. You're still uncomfortable with what happened last night. Aren't you?"

Flushing, she turned and started walking again. "Maybe," she admitted softly.

"Well, don't be," he said easily, falling in step beside her. "If it makes you feel any better, I've never turned down anything I've wanted more."

"Oh, brother." This was not really what she wanted to hear. She didn't need anyone's pity. "I don't need to be stroked, Jake," she told him coolly. "My psyche has not been harmed." Brave words. She only hoped they were true. "I'm okay. I'll get over it. And anyway, that's not what I want to talk about."

"Okay. What do you want to talk about?"

She drew in a deep breath and let it out, choosing her words carefully. "You're going to see Kenny soon."

"Am I?" he said dryly.

"Yes. And I . . . I thought we ought to talk about it. I just want you to be prepared. After all, he's not the little eight-year-old boy you left behind."

His eyes darkened and he looked out at the passing traffic. This was the time to tell her he knew what Kenny was like now.

If he didn't . . . If he let her go on thinking she was telling him things he didn't know, how was she going to feel when she found out he'd been lying? It seemed that every move he made was guaranteed to make things worse between them. But right now, he didn't see any alternative. He made his choice.

"Of course he isn't the eight-year-old boy I left behind," he said shortly. "I know that."

"He's going to be thirteen," she said. "A teenager."

"So?"

She swung around and looked at him again, stopping him beneath a spreading oak tree. "Doesn't that make you think twice? I mean—what do you know about teenagers? What are you going to do with one hanging around, going through puberty, getting sassy, doing all the things teenagers do?"

He shook his head. "I'm not going to put up with any of that nonsense," he scoffed. "He'll live like I do, lean and mean."

Lean and mean. Paige groaned inside. Boy, did he have a lot to learn. And then an idea struck her. "Tell me, Jake," she said brightly. "Do you have cable television?"

"No. Never stayed long enough in one place to get it."

"Ah-hah." She nodded, pleased with herself and her line of questioning now. "A compact disc player?" she added archly, smiling at him.

"Good old long-playing records are good enough for me. I do have a stereo," he added, as though he thought that would give him extra points.

"Right." She threw him a pitying look and almost laughed aloud. "To a teenager, you might as well be driving Henry Ford's original model. How about a computer?"

"Sure, I have one of those. I got it about three years ago. With word processor, for writing up research papers."

"Three years ago?"

"Yup. I got a good used one."

"Oh, no." She had to hold back the chortle. This was getting better and better. "I'll bet you're completely outdated. Do you have enough memory for the latest games?"

He almost growled loud. "I haven't the slightest idea."

"You'll know soon enough." Her face was sunny with confidence. "And that will be just as soon as Kenny gets a look at your machine. He'll know. And he'll raise a ruckus if he can't play his games."

Jake's face was stormy by now. "Too bad. I got along without all those things when I was a teenager."

She waved a casual hand into the air. "It's a new age, Jake. And that's just the point." She grinned. "You don't have a clue."

Her sense of superiority was beginning to annoy Jake. "Kenny will enjoy going back to the simpler things. Getting back to the basics." He gestured grandly. "He doesn't need all that electronic junk. I'll take him fishing in cold mountain streams. We'll sleep out under the stars and watch for comets. We'll play touch football in the yard. I'll take him caving."

"Great. Really, that does sound great." She smiled encouragingly, then gave him another pitying look. "But once the weekend is over, he'll be sitting around the house whining for his favorite program or something to play his music on. You just wait and see."

She put a hand on his arm. It was working. He actually looked worried. She almost felt sorry for him, but this was what she wanted, wasn't it? To wake him up to reality.

"Jake, I know those are only superficial things," she told him reassuringly. "But there's more, much more. I want you to think about what a boy that age really needs. About what you needed at that age."

He did think for a moment, and then he looked at her again. "I needed a father," he said bluntly.

She winced. She'd forgotten that. "That's right. Your father left when you were young, didn't he?"

She'd never known the details of his childhood. He'd always seemed a man who'd sprung up out of the earth and needed no background to cling to. But appearances were deceiving. She ought to know that by now.

He didn't answer right away. She took his arm and they started walking again. She didn't say a word, waiting for him to tell her what she'd asked to hear.

But the words didn't come easily to Jake. He'd buried his past under a lot of denial, and it took a little time to dig it out again.

"My father was a drunk," he said evenly at last. "He took off when I was about nine, and I never saw him again."

"Oh." She cringed inside. This wasn't easy for him. "But, as I remember, you still had your mother."

"I had a mother who worked too hard to keep a roof over our heads. A sad, withdrawn woman who started hitting the bottle herself to get through the long, lonely nights." His voice was bitter now. "Needless to say, my family didn't have the best of reputations. And because of that, I grew up in a town that treated me like dirt."

She turned and looked at him, distressed by his simmering anger. Maybe she shouldn't have brought all this up. "I've heard you say that before, but I don't remember it that way."

He glanced at her. "You don't remember the way I was always considered a second-class citizen?"

She shook her head. He'd always seemed a sort of golden boy to her. "Not at all."

He barely smiled and didn't answer.

"Tell me," she coaxed, sincerely interested. "What did they do?"

"Oh, little things. In elementary school I was always in fights. Kids called me names. I defended my family honor. Small change in the vast scheme of things. But I wouldn't call it a happy childhood. I always felt like I had to run twice as far and twice as hard to keep up with the others."

Of course, she hadn't known him then. "By high school, it seems to me you were quite popular."

He grunted. They'd reached the park and instead of turning back, they both sank onto the park bench at the edge of the playground.

"Popular is a strange word," he said sardonically. "It means different things to different people."

She nodded as a neighbor passed them, calling out her name, then she turned to Jake. "You certainly had enough admirers. As I remember it, the girls were falling all over you."

His mouth twisted. "Yeah. Big deal. That isn't really what gives a kid self-esteem, you know."

"No?" She knew that very well, but she wanted to hear his explanation. "Then tell me, what does?"

He thought for a moment, then answered. "Working for something. Working for something and finding out you can get it if you really try. Knowing you did it yourself."

Watching him dig down into himself to struggle for answers, witnessing how hard he was trying to find the truth, letting the compassion she felt spill out of her, she was hit by an undeniable truth. She had fallen in love. This man—sometimes arrogant, sometimes tender—had taken her heart and walked away with it. Now she had to keep him from knowing what he'd done.

She looked away, hiding her secret behind lowered lashes. She ached to put her arms around him, to hold him close, to shield him from a past that still hurt him. But she couldn't do that. She didn't have any right to him or his memories, especially knowing that she intended to take Kenny from him.

"And how did you discover that? Finding out about working at something, I mean."

He stretched back on the bench, his long legs out in front of him. "I didn't really discover it until I went away and worked in the mines. I worked side by side with other men and I found out I could be pretty good at a lot of things if I tried." He looked at her. "Self-esteem isn't people smiling at you and telling you how cute you are. It doesn't come from girls putting out for you, either. Telling you how cool they think you are, and at the same time, hiding you from their mothers." His eyes narrowed. "They'd hear my name and they'd say, 'Now, you stay away from that Winslow boy, honey. You know he's trash.'"

The pain was obvious, the anger leashed but still raw.

"Okay," she said, turning on the bench.

"Okay?" he responded, surprised.

She nodded. "I mean, I get it."

He looked startled for a moment, then gave her his slowest sexy grin. "Ah, she finally gets it."

"Don't mock me, Jake, I'm trying hard to understand here." But she smiled back, resisting the impulse to touch him, put a hand on his arm, his cheek, kiss his lips. "You were kind of a Huckleberry Finn kid."

He shrugged. "That's one way of putting it."

She sat a little straighter on the bench and scolded herself once again. She had to control her feelings and to remember she was only here to try to wrestle Kenny from him. Inhaling deeply, she went on.

"You grew up with hardly any parenting from anybody. But Jake, you've got to admit, you turned out pretty well."

He nodded. "I was lucky. Very, very lucky. I met some people who believed in me."

"And your parents—"

He cut her off before she could begin. "They hardly count. Life defeated them."

She examined his dark face for a moment. There was not a doubt in her mind that life would never get the upper hand on this man. Tentatively, she suggested, "And maybe seeing that made you as strong as you are."

"Maybe." He looked at her and smiled. "Who knows? Human beings are complex machines."

She nodded, then added softly, "And then there's Kenny."

"Yes." His face clouded again. "The hell of it is, I put him in the same situation I'd been in—no parents. I can't believe I did that so blindly, never thinking about anything but myself."

She jumped to his defense without even thinking about it. "Well, Jake, you'd just lost Carol—"

He moved impatiently. "Losing Carol...hell, Paige. You were right the other night. Our marriage was just about over. Yeah, I was upset at the way Carol died...."

He turned away, his face twisted, and she bit her lip. No matter what he said, he still missed her. He still loved her. Would it always be this way? Paige wondered.

"I don't think your marriage was just about over," she said gently, staring out at the mountains in the distance. "You and Carol would have patched up your differences. You would have made it."

He grunted. "I don't think so," he said gruffly. Abruptly, he got up and started walking out of the park. Concerned, Paige followed him.

"Sure you would have. Once you had a steady job and more money was coming in..."

"You think it was the money?" His laugh held no trace of humor. "I guess you *are* a lot like your sister, aren't you?"

"No." She stopped and glared at him, furious. "No, I'm not a bit like Carol. All we had in common was blond hair and dark eyes and a set of parents. The rest was very, very different." She took a deep breath and threw her head back. "Face it, Jake. Carol is dead. She doesn't live in me, or anywhere else."

He was gazing at her levelly, as though he could hardly believe what he was hearing. "Calm down, Paige," he told her quietly. "I don't need a lecture."

She opened her mouth to go on, because it was swelling inside her, the resentment, the fear. But she closed it again and turned away, walking quickly now. He came up beside her, but she didn't acknowledge him right away. She was too busy rebuking herself for her outburst. Once again, she'd taken the focus off what was important. She had to stop doing that.

"Anyway," she said coolly, forcing herself to go on with the conversation she'd interrupted a moment before, "you were despondent over losing Carol. So your judgment wasn't exactly crystal clear at the time."

He shook his head. "I had no excuse for leaving my son the way I did."

She glanced at him. "But you wanted to get an education."

"Yeah, I 'wanted'...big deal what I wanted. I had a responsibility to Kenny, and I blew it."

She shook her head slowly. "I don't think you did. I think your leaving him with us was the best thing you could have done for him." She went on quickly when she could see he was about to contradict her. "Look at it this way. We gave him a stable environment you couldn't possibly have given him at the time. He has a home. He has friends. He has a school. He has continuity in his life. Stability. And lots of love."

He knew very well what she was trying to do, and he knew she was right, as far as she went. But he also knew something else. Nothing was going to keep him from doing his duty to his son this time. Now that he'd seen him, he knew he would never leave him behind again. "Paige—"

"Jake, hear me out." She spoke quickly, nervously, but her eyes were entreating his, and her voice was full of ardor. "Leaving him with us would guarantee him that stability, that continuity, that he so desperately needs. And at the same time, having you back in his life, as a regular visitor, say, would give him that masculine role model he needs, too. You could come visit him any time you like. That would be wonderful for him. He would have his father back. But he would keep his home, his friends, his classmates, everything he has here. He lost his mother, and I...I won't claim to have taken her place, exactly, but—"

He grabbed her hand and pulled it close. "Paige, I know what a good job you've done with him, and I thank you for it from the bottom of my heart."

Her fingers curled around his hand, but she couldn't stop, running on like a train without brakes. "But, Jake, let me finish. About Kenny. Although he misses Carol, I don't think he feels the lack of a mother as strongly as you might have felt the lack of a father at his age. And if you come back into his life, he'll have his real father and at least a pretend mother. He'll have both the things he needs so badly. But if you take him away, he'll have the father...but no mother at all. And I think kids need both."

"You make a good case, Paige. I wish there was some way we both could win here."

"But we can." Now she wanted to shake him. "Don't you see?"

He shook his head, his eyes as cool as ever. "Bottom line, I'm his father, his real father. And I've neglected him too long. I'm going to take care of him now. There's just no other way."

"What if he wants to stay?" she asked desperately.

"What makes you think he does?" Jake was wiser now, and he knew the ground he was walking on.

"I'm not saying that he does," she hedged. "But what if?"

His wide mouth twisted. "I don't believe kids necessarily know what's best for them. There are some times when a parent has to step in and make the rules. That's what parents are all about."

He had her over a barrel, and she knew it, but before she could react, he pulled her closer and looked into her eyes. "Paige, Paige, you're making me feel like a monster. I don't want to hurt you, but I'm afraid I'm going to have to."

She turned her face away. "Please don't do this," she said softly. "I . . . I really don't think it's the right way."

He held her for a long moment, not moving, not speaking. "Paige, look at me," he said at last. "It's got to be my way."

She looked up at him, her eyes dark with sorrow, slowly shaking her head.

He hesitated, then said firmly, "Don't make it hard for Kenny."

"Oh, I wouldn't do that." How could he even think such a thing? She flushed and pulled away from him.

"No," he said calmly, knowing he shouldn't have said it. "I know you won't."

She looked back at him, her eyes dry, but her heart broken. "I'll admit I'm being completely subjective. I want to keep him so badly, I can hardly stand to think of losing him. But there's more. I wish you would think, really think, about what would be best for Kenny."

"I am, Paige. Believe me," he said firmly.

They were at an impasse, and she knew who lost in the event of an impasse. Closing her eyes in a moment of pain, she turned away again.

"I'd better get back to the shop," she murmured, beginning to walk. "Sara will want to get home."

He followed her. It was strange how much he'd come to care for her in the last few days, how much it hurt him to know he was going to have to hurt her. But he didn't see anything he could do about it. There was no way out.

He walked beside her, and as they went, suddenly the street seemed to be full of people she knew. Losing her air of tragedy, she smiled and waved and seemed to grow happier with every greeting. He watched it happen and suddenly realized why she'd wanted to walk this way. She never gave up. This was another weapon in her arsenal.

And she was using it well. She was obviously tied to the neighborhood, to the heart of it, in ways he could never be. And this was the atmosphere in which she was raising Kenny—the warm, comforting center of a loving community. That was something he couldn't give Kenny.

And he was sorry about it. Damn right, he was sorry. But what had to be, had to be. And when they reached the door to her shop and she turned and looked hopefully into his eyes, he had to disappoint her once again.

"Sorry, Paige," he said softly. "Nothing is going to change my mind."

CHAPTER TWELVE

SARA WAS looking out for them when they got back, and she hurried toward them as they entered the shop.

"You've had a phone call," she told Paige, looking anxious. "I took the number if you want to call back." She held out a piece of paper.

"A phone call?" Paige looked surprised. "From whom?"

"Here." Sara shoved the paper at her.

Paige snatched it and disappeared into her office. Jake sank onto a chair.

"Careful," Sara said with a grin. "That one's eighteenth-century French provincial, and I don't think they had men as big as you back then."

"Sure they did," he protested, though he did try to take some of his weight off the chair. "Think of Daniel Boone and John Henry."

"Oh?" She made a face at him. "How tall were they?"

"Big." He nodded knowingly, making her giggle. "Very, very big."

He would have gone on, but at that moment, Paige burst into the room. Her eyes were dilated with shock and she looked at Jake wildly. "I . . . I have to go. Uh . . ." She stared at Jake as though she wasn't sure what to do with him.

He rose from the chair and erased the distance between them with one large stride and took hold of her shoulders. "What is it, Paige? Is it your parents? What can I do to help?"

"No, Jake. It's...it's..." She put her hand to her mouth and stared up at him. She had to tell him. She had no right to keep this from him any longer.

And once she'd made that decision, she grabbed him by the shirt lapels as though to command his complete attention. "It's Kenny. He's had some sort of seizure, or something. I...we have to get out there..."

For just a moment, shock sizzled in the air and time hung suspended. Then Jake sprang into action. "Right," he said firmly. "Sara, can you stay a little longer?"

Sara nodded, looking from one of them to the other, her eyes huge with distress. "Of course," she said. "Don't worry about a thing. I'll close up."

"Come on." Jake put his hand into the center of Paige's back and began to propel her toward the door. "I'll drive to the hospital. Let's get a move on."

And they were off, almost running to his truck. Jake yanked open the door for Paige and she swung into the high seat before she realized what he'd said.

Whirling, she stared at him as he entered on the driver's side. "You know?" she demanded.

He threw her a look of pure exasperation as he started the engine and put the vehicle into gear. "Oh, Paige, don't be dense. Of course I know. Do you think I would have left one stone unturned until I found him? That story about the Boy Scout hike didn't fool me for a moment."

She fumbled with the seat belt, but all her attention was on him. "And you let me go on making a fool of myself?" she muttered, outraged.

He barely wasted a glance on the subject. "Of course. Hang on. We're going to fly. And you're going to tell me exactly what the doctor told you."

She tried, but it was all such a jumble in her brain by now. Fear had turned the information incomprehensible.

"I don't know. I didn't talk to Trent. Oh, Trent is his doctor. But maybe you know that."

Jake grunted as he wheeled the truck around a corner, going much too fast. "Go on."

"The doctor I talked to didn't know exactly what was going on." She had to stop for a moment to steady herself and keep from hyperventilating. "He said there was something wrong. Kenny had an attack or seizure, or something. He said something about the concussion." She turned toward Jake, her eyes wide with fear. "But Trent had said he was okay. He was ready to let him go home this morning. What could have happened?"

Jake let go of the steering wheel with his right hand and took hold of her left one, squeezing tightly. "He's going to be okay," he told her resolutely. "Don't worry."

She sighed. She couldn't relax, but it was good to have him with her this way. "I . . . do you know about Kenny's accident?"

He laughed shortly. "The excellent adventure in the mine? Yes. He's told me all about it. Including details about the owls and the bats."

"Oh." She glanced at him curiously, not sure what to think, too full of anxiety and remorse to make sense of much of anything. "Then you've been to see him."

"Of course."

She stiffened, realizing what that meant. "And no one told me?"

He squeezed her hand a little more tightly. "Just like you didn't tell me, Paige. Let's call it even and forget the recriminations. Okay?"

There was no time for recriminations now, anyway. She had to think about Kenny. She had to worry. If she didn't worry hard enough, who knew what might happen?

The tires screeched dangerously as they careened into the parking lot and came to a sudden stop in front of the entrance. They both jumped out and ran for the building.

The hospital hallway looked longer and colder than ever. Paige ran ahead, and swung open the door to Kenny's room.

The bed was empty. Adrenaline shot through her and she turned and flew back to the nurses' station, Jake right behind her.

"Where's Kenny?" she demanded, her eyes wild. "Where is he?"

The nurse smiled reassuringly, shaking her graying head of hair. "Now don't get all het up, honey. Dr. Holmes has taken him for magnetic resonance imaging. It's nothing to be alarmed about. It's just like having an X ray."

Paige whirled, ready to run in a new direction. "Where is he? I have to be with him."

"No. Now, honey, be reasonable." The nurse came around the counter and patted Paige's arm. "They'll be finished in just a few minutes. You go wait in his room. Doctor will be along in a minute or two."

"What happened? Why did he need new tests?"

The nurse looked uncomfortable. "Well, honey, it was like this. Kenny's been acting funny. And today, he started swearing at the nurses."

Paige shook her head, confused. What did this have to do with anything? "Swearing? That doesn't sound like Kenny."

The nurse wagged a finger at her. "You're going to meet a new Kenny, my dear. He's been a terror all day. Doctor said it might be mood swings."

"Mood swings?" she repeated. "Jake, what does it mean?" she demanded, clinging to the lapels of his denim jacket.

He looked down at her, surprised by how close she was to losing control. This was Paige, the one who always had it together. He'd never seen her this vulnerable before. He put his hands on her shoulders, trying to comfort and soothe her.

"We won't know what it means until the doctor comes and tells us," he told her. "Let's do as the nurse suggested and go wait in Kenny's room."

She stared at him for a moment, torn. Then she seemed to lose some of her frenzy. Nodding, she followed him down the hall. They sat in chairs and counted the seconds, listening to the normal hubbub of the hospital, jumping up whenever they thought they heard Trent coming back. The wait seemed to stretch forever.

"If he doesn't return soon," Paige said at last, rising to pace the room, "I'm going to go hunt him down."

"He'll be back as soon as he knows something," Jake said, then gave a self-deprecating grimace. How did he know what Trent would do? But he didn't say anything aloud. He didn't want to make Paige any crazier than she was already.

"If anything happens to Kenny," Paige began, stopping to look at Jake, wringing her hands. "Jake, if anything happens—"

"Paige, nothing is going to happen." He rose and took her in his arms, pulling her close and rocking her gently. "Kenny is fine. I'm sure it's nothing. Trent is just being careful. That's all."

She seemed to relax against him, and he smoothed her silky hair with his large hand.

"Do you really think so?" she whispered against his chest.

"I really do," he responded, burying his face in her hair and breathing in the full, spicy scent of her. "And just remember, Paige," he added softly, closing his eyes as he held her. "We're in this together. You're not alone."

Not alone. The feeling was unique. She clung to him, unwilling to lose it. Together, they would make sure nothing happened to Kenny. Together, they could do anything.

The door to the hospital room opened and they turned, still clinging to each other, and faced her parents, who were entering, their faces white with shock.

"You!" her father cried, raising his hands as though to protect himself from a blow. "What are you doing here?"

"Dad! Mother!" Paige pulled away from Jake and went to them. "Did Trent call you? Did he tell you anything?"

"Someone called from the hospital," her mother said, looking past Paige toward Jake. "We don't know anything. We came as quickly as we could."

"I want him out of here," her father demanded, pointing at Jake. "What's he doing here, anyway?"

"What is wrong with Kenny?" her mother asked, at the same time trying to hush her husband. "Do you know?"

Paige shook her head. "We don't really know anything. We were told that Trent took him for an MRI. That's all we know."

Her mother nodded, but Dr. Kenton was still sputtering. "We'll go ask at the nurses' station," she said, tugging on her husband's arm. "We'll be right back."

They left the room, her father still muttering threats, and Paige turned to Jake uncertainly. "Maybe you should leave for a little while," she suggested tentatively.

"Why?" he asked her bluntly, his eyes cold.

"Well, it's not going to be easy for them—"

"Paige, my sweet Paige." He reached out and touched her cheek with his hand, though he didn't smile. "Reality check. It's time for you to face it. I'm the father here. Kenny is mine. As long as there is anything going on with him, I'm staying."

He was right, of course. Her shoulders sagged. She couldn't protect him from her parents, nor could she protect them from him. She was just going to have to let things run their course. But she knew it was not going to be pleasant.

Her parents reappeared, with no real news, and her father grumbling because the nurses had refused to tell him anything. But his grumbling soon evaporated as he returned to his original gripe—Jake's presence in his universe.

Turning to his daughter, and gesturing toward Jake, he repeated his first question through clenched teeth, "What's he doing here?"

Paige steeled herself. "Dad, Kenny is his son."

That information didn't seem to sink in. "You said you'd take care of this," her father said accusingly, giving Jake another belligerent look. "You said to leave it to you."

Paige put a hand on his arm. "I'm doing everything I can, Dad." She hesitated, then decided to be blunt. "But Jake has to be here right now. After all, Jake has the power to do whatever he damn well pleases. So be nice to him."

Her father looked at her and suddenly his eyes were uncertain. But he still blustered, "We should get a court order."

"I've tried that," Paige said dryly, glancing at Jake. "Listen, Jake is Kenny's dad. He loves him just like we do. Let's try to get along, shall we?"

Her father turned away as though he'd been hit, almost reeling. Paige gasped and took a step toward him, but before she could reach him, he whirled and glared at Jake. "I can't stay in the same room with this bastard," he said angrily.

Jake sighed. He'd been deliberately letting Paige handle this, but he was about at the end of his patience. "You can call me names but it's not going to change anything," he noted.

Dr. Kenton snorted. "No, that's right, you'll never change. You'll always be the same old loser, won't you?" He turned to his daughter again. "What are you doing to get rid of him for good?"

Paige hesitated, glancing at Jake almost in apology. "I've talked to Judge Randall. He's looking into it. In the meantime, it would be best if we all tried to remain civil."

"Civil?" He spat the word out, still glaring at Jake. "You can't be civil to a rattlesnake. You can't say please and thank you." He made a contemptuous gesture with a toss of his head. "You take out your knife and cut off its head. Then it can't bother you anymore."

"Dad." Paige put a hand on his arm, shocked at his tone, his words. "Take it easy."

"I will not take it easy," he insisted, brushing her aside and turning to shake a fist in Jake's face. "You do nothing but ruin lives. You killed my daughter, now you want to take away my grandson. I want you out of here. I'll call the police if you won't leave on your own. One way or another, you're going to leave this hospital right now."

Jake stood easily, shifting his weight from one foot to the other. He didn't look at all threatened. "I'm sorry, Dr. Kenton," he said softly. "I'm not going."

"Not going?" The doctor reared back and stared at him. "Not going? We'll see about that." Turning, he nodded towards his daughter. "Paige, call the police. We'll just see about that."

She stepped toward him, her heart filled with pity for her sad, defenseless father. "Dad..."

"Get going, girl. The sooner you call the cops, the sooner we can get rid of this snake in the grass and be with our own family again."

Paige appealed to her mother silently, but she could see right away that Mrs. Kenton was going to be no help. Paige was going to have to do this on her own. Turning slowly, she faced her father. "Sit down, Dad," she said quietly. "I'm not phoning anyone. Jake has more right to be here than any of us do. He's not leaving."

He looked at her for a moment as though he didn't quite understand what she'd said, his watery eyes blinking rapidly. "Paige Kenton," he said ominously, "did you hear what I told you to do?"

She swallowed, looking from Jake to her father and back again. It tore her heart out to do this, but she felt she had no choice. "No, Dad," she said firmly, reaching out and putting her hand through the crook in Jake's arm. "Jake is Kenny's father. He's staying right here."

Her father seemed to crumble before her eyes, his back bowing, his shoulders sagging, his face falling slack and lifeless. "Has he taken you, too?" he whispered, his voice trembling.

"Dad!" Paige sprang to him but he pushed her away.

"You're not my daughter anymore," he said, shaking his head and moving away from her, muttering something as he turned. She couldn't quite make it out at first, but when she realized what he was saying, she drew back.

"Carol, my sweet Carol," was the mantra he was chanting under his breath. Tears welled up in his eyes and he turned and left the room. Her mother hurried after, but Paige was frozen where she stood, her heart like a stone in her chest.

Her father had disowned her, but he would cling to Carol forever. Carol. It was always Carol.

Finally she came to life again. "I'll be back," she promised Jake, and hurried out of the room after her parents.

He stood where he was, staring at the door as it slowly swung closed. He'd felt like an observer through most of that scene, somehow detached, and now he wondered why. It wasn't that Dr. Kenton's words hadn't cut deeply. They had. But they were nothing new. Carol's father had said these things before. The only difference was, this was the first time he was beginning to wonder if the doctor might not be right.

Not that he considered himself a snake in the grass or a bastard. But it did seem that whenever he came near the Kenton family, things began to fall apart. When he was around, daughters betrayed their fathers and turned on each other and no one seemed to get what he or she wanted. Was he the catalyst for all this misery? Or just the mirror of it?

"I've got to get out of here," he murmured to himself. But this time it was Paige he was worried about, not himself. If he stayed much longer, her life would be changed irrevocably. And he cared too much for her to let that happen.

Paige returned, her face pale. "They've gone down to the cafeteria to have some tapioca," she told him.

"I'm sorry," Jake said simply.

She tried to smile. "It can't be helped." No. Some things never seemed to change.

Sighing, she sat down to wait again. She wanted to go back into his arms, where she'd been before, but he didn't give her any reason to think she might be welcome there right now, so she rested on the bed, and listened for Trent's return.

And then Trent was back, pulling off his sterile mask and nodding to them before he dropped onto the chair.

"Well?" Paige demanded impatiently, her heart in her throat. "What is it? What's wrong?"

Trent looked at her and for a moment he didn't seem to know what to say. Terror gripped her soul, and she could hardly breathe.

"What?" she whispered. "Oh, Trent, what is it?"

He shook his head, raising a hand as though to stop her fear. "I was a little worried about an hour ago," he told them. "The nurses were telling me tales, and when I talked to Kenny, I noticed the change myself. He wasn't the same Kenny. And I was very much afraid that he was experiencing delayed concussion syndrome."

Paige's hands went to her throat. "Is that bad?"

He nodded. "It could be. It might mean surgery to relieve pressure on the brain."

Her world was spinning away. "Oh, my God."

Trent shook his head. "Wait, now, don't get excited. I just ran tests, and I can't find any physical evidence for it."

Her world hung in the balance, waiting. "Which means...?" she asked, hardly daring to hope.

He hesitated, then shrugged. "It means I'm not going to operate. And we're going to have to look for another cause for his strange behavior."

She sank back onto the bed as though all her energy had been sucked out in one fell swoop. "Trent!" she wailed. "Tell me quickly. Am I scared? Am I nervous? Am I relieved? What? What the hell are you talking about?"

"Calm down, Paige," he said almost impatiently. "I'm trying to explain. I think it is very likely that Kenny's strange behavior has another genesis. I'm calling in a psychologist."

They both stared at him dumbly. "A psychologist?" Jake repeated at last. "What are you talking about?"

But Trent didn't answer. He held up his hand at the sound of the elevator hitting their floor.

"That'll be Kenny," he said, and Paige was out of the room like a shot, reaching the gurney before it had begun its trip down the hall. Kenny lay back, eyes closed. Quickly matching her stride to the pace of the rolling bed, Paige took his hand in hers.

"Hi, sweetie," she said, smiling down at him as the attendants pulled the bed along and then into place in his room. "How are you doing?"

"Paige!" He looked up at her and suddenly his eyes were swimming in tears. He was once again the little boy she knew so well. "Paige, where were you?"

With a small cry of love, she bent down and moving gently, she put her arms around him and held his body against her.

"It's okay, darling," she whispered. "Everything is going to be okay."

His skinny little arms reached up and curled around her neck, clinging, holding tightly. His eyes closed, squeezing out the tears, and they clung together, the two of them encased in their own world.

Jake watched. The love between the two of them was almost palpable. He felt very much an outsider, an observer. For the moment, he came second. That was only natural, and he didn't resent it exactly. But it did make him think twice.

The question was, would he ever be able to replace the love Paige provided for his son? Would he be able to give the boy everything he needed?

Perhaps not.

"Dad." Kenny had looked up and caught sight of Jake, and he wiped his eyes, looking slightly embarrassed that his father had seen what he'd shown so unselfconsciously to Paige. "Hi." His face changed and he looked from one of them to the other. "You're both here," he said wonderingly.

"We're both here," Paige agreed, patting his hand and beaming at him. "And we're both going to stay with you as long as you need us. Aren't we, Jake?"

She looked at him expectantly, and he hesitated. "Of course we are," he said hurriedly at last. "Of course."

IT WAS HOURS LATER when they got back to the apartment. They'd waited for the results of all the tests, waited while Trent made his diagnosis, waited through the visit with the psychologist.

The latter had been an eye-opener. The psychologist had talked to Kenny alone, Kenny with Jake, Kenny with Paige, and then the two of them without Kenny. The upshot had been, "Cut it out, you two, you're tearing this kid apart."

It had taken a while for that message to sink in. Paige had been preoccupied, trying to reassure Kenny, trying to keep her father and Jake apart, trying to get some answers out of Trent. And trying to analyze why Jake seemed to have become more and more silent, more and more morose.

But now they were back and she felt as though she could finally begin to relax a little and think over everything that had happened. "It's our fault, isn't it?" she said woodenly as she flopped down onto the couch and leaned back. "We put that poor kid through hell with our tug-of-war over him."

Jake didn't answer and she looked up to see him walking through the room and into the kitchen. Something about the set of his shoulders raised alarms through her system, and she rose and followed him.

He was filling a glass at the sink when she entered.

"Do you have any aspirin?" he asked without looking around.

Silently, she got down the bottle and handed it to him, and, as he took it from her, their eyes met.

His eyes were dark, the darkest blue she'd ever seen, almost black in the shadowed light, and deep as the ocean. Something in them made her draw back quickly, and a shiver traced its way down her spine.

He turned from her as he took the aspirin. And then he stood where he was, staring into the night beyond the kitchen window, his hands curled around the edge of the counter, his knuckles white.

"Jake?" she asked at last. "What's wrong?"

He didn't answer. He didn't move, or make any sign that he'd heard her. She came closer and put a hand on his arm.

"Jake?" she said again.

He moved away from her touch. He didn't exactly yank his arm away, but the effect was the same; it was evident to her that he didn't want her touching him. She drew back, closing her fingers into a small fist, and tried to control the apprehension that gripped her.

"Would you like me to brew some tea?" she asked, watching him.

Leaning against the counter again, he shook his head. "No, thanks," he said softly.

He wasn't going to let her do anything to make things better. Frustration rose in her chest. She had to do something. She couldn't stand the tension in the room.

"Shall we sit down and talk?" she ventured.

He looked at her, turning his head slowly, looking at her in silence before he spoke. "What do you want to talk about?" he asked.

She hesitated, but it was obvious, wasn't it? "Kenny. And everything that has happened today."

He shook his head slowly, his eyes still the same deep blue. "No," he said, his voice rough and husky. "I don't want to talk."

Paige stared at him. The air seemed alive between them, as though electricity were sparking off their thoughts. "Then what do you want to do?" she asked, holding his gaze with her own, and suddenly her heart was pounding in her throat.

He didn't really answer her question. Instead, he said, "It's been a long day. I think I'll turn in." He turned and left the room.

She sagged against the counter, finally breathing, heart running ragged. What on earth had that been all about? She leaned against the sink for a moment, catching her breath and trying to decide what he'd meant. A tiny, niggling fear quivered inside her, but she ignored it. She didn't want to think about it. In fact, she didn't want to think about anything much right now. He was right. It had been a long day. She was tired, too.

He was in Kenny's room, with the door closed. She walked past it to her own room and pulled out her nightgown and robe, then carried them to the bathroom. A nice, hot shower. That was what she needed.

She stood under the sharp spray for a long time, eyes closed, soaking in the healing heat. She couldn't think about Kenny now. She'd thought about Kenny so long and so hard, she was exhausted with the effort. Tomorrow she would think about him again—think about him and decide what to do.

And then there was Jake. She tried to make her mind go blank but she couldn't get Jake out of her thoughts. He filled her head, filled her soul, and she knew he would fill her heart, as well, just as soon as she let enough of her guard down to let him in.

And yet, what did she want from him? There was nothing in this world that he was prepared to give her, nothing she would allow herself to take. Was there?

All he saw in her was Carol. She was convinced that was all he'd ever seen. That was all anyone seemed to see lately.

But the fact was, she was in love with him, achingly, crazily in love. She loved his dark looks, the way his white teeth flashed when he laughed. She loved his sense of humor, his sense of pride and the way he wanted Kenny back.

Yes. She even loved that—despite the fact that he was going to break her heart when he took him.

She'd never been in love before, and it was taking some time to get used to it. After all, she'd always thought being in love was an end in itself—that once you fell in love, you got married and lived happily ever after. She hadn't realized there would be a lot of heartache involved instead—that you might fall in love with someone who had other things in mind.

So she'd fallen in love with a man who had always been in love with her sister. Not the brightest move she'd ever made. She should have seen this one coming. But she hadn't. And now she was stuck with the consequences.

In the meantime, she had to get through this night without letting on. Tomorrow, they would talk. Tomorrow.

She had just stepped out of the shower and begun to dry off when she heard the front door slam. Her heart jumped into her throat and she grabbed her robe, not bothering to finish drying, slipping into it and tugging the belt into place as she raced out of the room.

"Jake?" she called, panic rising in her.

But he wasn't gone. Not yet. The slamming door seemed to have signaled his return from outside, because he was in the living room, dressed in his denim jeans and leather jacket, his face wary.

"What are you doing?" she asked, her eyes a little wild. "Where are you going?"

"I just took some of my things out to the truck," he said simply. "I have to go."

Dread spread through Paige like a lethal shock. "What are you talking about?" she demanded. She was terrified to know the answer to that question, but at the same time, she had to hear it.

"You know I have to go."

"But . . . but why?"

He grimaced, almost as though he were in pain. "Can't you tell, Paige? Can't you feel it?"

Of course she could. She stood before him, breathing as though she'd just been running hard, and she tried to conjure up enough nerve to pretend she didn't know, couldn't feel it. But it didn't work. She couldn't lie to him. He could surely read the truth in her face.

"Stay," she whispered, her eyes begging him.

He groaned, throwing back his head. "Don't, Paige."

"Please stay."

"You know I can't. If I do—"

She nodded, finishing for him. "We'll make love."

He winced. "Yes," he said so softly she could hardly hear him.

She shrugged, holding out her hands, palms up. "Is that so bad?"

His dark face was tortured. "You know it's impossible."

Why? Because of Carol? Because he still saw his wife when he looked at Paíge? She shook her head slowly. Just because that happened now didn't mean it would always be that way. Maybe they could change things. Just maybe. "No. No, I don't know that it's impossible."

He looked almost angry and his voice was rough. "Take it from me. It can't happen."

She refused to be bullied by his tone. "Why not?" she asked, her face open, trusting.

He merely shook his head, refusing to try to explain.

"You're scared," she said gently, her eyes luminous, as though she'd suddenly made a momentous discovery.

A flash of apprehension shot through him. "Paige..."

"I'm not scared, Jake." Her hand went to the belt of her robe.

"Paige, cut it out," he ordered, and as the robe began to slip away from her shoulders, he stepped forward to stop it, to keep her covered, to keep her from making the biggest mistake of her life.

But he was too late. He seemed to be moving in slow motion, and by the time he got there, the robe was a pile of discarded fabric on the ground at her feet, and Paige was standing before him, her golden skin glowing, her full hips so round, her legs so long, her waist so small, her breasts so full, the nipples flat and soft as the pale petals of a rose, and something split open inside him, pouring out heat that filled his entire body. He felt a pounding on his chest, and he couldn't breathe, couldn't think, and her hand was on his face.

"Don't be scared, Jake," she was whispering, her breath hot on his cheek. "It's time."

It's time. Those words kept echoing in his head. *It's time.* He tried to turn away, tried to get back to the front door. If he could just get his hand on the knob, he could make it to his truck and get away before... before...

Her skin was so hot and he needed to touch it, needed to feel it against his own.

"Paige, no," he said raggedly. He heard the words, knew it was his voice saying them, but he was pulling her into his arms at the same time, crushing her soft, silky skin against the rough denim he wore, taking her against his body and plunging into her warmth, drowning in her.

She took him in as though she had been waiting for him all her life, as though she had been tightly coiled, frozen in time, and now, only his touch could unlock the sleep and let her blossom, opening layer upon layer, unfolding to the sun. He held her close, but she wanted to be closer, press harder, and she murmured as his mouth covered hers, murmured sounds of love, sounds of need, sounds that required no words to make him understand.

He felt hot, searingly hot, as though he were about to burst into flames, as though he needed her to quench the fire, needed her and nothing but her to keep him alive. He could feel her body making demands, hear the sounds of pleasure she made as he fulfilled them, and he felt a sense of power as he'd never felt before. With one touch, he could change her. With one kiss, one stroke, one thrust...

But at the same time, he was more vulnerable than he had ever been before, powerless before her beauty, helpless in the face of the thundering desire that was pounding in his head, in his heart, in his loins. If he took her now, would he ever be able to leave her? Still, that fear couldn't stop him. It was much too late for that.

The carpet was scratchy against her naked back, but she didn't care. She didn't really feel it. She did feel his lips, so hot, so slick, and his tongue, rough like a cat's, as they explored her breast, exciting her nipple until it tightened like a rock, making her cry out and lift her hips to entice him closer to where she needed him most. He stroked her with his hand, and she felt a growl growing deep, deep in her throat, an animal sound to match the animal urgency she was beginning to feel.

His shirt was hanging open now, and he'd shed his jeans. His body was long and sleek and powerful and she took him, drew him closer, gasping in wonder as he came between her legs and joined her.

She loved him. She loved him so much, she knew she would never, ever let another man close to her like this, not ever. This was it, her time, her only time.

"Jake," she murmured. "Make it last."

For a moment, he thought she meant the lovemaking, and he gasped out an expletive, because he wasn't going to be able to make it last much longer. But when he looked down into her face, suddenly he knew she meant something quite different, and he closed his eyes, unwilling to look at her any longer, unwilling to face what she had in her heart. It was no use. This was just for now. It couldn't last. It could only be what it was.

They came together at the peaks, rising higher and higher, clinging together as though they might fly apart and crash against the earth if they lost each other, holding tightly and finding the miracle at the end of the rainbow as though it were a prize to be held high and celebrated.

And then it was over, fading away, leaving only a sense of wonderful peace and lethargy that curled into them both as they lay together. Together.

Hot tears squeezed between Paige's lashes as she lay back, catching her breath, hot tears of joy, of sorrow, of regret and ecstasy. His arms were still around her and his body felt so right next to hers. She had never been so happy before. This was new. This was heaven.

And beside her, Jake lay back with his eyes wide open, staring at the ceiling. Though he didn't make a sound, he was swearing at himself, swearing in harsh, ugly obscenities. He knew this should never have happened. And now he could never take it back.

But he could cut his losses—and hers. Rising on one elbow, he dropped a kiss on her lips, then vaulted to his feet. She half rose, looking after him anxiously.

"Where are you going?" she asked.

"To get the rest of my stuff," he said shortly, pulling on his jeans again, feeling like a monster, but doing what he knew had to be done. "I told you, I'm leaving."

She swallowed the lump that had suddenly lodged in her throat. "But where will you go?"

"To a hotel, motel, whatever."

"Why?"

"Why?" He shrugged, avoiding her gaze. "That's not an easy question to answer, but I think you know why in your heart."

"Is it because of Carol?" she asked, hardly breathing.

"Carol?" He looked at her. "Well, Carol's probably part of it. But you know it's more than that."

She felt her throat closing, choking off. He'd admitted it. Carol was at the center of this wall that he kept erecting between them. He'd been searching for Carol, thinking he would find his lost wife in Paige's arms and he'd been disappointed. That was it, wasn't it?

She couldn't let him slip away so easily. If he would just let her be herself, if he would just let go of the past...

"Stay," she said imploringly, her eyes huge as they gazed into his. "Please stay."

He returned her stare for a moment, then turned away. As he walked toward the bedroom, he looked back at her. "I can't stay here. You can see that, can't you?"

"No." Rising, she reached for her robe and draped it casually across her shoulders. She was trembling, but there was too much at stake for her to let this fight be lost so easily. "No, Jake. I don't see it at all. I mean...we've done what you were trying to avoid. Haven't we?"

He came out of the bedroom with a case in his hand and stood before her, his eyes dark and deep again. "Making love, you mean?" He shook his head. "It was never the sex I was afraid of." Reaching out, he touched her cheek with the tips of his fingers, then let his hand drop again. "Don't you know it's more than just sex? Can't you tell?"

She stood very still, unable to think of a thing to say, and he left her, heading for the exit, saluting her from the doorway.

"Goodbye, Paige," he said solemnly. "I'll call you tomorrow. And we can talk about Kenny then. Okay?"

She didn't say a word and he left, closing the door behind him, left her standing there, staring after him. She didn't understand. She didn't understand anything. All she knew was that her world was crumbling. And there didn't seem to be a thing she could do about it.

CHAPTER THIRTEEN

PAIGE WAS ready to give Kenny to Jake. It seemed as if it was the only thing to do. She was going to force herself to give the boy up without any more fighting, without any more agony.

The most important thing was Kenny and his well-being. What she wanted, even what Jake wanted, didn't matter a hill of beans. Kenny wanted his dad, and though she wasn't sure just how she was going to work things out, she was going to make sure the child got him.

But she didn't tell Jake that when he called at six a.m. She wasn't ready to tell him anything. She still hadn't come to terms with the way he'd left the night before. She wasn't sure she ever would.

"Hi," he said, his low, husky voice sending a thrill through her, despite everything.

"Hi," she said more coolly than she felt. "What do you want?"

"I just wanted to talk to you."

"Well, here I am. Right where you left me."

There was a pause, then his voice, softer, lower. "Paige, I'm sorry."

Determined not to show any pain, she came back at him without a pause. "I'm not."

He laughed softly. "Okay. Tough girl."

"Damn right."

He sighed. "Listen, I just wanted to let you know, I'm going to go out and get some breakfast, and then I'll go by and see Kenny at the hospital."

"Good," she said briskly. "Then I'll run out and see Kenny now, and come back later for my own breakfast."

There was a short pause. "Are you trying to avoid me?"

Her hand tightened on the receiver until her fingers started going numb. "Isn't that the way you want it?"

"No, Paige. That is not the way I want it."

"I see." Her tone was definitely icy. "It's just the way it's gotta be, right? A man's gotta do what a man's gotta do. Sure. I understand."

He swore softly. "You don't understand a damn thing if you think I'm doing this with some sadistic desire to torture you."

"No, actually, I thought you were doing it to torture yourself."

He groaned. "Paige . . ."

"That's all right. I'm not going to fall apart over this. You don't have to worry about that. I'm a little too old for hysterics." She paused to take a breath, and he didn't say a word, so she went on. "But we'll have to meet sometime today. We've got to discuss Kenny and what we're going to do."

"That's right." He actually sounded happy about it. "Shall I come over at about two?"

She closed her eyes for a second and forced herself to fight back the temptation to tell him to come over right away. "Better not. We probably need to meet on neutral territory."

"Paige..."

"And don't worry," she added brightly, "I promise to keep my clothes on this time. There will be nothing to subvert your spectacular self-control."

"Paige," he said softly, "just thinking about you subverts my self-control. Don't you know that?"

His voice was so low and so provocative, she had to catch her breath in her throat and hold back her impulse to tell him things she shouldn't—things like, "Make love to me, Jake, because I don't think I can take the cold I feel without you."

Instead, she said stiffly, "How about the shop? Two o'clock okay?"

He paused, then agreed. "I'll see you later, Paige. Goodbye."

Her hand was limp as she hung up the phone. She'd thought she could fight this. She'd thought she could maintain a tough exterior. But one statement like that from Jake, and she was a quivering mass of female emotions again.

Damn. This was going to be hard to get over.

SHE WAS JUST ABOUT to leave for the hospital when there was a knock at her door, and her pulse leaped. Jake. He must have thought about their phone conversation and decided to come over, after all. She went to the door quickly, heart beating in dread and anticipation at the same time.

And then falling in disappointment. It wasn't Jake at all. It was Barry. The last thing she needed right now was a confrontation with Barry.

"Oh," she said. "It's you."

He stood in her doorway looking a bit sheepish, his handsome face wary, his eyes a little shifty. He looked at her, then behind her into the apartment.

"Is he here?" he asked.

She folded her arms across her chest. "Who?" As if she didn't know.

Frowning his annoyance, he said, "You know who I mean. Jake."

She shook her head. "No, he's not here."

The wary look left him and he began to relax. "Good. Did you kick him out?"

She stepped back to let him in. "No. He kicked himself out."

"Oh." He shouldered his way in and looked around the room. "Well, no matter."

"What do you want, Barry?" she said, hoping to hurry him along.

He turned and looked her over, then his face loosened into a bittersweet smile. "Paige, Paige, it's too bad we never really got together."

She sighed. It looked as if he was going to drag this out, so she fell in with the scenario. "Some things just aren't meant to be," she murmured, shaking her head in mock sadness.

"No. And I guess we were one of them. So, anyway, I came to say goodbye."

That surprised her. "Goodbye?"

"Yeah. I've closed down my office, put my place up for rent. I'm heading for Chicago. My cousin's got a jazz club he runs there. I might go in with him."

Barry leaving Aberdeen? It hardly seemed possible. And then she realized his going would create a complication. "But Barry, you can't leave me with the Gold Rush Days parade to plan all on my own."

"Look, Paige, I'm sorry. Someone else will have to help you. I've just plain had it with this town. I can't stay any longer. I've gotta go try something new."

The shadows in his eyes, the lines of his face, told her there was more to this than pure whim. She stepped closer, concerned. "Why, Barry?" she asked softly, searching his expression for clues. "Why now? Why so suddenly?"

"I think you know why," he said, his gaze haunted.

"No. I haven't a clue."

He stared at her for a moment, then turned and paced into her dining area. "The dream is over, Paige. Shattered. Gone up in smoke." He turned back and looked at her. "It's all over. She won't be coming back."

She hesitated, puzzled, then the realization of what he must mean hit her. She was horrified. "Are you talking about Carol?" she demanded.

"I really loved her you know," he said sadly, reaching out and touching her hair, his eyes deep and liquid.

"You and half the known universe," she snapped, pushing his hand away. "Are you telling me you only dated me because I was Carol's sister?"

He nodded slowly. "Sorry," he said. "I'm really sorry, Paige. I know it was a miserable, rotten thing to do. But I kept hoping..." He bit his lower lip and searched her face. "You know, sometimes I really could see bits of Carol in you. And I kept thinking..."

She was outraged, and yet not really surprised. This seemed to have become a pattern in her life. "You were hoping I would turn into Carol?" she asked.

He shrugged. "Stranger things have happened."

"That is sick."

He tried to smile in his old carefree way. "Then call a doctor, honey," he said drolly, "I must be terminal."

She stared at him, hating him, hating Jake, and anyone else who expected her to be like Carol.

"I'm me," she said vehemently, thumping her chest. "I'm Paige. I'll never be Carol. Never."

"I know. Believe me, I know."

She sighed, her anger fading. How could she be angry when he seemed to be so helpless? "You still can't get over her?" she said softly.

He shook his head. "It took Jake showing up to make me realize that I've been wasting my life here. I've gotta get out of this town. I've been wasting away here too long. Have a good life, Paige. You deserve one."

He started for the door. Paige hesitated, then followed him, stopping him before he'd pulled the door open by putting a hand on his arm.

"Barry, I'm glad you came and told me. I wish you good luck."

"Thanks." He grinned. "I'm going to need it."

"Barry, wait," she said as he turned away. "Tell me something. Do you remember that last night before Carol died?"

He turned back. "Your birthday?"

"Yes." Suddenly her hands felt very cold. "Do you remember the fight?"

His eyes seemed to flicker in the light. "You mean your father and Jake in the hall?"

"Yes, that's it." She licked her lips and forced herself to go on. "Tell me something. Who actually called the IRS?"

"The IRS?" He looked blank.

"About my father's practice. Who got the agents here the next day?"

He looked at her vacantly. "Jake did. Don't you remember?" His face changed. "Or is he trying to weasel out of it now?"

She wouldn't deign to answer that question. "How do you know it was Jake?" she demanded.

Barry shrugged. "He was the one who brought it up. Didn't you hear him? He was the one who threatened your father."

She stared at him for a long moment, biting her lip. "You didn't do it?" she said at last.

"Me?" He gaped at her. "Why would I sic the IRS on your father?"

Hope died. She could see he was telling the truth. "That's what I'm trying to figure out," she murmured, frowning.

Barry waved that away. "There's nothing to figure out. Jake did it. Everybody knows that."

Everybody knew a lot of things that weren't true. She only hoped this was one of them. "Who else was in the hall that night?" she asked him, prodding his recollection. "Do you remember?"

He thought about it for a second or two. "Sure. Besides your father? You, me, Jake. Oh, and Trent. And Carol."

She frowned. "No one else?"

He shook his head. "Not that I can think of."

She nodded. "Thanks, Barry. And—" she reached up to give him a quick kiss "—good luck."

She closed the door behind him and leaned on it. She had to admit, she wasn't going to be all that sorry to see him go. Every time she saw him now, she thought of Carol. She truly did hope he would make a new life for himself in Chicago. There was no reason any of them should be so thoroughly haunted by the past.

And yet they were, weren't they? All of them— Barry and her parents and Jake and Kenny and even herself.

There was no getting away from it. Carol had been a strong, vibrant element in all their lives. She'd been the sort of woman who made waves. And those waves were still throwing out ripples after all this time—ripples from the past—a past that had put Kenny into her life, a past that was now going to take him away. She sighed, closing her eyes, feeling almost too weary to move. But she had to get on with her day. Kenny was waiting.

Pushing herself away from the door, she looked around her empty apartment dully. Her heart ached. Her body ached, too. But she was afraid the real pain was just beginning.

THE SMALL CAFÉ was half-empty, but someone had put a quarter in the jukebox and now Garth Brooks was blaring throughout the room. Jake grimaced and went back to attacking his scrambled eggs. It seemed a bit early in the day for Garth to him, but he supposed it was a matter of taste.

"Yeah," he muttered to himself crossly. "Some people have none."

It had been a cold, lonely night in the Hibernating Bear Inn. He would have given just about anything to have spent the night in Paige's arms instead...in Paige's bed. But that would have made a very bad situation even worse.

Of course, he could have tried to stay, and stay away from her. But that had already proved impossible. It was one thing to tell himself to keep his stupid libido in check. It was another to act upon it.

And so he'd left Paige right after making love to her. What sort of jerk was he, anyway? But he'd had to leave. He'd had to leave in order to be able to breathe.

Now he had to decide what to do about Kenny. He'd come to get him, and that was still what he wanted to do. But he hadn't counted on getting so close to Paige. In fact, he'd fought against it. And not only because it complicated everything. The truth was he didn't deserve someone like Paige.

He took a long sip of very hot coffee and stared at the clock on the wall. The thing with Paige was over now. It had to be. He'd left her so that he could get his head straight and think things through, but so far it hadn't worked.

How had he ended up at this point? Where had it all begun? Over the years, he'd grown used to putting the blame on Carol. But was that really true? Staring down into the depths of his murky coffee, he narrowed his eyes and confronted Carol as she had once been, all those years ago. He saw her again as she'd been in high school, her blond hair flying behind her, laughter always on her lips, the urge to do something mischievous in her eyes and a smart-alecky comment for every occasion. She'd been a lot of fun and they'd had some great times together.

And then he'd left, and if the truth be known, hadn't thought too much about her. He'd been busy going to school and working in the mines. She'd visited him once, and written. But it had been quite a shock when she'd shown up at the mining camp in Tailings almost two years after he'd left town. There she was, so fresh, so beautiful and vivacious, and there he was, lonely and discouraged. He'd been glad for the companionship. She'd seemed like a dream girl to him then, everything he could possibly want in a woman.

But that hadn't lasted too long, because he and the life he'd led were not at all what she wanted in a man, and she soon made that very clear. But Kenny had come along and he'd been such a cute, winsome child, they'd been enchanted with him from the first. Carol had even enjoyed playing mommy for a few years. He'd always known it couldn't last. Carol had been made for more exciting things than homemaking and Little League.

She'd been bored, and that was why she'd been involved with Barry, and with a few others he would never tell Paige about. Carol had always danced right to the edge of the cliff—many times she had been so close to stepping right over. But she always seemed to pull back just in time to avoid disaster. And then had come that awful day when she'd miscalculated and gone right over. And so many lives had lain in ruin.

If he told the truth, he would have to admit he had often blamed everything on her. Now that he looked

back, he knew that it wasn't really her fault. Carol was
what she was. She couldn't stop being that way any
more than a hummingbird could sit still. He'd been the
one who could have stopped things from moving along
their fateful path.

He didn't have to marry her. And once he'd realized what a mistake it was, he could have done something about it. More than that, he could have stopped
living the life she hated. After all, he'd done it after
she'd died—quit mining and gone back to school. She
would have liked that. Why couldn't he have done it
when she was alive? Because half of their relationship
had been a tug-of-war and quitting would have been
conceding to her.

Most of all, he could have avoided what he'd done
to the Kenton family. They were a nice, happy bunch
before he'd married one of their daughters and started
on the downhill slide that had ended here. Now, here
he was, about to hurt them again. And he knew he
could avoid it. He could go and leave Kenny behind.

He winced, the pain almost physical. Could he do
that? He struggled inside, struggled so hard that he
bent his coffee spoon in half without realizing what he
was doing. Was he brave enough? Was he man
enough?

Paige deserved it. God knew, she deserved that and
more. She'd loved Kenny and she'd been a mother to
him for four years. What right did he have to tear
apart that relationship?

Unlike Carol, Paige was a giver. She gave everything, didn't hold back anything. She'd given to him
the night before, and he'd let her. He'd taken, taken

as though he had a right to, as though he hadn't hurt her enough already.

But he wasn't going to hurt her anymore. Putting down the bent spoon, he made a silent vow. Paige was not to be hurt again.

PAIGE STOPPED IN to see Trent before visiting Kenny in the morning.

"He's been doing great," Trent told her, frowning thoughtfully. "I'm thinking of sending him home this afternoon."

"But..." She shook her head. "Just yesterday, you were almost in a panic over his condition. And now he can go home?"

Trent nodded. "My panic was somewhat premature. I'm convinced now that his symptoms were psychosomatic. If you and Jake can present a united, congenial front to him, I think he'll be okay." He pointed his pen at her. "But I want you to call me immediately if Kenny shows any signs that disturb you."

"Oh, I will."

She left his office on air, bubbling with the news when she burst into Kenny's room. "Hi," she said, eyes sparkling. "How's tricks?"

"Great." He looked at her expectantly. "Where's my dad?"

Her heart lurched. Whatever you do, she told herself silently, don't show him that you're in any way disappointed. The grin became strained, but much wider. "He'll be along a little later," she said.

"Why didn't he come with you this time?" he asked suspiciously.

"He's having breakfast," she said with a forced smile.

"Did you fight again?" he asked, eyes apprehensive.

"No." She took his hand and stared down at him. "Kenny, what gives you the idea that we've been fighting?"

He looked away. "'Cuz it had to be a secret. I mean I wasn't supposed to tell you I saw my dad." He looked at her again. "How come I couldn't tell you that I knew he was here?"

She sank into a chair beside him. This was getting tricky. "Kenny, it's true we were having a...bit of a disagreement at first."

"Because of me?"

She groped for a good cover story, but then she stopped herself. There had been too many lies, and they did no good, because Kenny could see through them. He could feel them in the air. She had to tell the truth, and he would have to learn to deal with it.

"Yes, Kenny. We were arguing because of you." Reaching out, she took his hand. "But not in any bad way. We're fine. Believe me."

"But..." He swallowed and looked very brave. "I love you both," he said in a quavery voice.

"Oh, Kenny." She leaned in and gave him a hug. "And we both love you. Don't you ever doubt it."

He nodded, but his eyes were clouded, and he said, "Then how come he was gone so long?"

She held his hand tightly. "Your father?"

He nodded.

"Kenny, your father loves you very, very much. You have to understand that he didn't want to leave you alone so long. He had to." She stroked his hair. "Do you have any idea why?"

Kenny hesitated. "He was sad about my mother dying?" he guessed.

"Well, that was part of it. But there was much more. You see, back when you were young, your dad worked hard, but he was very poor. He didn't have much money for his family. So when your mother died, he decided he had to go back to school and learn a trade that could provide a better living. He wanted to be able to take care of you right. So he studied hard and got a couple of degrees and then he got a very good job. And now he's ready..." She almost choked on the words. This was surely the most difficult thing she would ever have to do in her life. "He's ready for you to come and live with him."

"Really?"

He looked so happy, so eager. She had to fight down the lump in her throat.

"Kenny," she said, squeezing his hand tightly, "I want you to do one thing for me."

"What?"

She blinked back tears. "I want you always to remember your mother. Always love her."

His eyes were wide and candid. "Oh, I do."

Paige searched his gaze. "Do you remember her? What she looked like?"

He nodded. "She was beautiful."

"Yes, she was." She smiled at him. "And she was also funny and loving and lots of fun. Do you remember the adventures she used to take you on?"

"Yes." He smiled wistfully. "I think about her every day." His eyes widened, remembering. "Last night I had a dream about her."

"You did?"

"Yeah. She was sitting on a big white horse and she was smiling at me and she was saying, 'Your dad needs you, Kenny. Better go with him.'"

Better go with him. Her heart was going to burst open and spill out all her sorrow if she didn't hurry up and get this over with. If she could only get through it without sobbing in front of the boy, she would count it a victory.

"Do you want to go with him, Kenny?" she asked, forcing her voice to remain steady with a great deal of effort.

He nodded excitedly. "Yeah. I want to see his house. And he's got a dog."

"Does he?" A dog. And probably a white picket fence. She bit her lip.

"Yeah, a big golden retriever. His name is Chance."

It was obvious Kenny didn't have a problem with the transition. The only ones protesting the move were Paige and her parents. And they didn't carry much weight.

But she wasn't going to fight it. Jake should be with Kenny, and Kenny should be with Jake. That was very clear. That was the way this story should end, with the proper order back into this boy's life. And in some ways she was grateful to Jake. After all, he'd given her a gift—four years with Kenny, four of the best years of her life. For that, she would never have enough to repay him.

SHE MET JAKE at the shop at two. He came in through the glass door and she locked it behind him and turned the sign. They needed a little privacy for this.

"Do you want to come into the office and sit down?" she asked.

He shook his head, gazing at her warily. "No, I'm too restless," he said gruffly. "I'd rather stand."

She nodded, understanding. She felt the same way. "Okay. Where do we start?"

He hesitated, then looked at the toes of his boots. "About last night—"

"Stop," she said sharply, putting up a hand. "We're not going to talk about that."

He looked up at her, surprised. "But I just wanted to apologize—"

"No," she said, shaking her head adamantly, her eyes flashing fire. "Don't you dare, Jake Winslow. Leave last night alone. I don't want to talk about it."

He seemed nonplussed, staring at her. "Then I guess we go straight to talking about Kenny," he said doubtfully.

She nodded. "Okay."

"Okay." He paused, getting his thoughts in order. "He's a great kid, Paige. I couldn't have left him with anyone who could have done better with him."

She shrugged. "Like you say, he's a great kid. That came mostly from you and Carol. I just fed and clothed him for four years."

"You did a lot more than that. You were there for him when I wasn't." He closed his eyes for a moment, then opened them and looked her squarely in the eye. "This is no good what we've been doing to him this week, putting him in the middle."

"I know," she said softly.

"We've got to do something about it."

"I know," she said again, then lifted her chin, trying to feel brave. "I . . . I'm ready to do it."

He blinked at her for a moment, then shook his head. "I'm the one who has to do it," he said, his voice rough. "I'm the one who caused the problem." He turned away, looking out the window into the street. "I'll get out of here, Paige. And your life can get back to normal."

She stared at him for a moment, not sure she understood. "But Kenny won't be able to go right away," she said tentatively.

He turned to look at her again. "No, Paige. I won't be taking Kenny with me. I'm going to leave him here with you."

Her heart stopped. This was exactly what she'd wanted, prayed for, worked so hard for ever since he'd arrived in town. He was handing her what she wanted most in the world. The only trouble was, she couldn't take it.

Slowly, she shook her head. "No," she whispered, her eyes dry but burning. "No, Jake. You can't leave your son behind. Don't you see? You have to keep your promise to him. It's the only way. The only way."

He fixed her in his gaze, not saying a word, and she laughed softly, laughed at the irony, laughed at fate.

"Your son adores you," she told him. "He needs you so badly. He needs to pattern himself on you, learn how to be a man from you."

"But he needs you, too."

She smiled. "He's had me for four years. And I treasure every moment. But now he needs you." She steeled herself, head held high. "Take him with you, Jake. Keep your promise."

Jake nodded slowly. "Thanks, Paige," he said, his voice soft, his eyes luminous. "There's no one like you. No one."

She shivered, wishing she could believe he really meant it.

CHAPTER FOURTEEN

"WHEN DO I get to see my dad?"

Kenny was standing in a pile of shiny wrapping paper and ribbons, sifting through to see if he'd lost any of his many presents in the mad scramble to get them all opened. His friends had come, consumed ice cream and cake, watched him open the packages and departed again quickly so as not to tire him out on his first full day home from the hospital. But he looked like anything but an invalid. His eyes were glowing and his cheeks were flushed.

Paige held out a bag for the trash and began helping him put the refuse in. "Your dad's coming," she said. "He'll be here in about an hour."

Kenny looked up eagerly. "Is he bringing me my birthday present?"

She grinned. "Haven't you had enough presents for one day?"

"No! It's my birthday."

"Oh," she teased. "I almost forgot." She tousled his hair, then looked at him. He was shooting up like a weed. Soon he would be too tall for her to muss his hair. Was she going to miss the changes as he turned from a boy into a man? She couldn't stand to think of it, and she pushed the thought away. "Yes, he's bringing you a present," she reassured him quickly. "Don't you worry."

He sat back and gazed at her eagerly. "But when do I get to go with him?"

His question struck a blow to her heart, but she managed to smile at him. She ought to be used to it by now, he'd asked it often enough. "As soon as the doctors say you are completely out of danger."

"Then I'll be going with my dad." It was almost a chant to him by now.

"Yes. You'll be going."

And she would be staying. Looking away, she swallowed her agony so that he wouldn't see it.

The doorbell rang.

"It's him!"

Kenny was racing toward the entryway before Paige could take a breath. She laughed ruefully, following him, wondering what Jake would do if he knew she was just as excited about seeing him as his son was. But she waited, hanging back while they hugged and Kenny showed off his favorite presents. After all, she wasn't really a part of what they had. She was just the caretaker, when you came right down to it.

Jake did have a present for Kenny, and he looked up and met Paige's gaze as he handed it to him.

It was a video game system, the newest and the best, and he grinned over Kenny's head as the boy was exclaiming his excitement. "I'm learning," he said to Paige with a crooked grin. "Do I pass this one?"

She had to admit he did. "Better go get it set up in his room," she said. "I won't have it out here."

She watched them go, laughing and joking like buddies. "His room," she repeated softly to herself.

But for how much longer? It broke her heart. Everything was bringing tears to her eyes and she hated that. She went into the kitchen while they worked on Kenny's new toy. Someone had to clean up the mess of ten boys' careening through the place for an hour.

She did the dishes and swept the floor and was about to leave the kitchen, when Jake appeared in the doorway, making her jump.

"Sorry. Did I scare you?"

She put a hand to her chest and shook her head. "No, I'm just a little jumpy tonight."

He came into the room and leaned against the door to the pantry, watching her through narrowed eyes. "Do I get a piece of birthday cake?" he asked.

"Of course." Turning, she pulled the cake out of its hiding place and opened a drawer, searching for the right knife. "Do you want ice cream with it?"

"No." He gave her his slow grin. "I'll take it straight up."

With a baleful look, she began to cut the cake. "Would you get down a plate, please?" she asked.

He did as requested, coming to where she was working and holding the plate out for his piece. She lifted the slice on the knife and tried to get it to the plate, but it began to wobble.

"Oh, no!" she cried, fighting for control.

"Hold it," he said, steadying her arm and sliding the plate under the cake. "There we go."

Dessert was saved, but they'd ended up very close— too close for comfort. If he just turned his head a little, he could catch the scent of her hair, feel the warmth of her body. Instead of backing away, he stood where he was and let her fill his senses.

She knew what he was doing and she stood very still, staring down at the cake, her heart beating a crazy tattoo in her chest. When he touched her, his fingers brushing back the hair that fell against her neck, clearing a space behind her ear, she closed her eyes for a moment. It was tempting to float here, let it ride, let whatever was about to happen, happen. But she knew she couldn't do that. Not after what had occurred the other night.

She opened her eyes and turned her head to meet his smoky gaze. "No, Jake," she said, her voice just a little more shaky than she would have liked. "You're breaking the rules."

He raised one eyebrow and his fingers didn't retreat. "We've got rules now?" he asked.

Indignation flared and she grabbed his hand, pushing it away. "You should know," she said, eyes blazing. "You're the one who set them."

He shrugged, looking at her sardonically. "Then I should be the one who breaks them."

"No." She shook her head. "It doesn't work that way. Your rules have created a structure around our relationship. If you want to tear that structure down, you have to put up something new in its place."

He stared at her, not sure he knew exactly what she meant. She saw his hesitation, and she sighed, pushing him firmly away from her.

"Go eat your cake," she said briskly. "I'm going to check on Kenny."

Kenny was doing just fine. He barely looked up. "This is so rad, Paige," he cried. "I'm winning."

"Radical, dude," she said with a grin. "I'll check on you later."

She paused for a moment before she went back into the kitchen. She had to prepare herself every time she came near Jake. It was no easy task to hide the way she felt. Taking a deep breath, she entered and walked right up to the table where he was sitting, flopping down into a chair.

"So," she said in a bright and cheery manner, "how are things going for you?"

"Not so good," he said quietly, taking his last bite of cake. "In fact, I've come to a decision. I've got to get out of here."

"What do you mean?" she asked, startled. She hadn't faced the departure yet, not really. And suddenly she knew she was going to be as upset over his leaving as she was going to be over Kenny's. Double the pain. What a prospect.

Jake leaned back and looked at her levelly. "Kenny's going to be recuperating here with you for at least a week. I can't just hang around like this. So I'm taking off."

"Taking off?" Why didn't that bring a measure of relief? It didn't do any such thing. In fact, it only brought a sense of desolation.

"I'm going to spend tomorrow wrapping some things up," he went on. "I have some business I have to attend to. And then I'm out of here. I'll be back next Sunday to get Kenny."

She nodded. That was about what she'd expected.

He was gazing at her searchingly. "You're not going to give me any problems?" he asked her softly.

"What can I do, Jake? You hold all the cards. This hand belongs to you."

"You're not going to try any tricks? Not going to run away with Kenny and go hide in a cave or anything like that?"

She shook her head, feeling suddenly very weary. "No. I wouldn't do that to him. You know that."

He nodded slowly. "Yes. I do know that. I know you only want what's best for him. We just have a different opinion of what that is."

"No," she said vacantly, shaking her head and staring into space. "Not really, Jake. We're pretty much in agreement. He needs you. I know that. And... well, maybe he's had enough mothering for a while." She turned and smiled at him, holding back tears, fighting to keep her voice steady. "He'll do real well with you, Jake. I know it. He's yours. And you'll take good care of him. Won't you?"

His face changed. "Ah, Paige," he began, reaching for her.

But she stiffened and pulled back, away from him. "I'm okay," she said firmly, though her lower lip was quivering. "I know this is for the best."

"I wish things didn't have to end like this," he said.

"So do I." She dug into her pocket for a tissue and blew her nose. "So do I." She gave him a watery smile. "But life goes on, I'll make it. Don't you worry about me."

She turned in her chair, looking for the wastepaper basket, and he said awkwardly, "You could always come with us, you know."

She turned back, but he'd looked down quickly and was playing with his fork on the empty plate.

She stuttered, stunned by what he'd said and not sure how to take it. "I . . . my whole life is here. And I couldn't leave my parents . . ."

And then she flushed, realizing she was taking his offer too seriously. He hadn't meant it, any more than he'd meant it the time he'd said, "Marry me." She should have given it the lighthearted response it deserved. She had to make up for that blunder, fast.

"And anyway, three's a crowd," she said brightly, rising from her seat, desperate for an escape. "I'm going to go check on Kenny."

She left so quickly, he could almost hear the wind whistling past his head. He sat right where he was and stared after her. He couldn't believe he'd said that. What if she'd picked up on it? What if she'd said, "Hey, great idea. I'll go pack my things."

But she hadn't done that. Instead, she'd mumbled a handful of excuses and vacated the scene as quickly as possible. She didn't have any long-term designs on him. He should quit worrying.

But some little doubt still niggled at him. It had nothing to do with fearing commitment, or wanting to disentangle himself from relationships. It had even less to do with being wary of women. It was something completely different, and finally, he faced it. He was disappointed that she hadn't jumped at the chance to go with them.

But that was stupid. He didn't want her tailing along, did he? That had never been a part of the plan. Besides, he'd done too much disrupting of her life as it was. She needed to get back to whatever it was she wanted to do. She should be dating, finding the right man and moving on. And right now, he was going to head back to corporate headquarters and make his report, then he would be back to get Kenny, and all this would be over. Forever.

Well, maybe not forever. No. Kenny would want to see his aunt, to keep in touch with the woman who'd been a mother to him for the past four years. And, to be honest, Jake would look forward to seeing her as well. She was so loving and open and centered in her way. He liked being with her, loved touching her, craved making love with her. He'd held off when he'd first begun realizing how attracted he was to her because he hadn't wanted to get involved with another Kenton. He'd wanted to avoid ravaging another member of the Kenton family. Despite everything, his mere existence had done enough to them. They deserved to be left alone.

He was right to get out of here before something else happened to gum up the works. Still, there were a few loose threads he had to tie up. For instance, Paige's parents. He was going to have to make an effort to patch things up with them. He couldn't leave things the way they were. They were his son's grandparents, after all.

He rose slowly, as though all his muscles were sore, and walked, stiff-legged, into the hall and down toward Kenny's room. He didn't have much time left, and he wanted to spend it with people he cared about.

IT WAS almost two hours later when Paige came out to walk him to the door of the apartment. The three of them had had a wonderful time playing games on the new system, laughing, teasing one another. Sort of like a real family, Paige thought as she led him through the room toward the front door.

But when they reached the living room, something made them both stop and stare down at the patch of carpet where they'd been together a few nights before. Paige flushed and tried to move on, but Jake looked at her and grinned.

"Next time, I promise, we'll make it to the bedroom," he said, catching hold of her hand.

Her heart lurched in her chest. "There's not going to be any next time. Remember?"

But she didn't pull her hand away. They walked toward the door and when they reached it, he drew her close and dropped a quick kiss on her lips.

"Thank you, Paige," he said. "Thank you for letting me be a part of this with you two. And for accepting me as Kenny's father. I know the way you're treating me in front of him is having a major impact on him. And I appreciate it."

"It comes naturally, Jake," she said softly. "You're a pretty good guy, you know. You deserve it."

He looked down into her dark eyes, a feeling of wonder growing in his chest. She meant it. She really had gotten over thinking of him as a jerk trying to ruin everyone's life. He wanted to tell her how that made him feel, show her, maybe. But to do that would lead them into danger so he pulled back, forcing himself away from her, saluting and going off into the night.

It was better this way, he told himself. Much, much better. If only it weren't quite so cold and lonely.

CHAPTER FIFTEEN

SHE WAS GOING through Kenny's things, packing clothes in boxes, putting away toys he'd outgrown, when the phone call came. Kenny had gone to the movie with a friend and his family. She was alone and rather sad when the phone rang. But she snapped to right away when she heard the panic in her mother's voice.

"Paige, you've got to do something, you've got to come quickly, he's here!"

She gripped the receiver tightly. "Who? Mother, what are you talking about?"

"Jake. He's here." She sounded at the end of her rope. "He and your father are shouting at each other. It's horrible. Your father is going to have a heart attack if they keep on like this."

So this was the business Jake had to wrap up, was it? Paige swore under her breath. Why hadn't he let her know? She could have gone with him, she could have smoothed the way. Why did he have to be so stubborn?

But she knew what she had to do immediately. "I'll be there right away."

She ran down to her car, started it up and raced out into the countryside and up the mountain to her parents' place. It was set back among the hills, the white frame house sitting among a grove of aspen that sent their silver messages into the wind at all times of the day or night.

But, as she drove the driveway, she could see no sign of Jake's truck.

She ran inside and looked around wildly. "Where is he?" she cried. "What happened?"

Her mother came toward her, wringing her hands. "He's gone. Oh, Paige, it was awful. Your father's lying down."

Paige let herself relax, just a little bit. She inhaled deeply and shook herself. "How is he? Have you taken his blood pressure?"

Her mother flapped her hands in the air like shadow birds. "Oh, yes, yes. He's all right now. But he's so upset. They said such awful things to each other." She shivered. "It was terrible."

"They are going to have to learn to tolerate each other, the both of them. For Kenny's sake."

"Yes, dear, I know that. But try telling your father."

Paige shook her head. There was very little use in telling her father anything and she knew it. But one always had to try.

She went into his room and found him lying on the bed, one arm flung across his eyes.

"Dad," she said softly. "Are you okay?"

Pulling his arm back, he raised his head and looked at her. She jammed a pillow behind him for support. "No," he said bitterly. "I'm not the least bit okay. And you can thank that hellion you brought back into the family."

"Jake?" She sighed. "He's Kenny's father, Dad. There is nothing anyone can do to keep him out of the family. It's a little late for that."

"He's no good, Paige. Never has been, never will be. He and that no-account father of his."

"Did you know his father?"

He nodded. "Yes, I knew his father. He sold us this very land when we first came to Aberdeen, when I first started my practice. That was before you and Carol were born. He sold me this land—land that had been in his family for generations—and then he went on a binge of drinking and gambling and squandered the money in two years. Destroyed his family. Put his wife out to work to support them. And then he ran off, never to be seen again. A deadbeat if there ever was one."

"So it seems. But Jake isn't like that," Paige said.

He jerked around to look into her face. "Oh, no? Look what he did, taking Carol out of school, luring her to follow him into the mining camps, always searching for gold instead of making an honest living. Even after they had Kenny, he wouldn't settle down."

"But he has, now. He's got two degrees—one in geology and one in geochemistry, and he has a job with an important corporation."

He snorted, rolling his eyes in derision. "So he says."

"Daddy..." She took his hand and looked into his face. "He wasn't the one who called the IRS. He wasn't the one who turned you in."

"That's what he claims now. But tell me this, if not him, who?"

She hesitated. She still didn't have the answer to that question.

"And now he's taking Kenny from us." His anguish was written on his face. "That man, raising Kenny. The idea is intolerable."

She hurt for her father, knowing a lot of his anger was directed at fate as well as Jake. If he'd still been practicing medicine, if he'd still had his income and his self-respect, he wouldn't be holding on to his bitterness so desperately. It was always easier to blame outside forces for the miseries of life.

She gave her father a hug and left the room. If he was all right, lying down and getting some rest, her next priority was to find out what had happened to Jake.

"How long ago did Jake leave?" she asked her mother. "Do you have any idea where he went?"

"Oh, yes. Yes, he said he was going to the mine."

"The mine?" Paige frowned. "Why would he go there?"

"He said . . . now what was it? Oh, yes, he said he wanted to see where Kenny had the accident."

"I see." She turned. "Just keep Daddy calm, Mother. I'll go see Jake."

Her mother clutched at her arm. "I don't think you should. He was in a terrible mood when he left here."

She patted her mother's hand and smiled. "Don't worry. I can handle him. Leave it to me." And she headed out the door.

On her way to "handle" Jake. What a laugh. What a joke. She couldn't even handle herself, much less Jake.

But she had to go see him. If he was hurt . . .

She stopped for a moment. The thought of Jake hurting was too horrible to contemplate.

She took the rough road much too fast, but she was in a hurry. It was a warm spring day and the mountainside was covered with golden California poppies. She saw his truck parked at the end of the road. Pulling her car up next to it, she got out and began the hike up to where the tailings of the mine spilled out over the hillside. Suddenly, Jake appeared, standing high on the hill above the mine opening, climbing on some leftover scaffolding. She had to lean her head back and shade her eyes to see him. He'd pulled off his shirt and tied it around his waist, and his hard chest muscles rippled in the sunlight.

"Look at this view, Paige," he called down to her, flinging an arm out. "Look at the wide expanse of history stretching out in front of you." He looked down at her. "Doesn't it excite you, Paige? Doesn't it turn you on?"

In a way. But what excited her more was him, tall and strong up there on the scaffolding, like a conqueror, master of all he surveyed. She stood below and watched him, her pulse racing, her breath coming too fast. Slowly he climbed down and came to meet her.

"Hi," he said as he dropped in front of her, jumping from ten feet above. His eyes seemed to burn into her, melting her heart even further. "You came."

She nodded, speechless.

"I'm glad." His skin was wet and shining and gorgeous and he seemed big, bigger than life, bigger than dreams. "I messed up the meeting with your parents," he added simply. "I'm sorry."

She wanted to take him in her arms, but she held back, looking away so he couldn't read the impulse in her eyes. "What exactly did you and my father fight about?" she asked, instead.

He shrugged, turning away restlessly. "The usual. Carol. That night. Who said what. Who did what. Who held who back." He turned back and shook his head. "It's always fascinating how two people can go through the same situation at the same time and see it so differently."

"Did you tell him that you didn't call the IRS?"

He stared at her for a long moment, then sighed and looked away. "No," he said quietly.

"I did."

"And what did he say?"

She shrugged. "He didn't believe it. But he'll have to start thinking about the possibility, anyway."

He shook his head. "Leave it alone, Paige. He'll never come around. And maybe it's better that way."

"But Jake, he has to know. Would you like to tell him yourself?"

He shook his head again, slowly, avoiding her eyes. Bending down, he picked up a stone and tossed it high out over the canyon, so that it fell into the mass of poppies that spread out before them. "I can't tell him," he said. "I just can't do that."

She frowned, not sure she knew what he was talking about. "I think you should have told him. He might actually believe you." She paused for a moment. "Jake, we've got to get to the bottom of this and find out who really did turn my father in. I've been trying to reconstruct that night. But I can't think of anyone who might have done it."

He didn't answer. Instead, he picked up another stone and threw it into the air.

She took a step so that she was positioned where he couldn't ignore her. "Who do you think did it?" she asked.

He turned slowly and stared into her eyes. "Can't you figure it out?" he said softly.

A shiver of shock snaked its way down her spine. Suddenly, a premonition of doom filled her with dread. "What do you mean?" she said, her hands to her throat. "Jake, I don't know what you mean."

He stared at her and she wasn't at all sure he was going to tell her. And then it was too late, because the sound of wheels on gravel turned both their heads. Her mother's car came into view.

"It's my mother," she said quickly. "I don't want her hiking up here." She turned and began walking down the road.

Jake came more slowly behind her, pulling his shirt from around his hips and shrugging into it.

Her mother came toward them, talking as she came. "I just had to see if you two were all right," she said anxiously. "I didn't know. Jake left in such a tear and then, you, Paige..."

"How is Dad?" she asked.

Her mother waved a hand in the air. "Your father is all right. He's sleeping now. He'll be calmer when he wakes up." She glanced at Jake and shook her head. "He'll get over this. It will be all right."

"I hope I didn't upset him too much," Jake said. "I didn't mean for things to go that way."

"I know." Her mother smiled at him. "I know that." Then her smile faded and she looked unhappy again. "I know a lot of things, my dear," she said to Paige. "Some things I think you should know, as well."

Paige gave her a bewildered look. "What are you talking about?"

Her mother came closer and took her hand. "I just wanted to say something to you, Paige. It's about that day, when the government agents arrived and shut down your father's office and Carol drove off in the rain."

Paige went cold. Here it was again. Suddenly, she wasn't sure she wanted to know the truth, after all.

"I know you've thought, along with everyone else, that Jake was the one who turned your father in," her mother said, speaking haltingly. "Well, it's not true. I know who did it. I've known all along."

Jake turned away, walking a short distance from where they were talking. Paige looked from him to her mother, feeling sick to her stomach. "Mother! You didn't . . ."

"No, of course I didn't do it."

"Then who?" Paige asked weakly.

Her mother seemed to be gaining strength as she talked. "You remember that Carol wanted to see me alone the night before? She had a proposal for me. Big plans." She closed her eyes for a moment, but when she opened them again, her voice was as strong as ever. "She wanted to leave Jake at the mine, leave Kenny here with your father and me and take off for San Francisco. She actually asked me to set her up in an apartment—nothing simple, of course, but a nice one near the Presidio so that she could live in the style she thought she should have been living all along. She said we owed her, since she hadn't finished college and that had saved us all sorts of money. And she wanted the payback right away."

Paige was stunned. This was a nightmare. "Mother. I can't believe it."

Her mother smoothed her blouse with two hands. "Well, Carol was always a demanding child, and I suppose we indulged her too often. Especially your father. She was really his pet. But you know that."

Paige nodded numbly.

"But I put my foot down this time. I told her in no uncertain terms that she had been spoiled too long. We weren't going to give her any more money. She'd set her life up and she was going to have to live it out the way she'd determined it. It was her responsibility to be a good wife to Jake, a good mother to Kenny and a good person. She had no business running off and doing something else, just because she felt like it." Mrs. Kenton sighed, shaking her head. "She threw a fit. You know how hysterical she could get. Well, she thought she had an ace up her sleeve. She tried to blackmail me. She told me that if I didn't do what she'd asked, she would call the government on your father."

There it was, the truth Paige had been dreading. And yet, when it finally came, she felt curiously detached.

"Oh, no. No, not Carol," she said, but she said it without much emotion. All her emotion was tied up elsewhere.

"Yes, my dear, I'm afraid she did it. I didn't believe her. I thought it was just another of her crazy threats. But then the next day, there were the agents. I confronted her. She admitted she'd done it."

Paige closed her eyes. Carol. Her beloved, evil sister. She'd loved her and hated her. But she'd never dreamed Carol could do something like this. Opening her eyes again, she looked at her mother.

"But then, why did she drive off?"

"We had a dreadful row. She was very upset and said she was going to San Francisco anyway, and to hell with us all. And she raced off into the rain. Carrying, by the way, all the money she could steal from my dresser drawer."

Paige rocked herself, seeking comfort. "Why did you let everyone believe it was Jake?" she asked dully, staring into the sky.

"What else could I do? Carol was the apple of your father's eye. It would have killed him to know she was the one."

Paige knew her mother was right. "Are you going to tell him now?"

Finally, her mother's voice began to show the strain of her confession. "I'm going to have to, aren't I?"

"No." Jake moved back into their circle, looking at Paige and then her mother, his face hard and emotionless. "I'll take the rap."

Mrs. Kenton started to say something, and then shook her head, holding back. "I'm not going to do anything right away, so the two of you make the decision. You do what you think best, but I'm not going to talk anymore about it. I'm tired and I want to get back before your father wakes up. Goodbye."

She turned, and Paige let her go without another word. What was there to say? She and Jake trudged back to the mine, walking without speaking. When they got to the cleared area, they both sank to the warm earth and sat in the sun.

"Are you okay?" Jake asked at last.

She smiled at him. "I'm a little stunned. But all in all, I'm not that surprised."

He nodded. "It has nothing to do with you, you know. Don't start putting the guilt on yourself."

"No." She shook her head. "No, I won't do that." She looked at him curiously. "You've known all along?"

"Carol talked about doing exactly what she did for months before that night. It wouldn't have been in my mind in the hallway if she hadn't been on and on about it all the way over in the car."

"I see." She sighed, leaning back against a rock. "Well, it's all over now. I just want..." She looked at him seriously. "I don't want Kenny to know about it. Not until he's old enough to deal with it. Okay?"

"There's no reason at all to tell him," he agreed.

"He's got to have a good image of his mother," Paige insisted.

"Of course."

She sighed again, this time with relief. "How could she have done it, Jake? I really don't understand."

"Carol was wild and beautiful and fun to be with when she wanted to be. But she was also willful and selfish and cruel. That was just the way she was."

Paige sat still for a long moment. "Maybe you're right," she said at last. "I hate to think it. But I don't have a lot of choice anymore, do I?" She sighed. "I was always wary of criticizing her, you know. I was always afraid that maybe I was just jealous."

"Jealous?"

"Sure. She was so much more popular." She laughed softly. "My father always loved Carol best. He made no bones about it."

Jake looked at her. "Did that bother you?"

"Not in the way you mean. It was always that way. I just thought of it as the natural order of things. That was the way it was while I was growing up." She squinted, remembering. "Everyone has always loved Carol best."

Jake made a noise deep in his throat. "That's crazy," he said.

Paige shrugged. "Crazy but true."

"No," he said roughly. "You're ten times the person Carol was."

She turned to look at him, shocked by his words, surprised by the vehemence of his tone, but he was staring out into the hills. She couldn't read the expression in his eyes. How could he have said such a thing? But maybe he'd just wanted to make her feel good. Maybe that was all it was.

"Jake, promise me you'll always speak well of Carol," she said quietly. "Never, ever say anything critical of her. You never know when Kenny might be listening."

"Is that what you've done?" He turned and looked at her. "Pretended all these years for his sake?"

"I . . . I don't know what you're talking about."

"Oh, come on, Paige. Let's not play games any longer. Carol was exciting and beautiful. She was also lovable, in her way. But at the same time, she was selfish and demanding and very easy to hate."

"Jake . . ." She shook her head. "Don't say that."

He leaned toward her and took her shoulders in his hands. "I won't, Paige. I'll put on the act for Kenny's sake. But for now, right here, with only the two of us, we can be honest, can't we? I loved Carol when we were first married. But by the time she died, I hardly even liked her any longer."

She stammered, confused. "But, I thought...I was so sure..."

"That I was still pining away for Carol?" He released her, grimacing. "Sorry, Paige. I can't pretend that. It's not true. But I still don't think your father should be told about what she did," he went on slowly. "I know how he felt about her, and I don't think he needs to be hurt that way."

She looked at him wonderingly. Every day she was learning new things about him. She was finding out how different he was from the image he'd carried like a weight around his neck since he was a kid. "So you're willing to fall on your sword for him? After the way he's treated you?"

"He's your father. And Kenny's grandfather." It was as simple as that.

"I don't agree. I think he has to know the truth," she insisted.

Jake hesitated. "He's your father," he said at last. "It's up to you, I guess. You know him best."

She nodded. "I'll tell him later. After he gets used to Kenny's absence."

"I'll do it for you, if you want. Then he can take his anger out on me."

She stared at him, dazzled by his sense of integrity, his generosity, then grinned. "Hey, pretty fancy footwork. One week from scumbag to hero."

He winced, his blue eyes flashing. "I'm not a hero, Paige."

Reaching out, she took his hand. "I don't know, Jake. You look pretty heroic to me." She smiled at him.

Their gazes met and held. He saw the feeling in her eyes, read her mind, and every instinct inside told him to get out while the going was good. If he stayed, he was going to take another step in the direction he'd been avoiding all this time.

But she looked so beautiful with the sun in her hair, and he felt so good having her here, and suddenly he was springing to his feet and pulling her along with him.

"Come on," he said. "I want to show you something."

She followed him, still wondering, still bewildered by the things he'd said about Carol. He didn't think he still loved her. But was he telling himself the truth? That was the problem. She wasn't so sure he understood his own motivations. Only time would tell.

He led her down the hillside, into the poppy field, until they reached a place where the flowers came to above their knees.

"This is it," he said, throwing out his hand.

"It's beautiful," she agreed, delighted.

He turned and curled her closer into his arms. "So are you," he murmured, burying his face in her silver-blond hair. "You belong here."

She laughed and pressed her body against his, shivering with the sense of him that gave her. "We both do," she murmured thickly.

He kissed her slowly, deeply, then drew back and pressed his face against hers.

"Have you ever made love in a field of poppies?" he asked her softly.

"No," she said breathlessly, clinging to him.

"Want to try it?" he asked, dropping tiny, nibbling kisses on her neck and behind her ear.

"Why not?" she whispered, sliding her hand inside his open shirt, half-drunk with the sense of his masculine power.

He groaned, shuddering at her touch, and then he looked down, laughing softly. "I promised you a bed," he reminded her.

She smiled, rubbing against him like a cat. "I don't need a bed," she whispered, her eyes closed, her lips barely grazing his skin. "All I need is you."

His arms wound more tightly around her, his hands plunging deep into her jeans, taking her into his grip, drawing her into the strength of his body. His mouth found hers and took it as his own, and she left sanity behind, dropping gladly into the magic world of sensation only he could conjure up for her.

She was nothing but love, nothing but senses, feeling, tasting, hearing, crying out with need and desire, urging him to hurry, then to slow, then to come much, much harder, flying higher and higher until she thought she would crash into the sun.

And then, lying half-naked among the flowers, she felt the incredible power of his thrusts as he came inside her, and she cherished him, held him with her legs, held him with her hips, and shared his moment of ecstasy. Taking in every sensation with a greed she didn't know she possessed, even reveling in the heaviness of his hot, slick body as he lay atop her, she smiled, pure joy curling inside her like smoke from a fire. This was happiness. This was love. This was something so rare and precious, she would keep a part of it with her forever, keep it locked in her heart where only she could find it, take it out and remember.

They lay together in the flowers, talking softly, laughing, savoring the moment in the sun. But finally it was time to go, and they turned reluctantly, gathering their clothes.

"I'm leaving tomorrow," he told her.

She nodded without meeting his gaze. She knew that. She'd never expected anything else. He needed to go, needed to prepare for taking Kenny away.

"I'll let you know how Kenny's doing," she said. "You'll call?"

He nodded. He hated leaving her like this. He owed her so much, and yet he'd promised her so little. "Paige," he began, but she put a finger to his lips, knowing what he was about to say.

"Hush," she whispered, her love for him in her eyes. "Don't say a word. The only thing I want from you is to be a good father to Kenny. Will you promise that?"

"Of course." He pulled her close and kissed her soundly. "You'll come visit us, won't you?"

"Oh, sure," she said, knowing it would not be the same. They would be starting a new life, and she wouldn't be part of it.

"Okay." He let her go. "We'll miss you."

She laughed, throwing out her arms, letting her hair fly in the breeze. "No, you won't," she told him, turning slowly and memorizing the scene so she would be able to bring it up in her mind on cold, lonely nights. "You'll be too busy for that." Then she turned and sobered, searching his eyes. "Just don't forget me," she whispered.

He took her face between his hands and kissed her gently. "How could I do that?" he whispered back.

They stared into one another's eyes for a long moment, then began to laugh. Joining hands, they started back, out of the enchanted valley. But Paige looked over her shoulder at the last minute. And so did Jake.

CHAPTER SIXTEEN

IT WAS HER last week with Kenny and the days passed much too quickly. Suddenly it was Sunday, Kenny was packed and ready to go and Jake was at the door.

"Hi," he said, looking at Paige as though he wasn't sure what his reception was going to be.

"Hi yourself," she said, forcing a wide smile. "Come on in and have some lunch. Then he'll be ready to go with you."

She'd planned a lovely meal, thinking it would be a nice farewell, but the three of them were quiet and strained through the whole thing. She couldn't eat and Jake hardly seemed the man she'd been with in the field of flowers only a week before. Kenny spilled his glass of milk and dropped his fork and bounced up and down in his chair until she wanted to scream.

And then lunch was over and it had gone much too fast and they were on the doorstep, ready to go.

She didn't cry. At least she had that as a point of pride. She kissed Kenny goodbye and caught a very strange look in Jake's eyes and then they were walking to the car and she thought she would die. But she waved as they drove off.

And then she cried. Cried for days. Cried every time a sappy commercial came on the television. Cried when she heard a song she liked on the radio. Cried when she looked into Kenny's empty room. Cried when she felt the loneliness of her empty bed.

Fortunately she had too much to do to keep crying all the time. First there was the shop. With Gold Rush Days coming, everyone suddenly had to have something nostalgic, and her shop was the place to go for that. The place was full of people from morning to night. Sara worked as hard as she did herself, and together they pulled it off.

Trent was a big help, too. He was always around when she needed a shoulder to cry on, or someone to go out to dinner with. It would have been so perfect if only there could have been a spark of romance between the two of them. But for some reason, much as they liked each other, the passion just wasn't there.

Her biggest problem was getting the work done for the Gold Rush Days parade. With Barry gone, all the work was on her shoulders, and she was up past midnight on many a weary night, taking care of the details.

Meanwhile, Jake and Kenny were traveling. Jake was taking Kenny on a tour of gold country, in California and Nevada, showing him mines, teaching him the history of the area. Every night, Jake let Kenny call her from whatever motel they were staying in. And that was the best part of her day.

"This is costing you a lot of money to call every night," she chided Kenny on one of the first nights he called.

"It's okay," Kenny said confidently. "Dad said he can afford it. He said you're worth it."

"Did he?"

That was enough to give her a rosy glow for at least the next twenty-four hours. And then there was another call, and the next night another. And she blessed the man. Without those calls, her life would have taken on the consistency of ashes.

The two of them were having a lot of fun together, and she was glad. But she missed them both so much, it stung like crazy.

And yet, life did go on. The plans for the parade were falling into place and she was meeting new people, both at work and at committee meetings. And one night, in a weak moment, she actually accepted an invitation to dinner from a man who took her dancing.

And she caught flak for it the very next evening when Kenny called.

"Where were you last night?" he demanded right off the bat. "We tried to call."

She hesitated, then decided to take the plunge. "I was out on a date last night," she said carefully.

"You had a date?" The question was asked in a tone of incredulity, and immediately Kenny called out, "Hey, Dad. Paige had a date."

Then he came back to her. "You mean with a man?"

"Yes, with a man. That's the usual way dates go."

There was an odd sound on the other end of the line, and then Kenny was back, half whispering. "Paige... I don't know. I think something's wrong with Dad."

Paige blinked, startled. "Why? What's going on, Kenny?"

He was obviously cupping his hand over the receiver. "Dad's rolling around on the bed and groaning and making a horrible face..."

His narrative was interrupted by Jake's voice demanding, "Give me the phone, Kenny."

And then, in a much calmer voice, "Hi, Paige?"

"Hi," she said dryly. "Is something wrong?"

"Wrong?" He muttered something to Kenny, then returned to their phone conversation. "Oh, no, nothing's wrong. I just had a slight stomachache, that's all. Nothing to be worried about."

She grinned. Did she really dare believe he was jealous? "And that was why you were writhing on the bed?" she asked archly.

"Uh...yeah. That's it."

She smothered her laughter. "Is it over now?"

"Oh, yeah. I feel great." He coughed. "So—you had a date? Who with?"

"Someone I just met," she said. "You don't know him."

"So—what was he like?"

"He was very nice." That was probably an exaggeration, but Jake didn't have to know that. "A really dynamic, passionate sort of guy."

She could almost hear the fumes rising. "Oh, yeah?"

"Yeah." She grinned. "And I got a great kiss out of it, too."

"No kidding?" Was he clutching the phone as though he were about to strangle it? That was certainly what it sounded like.

"Yeah. A nice wet one—right on the cheek."

There was a pause, then Jake said, "What?"

"Uh-huh," she went on nonchalantly. "He brought his German shepherd along."

"Oh." He groaned, then took a deep breath. "Damn it, Paige, don't do that."

But he had to chuckle. She was laughing so hard, he felt more sheepish than ever. "Not that I care," he protested.

"Of course not," she agreed. "Why would you?"

"Why would I?"

She caught her breath. That last sentence had sounded strange. He'd said it slowly, lingeringly. "But you know, I'm going to have to start dating more often," she said quickly, just to keep the conversation going.

"Why? It seems like a lot of trouble to go to."

"It is. But I'm not getting any younger. And anyway, I'm thinking about getting married."

The air chilled again. "Who are you thinking about getting married to?"

"That's just it. I want to find someone. So I guess I'll have to start doing a lot of dating. What kind of guy do you think I should go after?" she asked him idly.

"I think you should join a convent," he muttered.

"What?"

"Nothing. Hey, wait until we get back, okay? We'll find you someone to marry. Won't we, Kenny?"

"No," Kenny protested in the background. "Why can't she marry you?"

There was dead silence for a very long time, and Paige tried hard to smother her laughter.

"I'm glad you're getting such a kick out of this," he said at last, his voice just a bit resentful.

"Who, me?" She forced herself to sober. "Not at all. It's a very serious subject."

And it was, she reflected later. The most serious in the world. She was in love with Jake, and she couldn't help but think about marriage now and then. But she knew there was no use in it. Carol had been there before her. And Carol had made the whole thing impossible.

And anyway, the entire question was moot, because Jake was not in the market for a wife. He'd made that clear. So what was the use in thinking about it?

After a few weeks, Jake took Kenny back to his house in Reno, and then the calls seemed to change in tone. This was Jake's home. Kenny was full of news.

"You know what? Jake's got a Corvette. And a swimming pool."

"He does?"

"Yup. And he took me in to where he works. It's cool. They've got neat computers. And the mine is all computerized. It's like a skyscraper built inside a mountain."

That was interesting. Very interesting. Because it confirmed what Jake had been telling her. This wasn't the Jake of old, the drifter, the guy with torn jeans and a pack on his back. He really did have a couple of degrees and a job with a major corporation. She was having a hard time assimilating these facts, but she couldn't deny them.

Then came the call she'd been dreading from the first, even though she hadn't let herself realize it until now.

"Hey, Paige, guess what," Kenny started off brightly. "Jake's got a girlfriend."

"What?" Her hands were suddenly cold as ice and she wasn't sure if she could still breathe correctly.

"Her name's Beth and she's real pretty. She came over last night and—"

"Give me that phone." Jake took over in the nick of time. "Hi, Paige," he said pleasantly. "How are you?"

Fuming, seething and petrified. "Jake Winslow," she snapped, "if you're having women overnight, with Kenny in the house—"

"Whoa. Hold on." He paused and she could tell he was taking the phone out of the room where Kenny was so they could talk. "It's not like that at all. Calm down, Paige. It's all perfectly innocent."

"Really?" She knew she was being irrational, but she couldn't calm down. "Kenny didn't seem to think so."

"Kenny was exaggerating. She's just a woman I work with, a geologist. She came over and had dinner with us, that's all."

"An old girlfriend?" she asked icily.

"No. A new employee. I'm breaking her in."

"Oh, great. That's very reassuring."

"No, now, I didn't mean it that way. Damn it, Paige, you're twisting everything around. Beth is a nice kid."

"Really. Is she your type?"

"My type?" He let out an exasperated breath. "No."

Paige closed her eyes for two seconds, then said, "What is your type?"

"I don't know. I sort of lean toward top-heavy blond strippers. Why do you ask?"

"Jake!"

"You asked for it, Paige. Anyway, Beth isn't anything like that. She's just out of college and engaged to a guy in law school. She probably has more in common with Kenny than she does with me. They both had a ball playing video games. And that's all there is to it."

Paige held her breath and forced herself to think rationally. "Okay," she said at last. "I believe you."

He let out a long breath. "I wish I could believe you really meant that."

"I do. No problem. Your girlfriends are your business, anyway, as long as you don't sleep with them when Kenny's around."

He groaned. "Paige, you idiot, the only woman I've slept with in months is you. So chill out."

Her heart sang. She believed him, and his words brought tears to her eyes. "Okay," she said in a very small voice.

IN THE MEANTIME, her parents were slowly learning to deal with Kenny's absence. Her mother was handling it best, but even her father was losing his bitterness. And finally, Paige decided the time was right to tell him about what Carol had done.

To her amazement, he took it without much surprise, as though he'd known it deep inside all this time. But he forgave her. Carol could do no wrong in his eyes. There were always excuses for everything she did. Some things would never change.

As for her own feelings, they had come full circle. She'd loved Carol, idolized her, forgiven her for many things. But this last thing she couldn't forgive, somehow. It had destroyed too many people.

But all that was in the past. Now it was the day of the parade, and Paige was running around making sure every last minute detail was taken care of. She was very busy—so busy, she should have been able to block out everything else. But that turned out to be impossible. It was, in many ways, her big day, and she wished—how she wished!—that she could have the two people she loved best with her.

She'd asked Jake to bring Kenny home for the celebration, but he'd had to decline. He was involved in some project at work and couldn't get away. And Kenny was registering for school in Reno. It seemed very much as though her ties to them were being cut, little by little, and that filled her with a sadness she couldn't begin to describe.

She tried to push all that into the background as she worked. But it was there all the time, a part of her she couldn't ignore.

Especially as the work wound down. By nine in the morning, the parade was about ready to go. The entries had to be lined up, and it was getting darn difficult to keep the acrobatic cheerleaders from breaking ranks and showing up in the meticulous lines of the Randstreet Band and Bugle Corps, teasing the boys who'd been ordered to stand at attention.

Trent called to her from the sidelines as she rode slowly by on a float made to look like a mountain stream. "Good luck, Paige. You look great in that getup. Very authentic to the time period."

She looked down at her boots, jeans, plaid shirt and leather vest. "I feel like Annie Oakley in this thing," she called to him, laughing. "But it comes with the territory."

He waved as she rode past, then he melted into the crowd. She looked after him, sighing, wishing...

She helped get the float into place, then stood back. It was over. It was done. There was nothing much left for her to do. She'd launched the ship and now it had to sail on its own wind. She could actually leave. No one would notice.

The thought hit her like a ton of bricks. She could leave. She could go to Reno, if she wanted to. She could drop in on Kenny—and just incidentally, Jake. Why not? She should be allowed to do that. After all, she was a friend.

Oh, heck, she was more than a friend. Yes, once the idea had popped into her mind, it took root and grew quickly, until it took over every part of her. She could go. There was nothing to stop her.

The Aberdeen Travel Office was just across the street, and as luck would have it, it was open today, hoping to capture the imaginations of people come to see the parade. She dashed across and went inside, asking breathlessly, her heart beating hard, for the next flight to Reno.

"Let's see. The next one leaves at ten-thirty from the Aberdeen airport. Would you like me to call and see if they still have an empty seat?"

Yes! She made the decision without thinking, because she didn't want anything to stop her. The salesperson called. There was a seat. She pulled out her credit card, and within minutes, she was running toward where she'd left her car, excitement shimmering through her. She was going to Reno to see Kenny and Jake!

JAKE WAS WANDERING through the crowd. At his height, he could see above most of them, but with hordes like this, it didn't help much. He'd found where Paige's parents had set up their chairs along the route, and he'd left Kenny with them. Now all he wanted was to find Paige. She had to be here somewhere.

"Let's go surprise her," he'd said to Kenny last night as he'd put the boy to bed. He'd just come home after a late meeting and he'd decided to go to Aberdeen, despite the fact that there was another meeting he should be attending right at the time the parade was scheduled to begin. "We'll get up before dawn and drive to Aberdeen. What do you say?"

"Really?" Kenny's obvious joy had given Jake a twinge. He'd kept him away from Paige for too long.

There were various reasons for that, reasons that had very little to do with work or wanting to have time to bond with Kenny, although those were the excuses he'd given at the time. There were other complications, other emotions that had to be analyzed and dealt with. For a while, he just hadn't been ready.

"But now I am," he muttered to himself as he scanned the crowd. "And now, where the hell is she?"

He'd been to the queuing area, where various people had said they'd seen her, but she hadn't been there. And now the parade was starting. Surely she ought to be around to see that.

He stood morosely, looking up and down the line of bands and floats. And then, suddenly, there she was, across the street. At exactly the same time, a huge marching band playing "When the Saints Go Marching In" moved between them.

"Paige!" he called, but of course she couldn't hear with all the racket the drums and horns were making. She turned at the corner, moving quickly, and disappeared down a side street.

"Paige!" he yelled out again, more in frustration than in the vain hope she might hear him. And then he plunged into the heart of the band, weaving in and out between tubas and trumpets, ducking as the guy with the bass drum made a swipe at him with a drumstick, ignoring the shouts of anger from band members and audience alike.

He was a little worse for wear by the time he made it to the other side of the street. He dashed down the street where he'd seen Paige turn, but she was nowhere in sight. And then he saw her car heading down the cross street, pointed toward the highway. She was driving out of town.

"Paige!" he yelled again, but the car kept right on going.

He gazed around frantically. His own car was parked at least a mile away. What was he going to do? How was he going to catch her? He couldn't run after her. He needed a car. Any car. Glancing down at the little foreign job he was standing beside, he saw something remarkable. The owner had left the window down, and the keys lying on the seat.

"Just as though it were meant for me," he would tell people later, when he recounted this story, year after year.

He didn't hesitate. He folded his large frame into the tiny shoe box of a car, started the engine and took off like a shot, heading in the direction he'd seen Paige take. Come hell or high water, he was going to catch her.

PAIGE WAS ALMOST at the airport when she began to notice the tiny red car behind her. The driver was acting very strangely, honking and coming up close, then falling back. He was making her nervous. She'd heard about holdups around airports, where crooks created minor traffic accidents just to get people out of their cars where they could be robbed. There was no way she was falling for that.

The sun was shining on the windshield of the back car and she couldn't see who the driver was, but she didn't know anyone with a car like that. She stepped on the gas.

The little red car stayed right behind her. The faster she went, the faster he went, and he kept on honking his horn. There was a red light ahead, and she was beginning to think she'd better run it. But quickly she thought better of that plan. After all, if she kept her doors locked and her windows up, she should be all right. And running the light was asking for trouble.

She pulled up to the light and stared stonily ahead. Don't make eye contact. Wasn't that what they said you should do?

But when she heard her name, her head whipped around and her gaze met Jake's, and her heart stood still.

"Jake!" she whispered, stunned.

"Pull over," he called to her, pointing toward the side of the road on the other side of the intersection.

The light turned and she did exactly that, turning off the engine and jumping out of her car to meet him halfway, her heart pounding. But as they came face-to-face, suddenly she was shy.

She stopped a few feet away from him, smiling.

"Hi," she said.

"Hi," he said back, stopping, too.

She shrugged, feeling awkward. "Well, what are you doing here? I thought you couldn't come."

He seemed uncharacteristically nervous. "Oh ... uh ... well, you know that project I've been telling you about? The theme park my company wants to develop? I came about that. They're ready to make a bid on your parents' land."

She had to think a minute to realize what he was talking about, but once it came clear in her mind, she was amazed. "You're kidding."

"No. Really. They envision a small theme park based on the gold rush. I brought papers for your parents to sign. This should make them very comfortable in their golden years." He smiled at her. "Since your father still hates me, Kenny is explaining it to them right now. Don't worry about a thing. They'll be well taken care of."

"Why didn't you tell me?"

"I didn't know if my company would go for it. I didn't want to get anyone's hopes up, in case it didn't come through. Believe me, it will be a good deal for them. They'll make out like bandits if they decide to sell."

Her parents financially secure at last. That would certainly take a huge burden off her shoulders. "That's wonderful."

But her mind dropped the subject as quickly as it had taken it up. "So that's what you came for?" she asked, slightly disappointed.

"Well, yes. More or less." He smiled at her and she smiled back, and for just a moment, they both hovered on the brink of coming closer together. But it didn't happen. And finally, he asked her, gesturing toward her car, "Where are you going?"

"Oh, nowhere." The ticket for Reno was sticking out of her purse. She moved her hand to cover it up. "Just taking a little drive," she said airily.

He frowned, looking skeptical. "While the parade is still in progress?"

That was a little hard to explain, but she did her best. "Well, I'm just about paraded out. You know I've been living with that darn thing for months."

He nodded as though she was making perfect sense. "It's a good parade. You did a good job."

"Thank you."

They were silent again, staring at each other. Finally, Jake took a deep breath and said, "So...do you want to come back with me?"

She blinked at him. "Why?"

"I don't know." For some reason, he was turning red. "I thought maybe we could talk some things over."

"Like what?"

He seemed to be about to hyperventilate. "Like... when you want to get married."

"What?" She was sure she was imagining things. He couldn't have said what she thought she'd heard.

He was shaking his head, grinning sheepishly. "You heard me."

She shook her head, her face full of doubt. "I don't think I could have heard you right."

Stepping forward, he took her shoulders in his large hands and shook her gently. "I love you, you idiot," he said loud and clear, right into her face. "I love you. Will you marry me?"

She could hardly breathe, and at the same time, she could hardly believe her ears and her eyes. This was what she'd dreamed of hearing him say and do for months now. And yet... and yet... There was something missing. She couldn't quite let herself enjoy this. There was still a problem.

"Jake," she said softly, reaching out to touch his dear face, "I don't know if I can believe you."

"What are you talking about?" His face clouded and he stared down at her.

She winced, the pain of what she had to say reflected in her eyes. "There's still another problem, Jake," she said, searching his eyes. "You were married to Carol..."

His blue eyes froze. "So?"

She shook her head and said softly, "I need to know that it's me, Paige, that you love."

His eyes widened and he pulled away from her. "What on earth do you mean?"

"Jake. In the beginning, you loved Carol so much. After all, you married her."

He kissed the top of Paige's head, ignoring the fact that they were still standing along the side of a busy highway. "I love you, Paige, like I've never loved any other woman, not even your sister," he whispered softly. "Just tell me what I can do to make you believe me. I'll do it. Anything." He pulled back and raised her face to his with two hands, kissing her lips. "Anything," he repeated.

She adored him. Couldn't he see it in her eyes? "Oh, Jake," she murmured, looking at him with all her love. "Kenny—" Her voice broke and tears filled her eyes.

"Yes, Kenny," he agreed, though he really had no idea what she'd been about to say. "Kenny, you and me. We can be a family in a way none of us has ever been a real family before." His joy came out in his smile.

She shook her head, dizzy. "Well, there's still my shop—"

"You want to live here? Fine. We'll live here. That might be better for Kenny, anyway. And my company has offered me the job of managing the development of the theme park. I could take the job. Then there would be no question about it."

Her head was spinning. It was all so perfect. Could it be true?

"You and me and Kenny," he was saying again, looking deeply into her eyes. "Do you see that? It would work. Wouldn't it?"

She nodded, hardly able to see him through her tears. "Yes," she said weakly. "Oh, yes."

He frowned. "Yes, what?" he demanded impatiently.

She shook her head, laughing and crying at the same time. "Yes, I love you. Yes, I will marry you. Yes, we'll make a family like no other family in the world. Yes!"

He sighed and pulled her close again, satisfied at last. And neither of them paid any attention to the honking horns from the passing traffic. They were lost in a world of their own, a world where dreams really did come true.

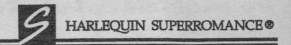

COMING NEXT MONTH

#618 MEG & THE MYSTERY MAN • Elise Title (*Class of '78*)
Meg Delgado goes undercover as a wealthy socialite on the
cruise ship Galileo. Her mission: to catch a thief. Her suspect:
Noah Danforth, who's got the looks, the charm and the wit of a
Cary Grant. But if Meg isn't who she seems to be, neither is Noah.
And together they discover that deception and disguise lead to
danger...and to romance!

#619 THE COWBOY'S LOVER • Ada Steward
Lexi Conley kidnaps rodeo cowboy Jake Thorn because she
needs him to manage her family's ranch while her father's in the
hospital. It doesn't help that Jake, her sister's ex-husband, may be
the father of Lexi's adopted son—or that he's still the only man
she's ever loved.

#620 SAFEKEEPING • Peg Sutherland (*Women Who Dare*)
An unexpected snowstorm traps Quinn Santori and her two young
companions in an isolated mountain cabin. A cabin that's already
inhabited—by a man toting a gun. They make an odd foursome—
Quinn, the two little girls in her charge and ex-con Whit Sloane.
And chances are their number will increase to five before the snow
melts. *Quinn's about to have a baby!*

#621 THE LOCKET • Brenna Todd
Transported back through time, Erin Sawyer is mistaken for her
double, the adulterous Della Munro, whose husband is a powerful
and dangerous man. But Erin finds herself attracted to his partner,
Waite MacKinnon, a man whose compelling eyes have been
haunting her dreams for what seems like forever.

AVAILABLE NOW:

#614 LAUREL & THE LAWMAN
Lynn Erickson

#615 GONE WITH THE WEST
Dawn Stewardson

#616 PERFECTLY MATCHED
Candice Adams

#617 JAKE'S PROMISE
Helen Conrad

Take 4 bestselling love stories FREE

Plus get a FREE surprise gift!

Special Limited-time Offer

Mail to Harlequin Reader Service®

3010 Walden Avenue
P.O. Box 1867
Buffalo, N.Y. 14269-1867

YES! Please send me 4 free Harlequin Superromance® novels and my free surprise gift. Then send me 4 brand-new novels every month, which I will receive before they appear in bookstores. Bill me at the low price of $2.89 each plus 25¢ delivery and applicable sales tax, if any.* That's the complete price and—compared to the cover prices of $3.50 each—quite a bargain! I understand that accepting the books and gift places me under no obligation ever to buy any books. I can always return a shipment and cancel at any time. Even if I never buy another book from Harlequin, the 4 free books and the surprise gift are mine to keep forever.

134 BPA ANRJ

Name _____ (PLEASE PRINT)

Address _____ Apt. No. _____

City _____ State _____ Zip _____

This offer is limited to one order per household and not valid to present Harlequin Superromance® subscribers. *Terms and prices are subject to change without notice. Sales tax applicable in N.Y.

USUP-94R

©1990 Harlequin Enterprises Limited

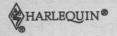 HARLEQUIN®

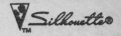 Silhouette®

The movie event of the season can be the reading event of the year!

Lights... The lights go on in October when CBS presents Harlequin/Silhouette Sunday Matinee Movies. These four movies are based on bestselling Harlequin and Silhouette novels.

Camera... As the cameras roll, be the first to read the original novels the movies are based on!

Action... Through this offer, you can have these books sent directly to you! Just fill in the order form below and you could be reading the books...before the movie!

48288-4	Treacherous Beauties by Cheryl Emerson		
		$3.99 U.S./$4.50 CAN.	☐
83305-9	Fantasy Man by Sharon Green		
		$3.99 U.S./$4.50 CAN.	☐
48289-2	A Change of Place by Tracy Sinclair		
		$3.99 U.S./$4.50CAN.	☐
83306-7	Another Woman by Margot Dalton		
		$3.99 U.S./$4.50 CAN.	☐

TOTAL AMOUNT		$	
POSTAGE & HANDLING		$	
($1.00 for one book, 50¢ for each additional)			
APPLICABLE TAXES*		$	_____
TOTAL PAYABLE		$	_____
(check or money order—please do not send cash)			

To order, complete this form and send it, along with a check or money order for the total above, payable to Harlequin Books, to: **In the U.S.:** 3010 Walden Avenue, P.O. Box 9047, Buffalo, NY 14269-9047; **In Canada:** P.O. Box 613, Fort Erie, Ontario, L2A 5X3.

Name: _____

Address: _____ City: _____

State/Prov.: _____ Zip/Postal Code: _____

*New York residents remit applicable sales taxes.
 Canadian residents remit applicable GST and provincial taxes.

CBSPR

"HOORAY FOR HOLLYWOOD" SWEEPSTAKES

HERE'S HOW THE SWEEPSTAKES WORKS

OFFICIAL RULES — NO PURCHASE NECESSARY

To enter, complete an Official Entry Form or hand print on a 3" x 5" card the words "HOORAY FOR HOLLYWOOD", your name and address and mail your entry in the pre-addressed envelope (if provided) or to: "Hooray for Hollywood" Sweepstakes, P.O. Box 9076, Buffalo, NY 14269-9076 or "Hooray for Hollywood" Sweepstakes, P.O. Box 637, Fort Erie, Ontario L2A 5X3. Entries must be sent via First Class Mail and be received no later than 12/31/94. No liability is assumed for lost, late or misdirected mail.

Winners will be selected in random drawings to be conducted no later than January 31, 1995 from all eligible entries received.

Grand Prize: A 7-day/6-night trip for 2 to Los Angeles, CA including round trip air transportation from commercial airport nearest winner's residence, accommodations at the Regent Beverly Wilshire Hotel, free rental car, and $1,000 spending money. (Approximate prize value which will vary dependent upon winner's residence: $5,400.00 U.S.); 500 Second Prizes: A pair of "Hollywood Star" sunglasses (prize value: $9.95 U.S. each). Winner selection is under the supervision of D.L. Blair, Inc., an independent judging organization, whose decisions are final. Grand Prize travelers must sign and return a release of liability prior to traveling. Trip must be taken by 2/1/96 and is subject to airline schedules and accommodations availability.

Sweepstakes offer is open to residents of the U.S. (except Puerto Rico) and Canada who are 18 years of age or older, except employees and immediate family members of Harlequin Enterprises, Ltd., its affiliates, subsidiaries, and all agencies, entities or persons connected with the use, marketing or conduct of this sweepstakes. All federal, state, provincial, municipal and local laws apply. Offer void wherever prohibited by law. Taxes and/or duties are the sole responsibility of the winners. Any litigation within the province of Quebec respecting the conduct and awarding of prizes may be submitted to the Regie des loteries et courses du Quebec. All prizes will be awarded; winners will be notified by mail. No substitution of prizes are permitted. Odds of winning are dependent upon the number of eligible entries received.

Potential grand prize winner must sign and return an Affidavit of Eligibility within 30 days of notification. In the event of non-compliance within this time period, prize may be awarded to an alternate winner. Prize notification returned as undeliverable may result in the awarding of prize to an alternate winner. By acceptance of their prize, winners consent to use of their names, photographs, or likenesses for purpose of advertising, trade and promotion on behalf of Harlequin Enterprises, Ltd., without further compensation unless prohibited by law. A Canadian winner must correctly answer an arithmetical skill-testing question in order to be awarded the prize.

For a list of winners (available after 2/28/95), send a separate stamped, self-addressed envelope to: Hooray for Hollywood Sweepstakes 3252 Winners, P.O. Box 4200, Blair, NE 68009.

OFFICIAL ENTRY COUPON

"Hooray for Hollywood"
SWEEPSTAKES!

Yes, I'd love to win the Grand Prize — a vacation in Hollywood — or one of 500 pairs of "sunglasses of the stars"! Please enter me in the sweepstakes!

This entry must be received by December 31, 1994.
Winners will be notified by January 31, 1995.

Name _____

Address _____ Apt. _____

City _____

State/Prov. _____ Zip/Postal Code _____

Daytime phone number _____
(area code)

Mail all entries to: Hooray for Hollywood Sweepstakes,
P.O. Box 9076, Buffalo, NY 14269-9076.
In Canada, mail to: Hooray for Hollywood Sweepstakes,
P.O. Box 637, Fort Erie, ON L2A 5X3.

KCH

OFFICIAL ENTRY COUPON

"Hooray for Hollywood"
SWEEPSTAKES!

Yes, I'd love to win the Grand Prize — a vacation in Hollywood — or one of 500 pairs of "sunglasses of the stars"! Please enter me in the sweepstakes!

This entry must be received by December 31, 1994.
Winners will be notified by January 31, 1995.

Name _____

Address _____ Apt. _____

City _____

State/Prov. _____ Zip/Postal Code _____

Daytime phone number _____
(area code)

Mail all entries to: Hooray for Hollywood Sweepstakes,
P.O. Box 9076, Buffalo, NY 14269-9076.
In Canada, mail to: Hooray for Hollywood Sweepstakes,
P.O. Box 637, Fort Erie, ON L2A 5X3.

KCH